Would it Kill You to Smile?

Philip Lawson

LONGSTREET
Atlanta, Georgia

Published by
LONGSTREET PRESS, INC.
A subsidiary of Cox Newspapers
A subsidiary of Cox Enterprises, Inc.
2140 Newmarket Parkway
Suite 122
Marietta, GA 30067

Printed in the United States of America

1st printing 1998

Library of Congress Catalog Card Number: 98-066372

ISBN: 1-56352-511-9

Jacket and book design by Jill Dible
Jacket illustration by David Turner
Typeface design by Jamie Bishop

For Ginger's mom & the Gurley Drive Kid
and
in memory of Ross

Would it Kill You to Smile?

CHAPTER 1

At least sixty people watched my father die. I did not number among the witnesses, but I learned of his death only fifteen or twenty minutes after it happened. Sixty spectators for his final performance: the club half full on a slow Thursday night. The old man would have been happy. Because he measured love by the size of the audience, a family of merely three spectators had never quite satisfied him.

I had not driven down to Columbus for his Thursday-evening gig at the Gag Reflex, the comedy club he owned with Satish Gupta. I had a calling I loved in the workaday world of people with mortgages, kids, and unpaid dental bills — though none of those three applied to me. Still, Fridays cut me no slack in the Speece County School System. So when Skipper Keats and his teakwood alter ego, Dapper O'Dell, collapsed in front of that audience like a sniper victim and his knee-riding child, I lay in bed dreaming of a school of neon blue parrot fish.

Kelli, my sixteen-year-old kid sister, telephoned me near midnight from the Gag Reflex's kitchen. "Will," she said, audibly on the edge of tears, "Skipper just crashed. For good. Dr. Sammons has pronounced him dead."

"Where?" The glowing red digital display on my clock radio read 11:43. I had slept maybe forty minutes, but the illusion that Kelli had spoken to me through the beak of a parrot fish persisted for several heartbeats.

"Here at the club," she said. "He had his military routine going. You know, Dapper in khakis and a service cap. A lot of visiting Canadian officers from Fort Benning in the audience.

Skipper had them hooting at him and the chip-block."

Chip-block. Received Keats-family terminology for any of the dummies that Skipper used in his act, with specific reference to Dapper O'Dell. Once, Skipper had hopefully applied the term *chip-block* to me too.

I turned on the lamp, sat up groggily in my sleep-creased birthday suit. "What happened, Kelli?"

"A vein burst in his brain. An aneurysm, Dr. Sammons says. Can you come, Will? I can't talk anymore over the phone." Her voice had begun to spongify, thickening and softening.

"Sure. Where to? The hospital?"

"The hospital can't do him or us any good. Come to the house, okay?"

I pulled on jeans and an oatmeal-hued sweatshirt with "Save the Kids" in crimson lettering, pocketed my wallet, then groped outside through the April chill to my car, a '92 Saturn S-1. My father, the quasi-famous Kevin "Skipper" Keats, had just died. With my key in the car's door lock, I covered my face with my hands and exhaled deeply. No one, it occurred to me, would now begrudge me Friday off.

Friday off: every worker's dream. A fine long weekend. Full of delightful arrangements to make.

LaRue would probably cringe before the responsibilities of mortality, but Kelli would soldier through. I could count on her and on Denise Shurett, Skipper's latest agent, and maybe on Burling Whickerbill, a family attorney. But most of the fallen sky's weight rested on my shoulders, and in my disoriented grogginess I felt like a roustabout trying to pitch a collapsed circus tent all by myself.

I looked up. Stars prickled the sky. Earlier, on the northern porch of my rented house, I had seen the comet Hale-Bopp, named like some old vaudeville act, streaking motionlessly over Georgia and Alabama like one of van Gogh's nimbused stars. How could it concurrently suggest fiery speed and self-possessed repose? Just as Skipper Keats had, I figured. Like a comet, he had come and gone, blazing through our family's life with a spectacular evanescense.

Driving, I lusted for hot coffee. What had my father felt as his brain spurted and he began to slide off his high, trouser-polished stool? He may have taken a greedy satisfaction from dying in performance, the jaunty Dapper O'Dell again on his lap, his hand clandestinely gripping the dummy's headstick. Skipper's lips as he fell would have still held the minimal twist that cast his reedy wiseacre voice into Dapper's spooky-looking chops. From the boozy crowd: titters, guffaws, and a few ungovernable belly-laughs, segueing into gasps.

His military routine, Kelli had said. For some Canadian army officers on a get-acquainted goodwill tour of the prettiest little city in the Chattahoochee Valley.

Imagine a tall, thin sixty-seven-year-old man with a silver pompadour, darting eyes, and a wide, slack mouth: Skipper Keats. Imagine, in his arms, a boy-sized wooden replica of himself with features similar to those in old photos of Skipper in his thirties (my own age now): Dapper O'Dell. Imagine both Skipper and Master O'Dell, the eternal Irish bad boy, in tailored U.S. Army uniforms, a captain's outfit for Keats and a corporal's khakis for Dapper.

Above the hum of my tires, I could almost hear the act. Tarted up with "contemporary" references already growing moldy, it had persisted intact since the Korean War. I had sat dutifully through it hundreds of times.

"The Pentagon appointed me an aide to General Ironbutt," Dapper says. "Right in the middle of our last run-in with the Arabs."

"I guess the general needed a swagger stick. Did he hold you by your ankles or your neck? Me, I'd choose the neck."

"Stow it, Keats! Or I'll stick *my* hand up *your* back and close that fat trap of yours!"

"Oh, Corporal Log has feelings, does he?"

"You bet I do! One more comparison to my inanimate cousins, and I'm out of here!"

"Okay, I promise: no more wooden jokes. Now, back to your military career. Is it true you once helped out the MPs?"

"Not that I recall. Say, you're not insinuating — "

"That you should change your name to Billy Club?"

"That did it! You and I are history, pal!"

"Now, now, settle down. I'm sorry. Go on with your heroic story."

Dapper fumes for a moment, and then proceeds:

"Well, one day our camp came under attack by five or six lost and starving Republican Guards. The general said, 'Give me my red shirt, Dapper!' 'How come?' I asked. The general replied, 'If I'm wounded, the blood won't show and my men won't get discouraged.' What a man! I thought. The next day word came that eight divisions of towelheads were on their way, with full armor and air support. Guess what the general asked me to fetch?"

"His red shirt?"

"No — his brown pants!"

"D'oh!"

Even passing the carnival-lit trailer of a droning diesel semi on I-185, I could see the entire scene: Skipper, Dapper, the appreciative crowd, cigarette smoke curling through the footlights and the beer-sign glow. The Gag Reflex jumping even as Satish Gupta, there only for solidarity's sake, stood at the head of the stairs inventorying the evening's take. At length, the laughter dies, Dapper swivels his head and looks directly at my father: original and reflection in a bizarre time-distorting mirror. Everyone knows what lumberboy intends to say, but everyone's accurate anticipation of this line fails to subvert its ritualistic bite:

"Come on, Keats: *Would it kill you to smile?*"

Driving around the shuddering eighteen-wheeler, I imagined the eruption that had greeted this shibboleth — that almost *always* greeted it — and imagined, too, Skipper Keats glorying again in this repetitive Podunkish triumph, sensing at that moment the failing vein in his skull, as he rocked on the toes of his spit-shined boots in a futile attempt to stand, then slumped to the dais as if from the impact of a rifle shot. Dapper O'Dell, rudimentary arms and polio-stricken legs frantically aflail, loyally following his master down to hell like a demon familiar. A stunned silence. Shrieks. Chair-scrapings. Free-for-all chaos.

How I hated show business. It robbed even death of its grim

dignity. And how I resented Skipper for suddenly nominating me by his death the head of our shambling family.

In reality, I soon learned, Skipper had dropped dead between punchlines, but still close enough to the end of his act to give his death a little of the curtain-falling drama I had imagined. Also, Kelli explained, he had just embarked on his and Dapper's one-armed-paratrooper routine, not the aide-de-camp shtick.

The Keatses — *sans* son — lived in a two-story white stone house on a hilly street not far from Weracoba Park, a recreational area locally nicknamed the Lake Bottoms. Even at half-past midnight, joggers in spandex, cutoffs, sweatsuits, or headband-accented combinations of these styles loped or trudged along the park's sidewalks. Three or four had dogs — Rotweilers or German shepherds or Labs — for company or protection, if not both. In a torpid daze, I cruised past them in my Saturn.

The house, which in the immemorial past my parents had christened "Skipper's Keep," blazed like a torch among the dog-woods and sycamores. Porch lights, driveway lamps, security spots — even some eaves-running yellow fluorescents on the car-riage-house-*cum*-garage — burned, flickered, or glowed, as did the lamps in windows upstairs and down. Now I truly believed that Skipper had died. Alive, the guardian of the family purse strings would never have allowed such a display. LaRue must have commanded this light show as a practical way to keep the haints and hobgoblins at bay. Death dispelled by the flick of a switch.

From the head of the driveway, engine off, I saw the black baby grand that my mother sometimes played — and played well — gleaming in the glass-walled conservatory between the carriage house and the drawing room. Stepping from the car, I thought I saw a young woman, gowned and face averted, seated on the piano bench. A family friend, here to console and mourn? Then I recognized the gown. LaRue had last worn it in her farewell stage performance, then permanently closeted it. Nearer, I saw that no one inhabited it. Its stiff layers of crinoline merely sat, propped in a lifelike way on the bench. And yet, hadn't I seen bare arms, a white neck, a thick chignon?

Kelli greeted me at the front door. Almost literally the trophy child of the Keatses' dotage (in both senses), she had turned out far more feistily independent than anyone would have expected. She clung to me wordlessly for a full minute, then led me inward to the parlor.

"He didn't suffer, Will. He didn't have time."

"You tell me that to comfort me?"

"Don't start, Will." Kelli brushed tumbling amber ringlets away from her face, disclosing several new piercings and adornments in her ear, miniscule cut stones and rune-engraved clips. Skipper must have mellowed considerably to let her wear those.

Call my sister striking rather than pretty. She had Skipper's thin nose and generous mouth and LaRue's astonished emerald-grey eyes. She wore a long-sleeved white satin blouse with flounces at the shoulder and no midriff to speak of. Above her hip-hugging flared black slacks, a silver navel ring glinted against ivory skin.

I dropped my gaze to this ring as Kelli told me how Skipper had died. To me, the piercing spoke of a showy self-rape, a cry of angry defiance and otherwise inexpressible hurt. Kelli failed to notice my distraction or my disapproval.

When she had finished talking, I asked, "Where'd they take him, Sis?"

"Straight to the Smittinger-Alewine Mortuary. Dr. Sammons hauled fanny to get to the club before the coroner — so Mama wouldn't have to deal with a stranger. Hospital was pointless by then. You didn't want us to bring him home, did you?"

"Not really. And LaRue?"

"Upstairs in the Prop Room, with Aunt Denise and Uncle Burling. You might've noticed she's got every light on, chandeliers, pole lamps, even that Madonna nightlight in the bathroom. And she has a fishbowl-sized snifter of brandy in her lap."

"Has she flipped?"

"Actually, I'd say she's hanging steady."

I paced away. The Prop Room had always steadied LaRue. It had the amenities of a library and the reassuring familiarity of a private museum of stage articles and career mementos. As a kid,

I had almost preferred it to my own room.

"Nice belly-button pull," I said without looking at Kelli. "When do the Oompa-Loompas get here to haul you back to the Chocolate Factory?"

After a beat or two, Kelli said, "Do you really want to pick a fight with me on the night our father has died?" The evenness of her voice, her refusal to send up fireworks, impressed and shamed me. I had wanted to provoke an airburst to match my own consternation, but she had stayed focused on the matter at hand. I could hardly deride Kelli's trendy yet ultimately harmless piercing if it meant that Skipper had learned something valuable about parenting from his manifold mistakes with me.

"Sorry, Sis. Apparently, even tonight I can't quite escape Skipper's psychic ventriloquism."

"No prob." Kelli walked over and gripped my forearms, then yanked on them, hard. "*Just don't do it again.*" Then she was all practicality. "Don't you want to go up and see Mama?"

"No. But it's the only decent thing to do."

CHAPTER 2

Duty — embodied in the Prop Room — beckoned. I climbed the curving marble staircase like a convict climbing a gallows.

LaRue, Denise Shurett, and Burling Whickerbill hovered like a quorum of grieving potentates among the leather-bound books, the scattered Oriental throws, the framed celebrity photographs, and the impish choir of Skipper's manikins. Each of Dapper O'Dell's brothers and sisters had a chair or davenport cushion of its own. Dapper himself, rescued from his ignominious stage-sprawl, sat on the floral-print sofa next to LaRue, his chin on his chest and one leg at an indecorous angle. He reminded me of a GI on a weekend pass, bumpkinish in the parlor of an off-limits cathouse.

"Will! I *knew* you'd get here quickly! Bless you!" LaRue, slender in an antique sleeping-gown kimono, snifter cupped in one hand, approached. She pecked me on the cheek and ran a crimson fingernail under each of my eyes, trolling for unshed tears. "An *angel* took Kevin." She lifted her brandy snifter in peculiar valediction. "*His* angel."

Whether from LaRue's lips or Skipper's, this belatedly adopted family theology always unsettled me. I could not help thinking that if an angel had taken my father, it was the Angel of Death. The marksman Israfel, maybe, trained to go for the headshot. Or the assassin Makatiel, prone to finishing off his victims in the most embarrassing manner possible. Anyway, whichever celestial creature had executed Skipper had sloppily overlooked an ancillary victim: Dapper O'Dell.

I looked around the room at the persistent figures of Dapper and his seldom-seen cousins, supporting players relegated to this Sunset Boulevard hermitage: Simon Smallwood, Letitia Crone, and the stupid but lovable duck, Davy Quackett. Davy, a particularly hoary example of faded star status, wore a coonskin cap, a leather vest, and a pair of deerskin boots in the exact shape of his fat webbed feet.

"How are you doing?" I asked my mother.

"All right, I suppose. Nothing except Kevin's translation to the Great White Light has sunk in yet. I still keep expecting him to come home any minute."

Denise Shurett, a small olive-complected woman in her mid-fifties, and Burling Whickerbill, a hulking contemporary of mine in a rumpled seersucker suit reminiscent of either prison garb or pajamas, had stood up upon my entrance, but I had paid more heed to my father's dolls than to his agent or his attorney.

"We can't begin to tell you how sorry we are," Denise said. "Your father always looked — "

"The picture of health," I finished for her. "But pictures can lie. And nobody ever succeeded in getting a snapshot of Skipper's sick soul." The words came out before my better judgement could stop them, and they dumbfounded everyone, including me. "Scratch that. And please forgive me. I can't say anything right tonight. First an uncalled-for jab at Kelli, now a gratuitous swipe at you good people." The others stared at me unreadably. "I *do* appreciate your coming. Obviously, so does LaRue."

LaRue nodded and steered me by an elbow to the sofa, where we sat down on either side of Dapper O'Dell. Denise and Burling, exchanging a wary glance, took their chairs again.

There we sat, three Keatses in a row: See No Evil, Hear No Evil, Speak No Evil. Technically, Dapper was an O'Dell, of course, but Skipper had "adopted" him long before my own birth, and that all-but-legal initiation into the clan made us brothers. If Edgar Bergen's Charlie McCarthy had had his own sister, Candice, then clearly Dapper and I shared a comparable siblinghood.

LaRue sipped again from her outsized brandy snifter — not brandy, however, but a homemade Margarita with half a lime marinating in it and a crust of salt around the rim.

"Spend the night," LaRue said, half command, half supplication.

"I didn't bring anything with me, LaRue. Just hopped half asleep in the car and drove down."

LaRue said, "What does one need to spend the night? Why, when I was on the road I packed all my possessions into a small satchel and took off at a second's notice. Will, we have tooth-paste, towels, even some of your old clothes. And never since puberty have you bothered with pajamas."

"I think you've made him blush," Denise said.

Of course she had. No one else in the world could activate my internal heatpump and send a rush of color to my cheeks as dependably as LaRue, who plainly relished her power.

Now Burling said, "Your father has just died. You can't go back to Mountboro."

"Skipper's past caring, and LaRue has Kelli and hundreds of lights to comfort her. Let me come back in the morning, rested and more appropriately dressed."

Burling said, "Rest? Who's going to rest tonight? That's not the issue. We're talking solidarity here. A united front."

Against whom or what? I wondered.

"Consider the wear and tear on your car, Will," Denise said. "And it won't do your mental condition any good either, rumbling alone up and down the freeway."

LaRue said, "I *would* rest better if you stayed, Will. Suppose in your grief and fatigue you had an accident? Two lost in one day? I'd never rest again! Please, Will, you grew up here."

Sufficent reason, along with Skipper's egotistical quirks and petty tyrannies, to run straight back to Mountboro. But in the end I relented, because another bout of driving held no allure, LaRue genuinely wanted me beside her, and the death of an immediate family member did require solidarity among the sur-vivors. Who should know that better than a college-trained school counselor?

"Good boy." LaRue drained the remainder of her margarita and set the snifter on the coffee table. "Bed for me. I can't think any-more about death certificates, casket purchases, or funeral hours.

They all seem so trivial next to Kevin's merger with the One."

"We'll do the thinking, LaRue," Burling told her, rising from his chair like a blue-and-white-striped hot-air balloon. "You just try to get your sleep." Denise rose too, less showily, and kissed LaRue on the cheek.

Despite heartbreak and drink, LaRue had to this point maintained her composure. But Denise's kiss caused her eyes to flood with tears. Quietly, she said, "Kevin rarely made me sleep alone these last years. How can I face that awful empty bed?" Tears channeled down the creases bracketing her mouth. She made no effort to wipe them, and almost in spite of myself I registered a pestering fraction of her pain.

Denise, also crying, used her own silk leaf-patterned scarf to blot my mother's tears. LaRue caught Denise's wrist and touched her lips to the agent's hand. She winked at me then, not conspiratorially or ironically, but as a signal to reassure me of her self-sufficiency and clarity of mind. Then, twisting on the sofa, she scooped Dapper O'Dell into her arms and nuzzled his cheek, incidentally knocking his service cap off.

Standing with him, as a parent might lift a fussy infant from its crib, she said to him, "You'll sleep where Kevin slept. And I'll sleep beside you. Goodnight, everyone." LaRue left the Prop Room, carrying a small and youthful facsimile of her dead husband of thirty-six years.

For a moment, no one spoke. Then Denise excused herself, and Kelli, a serape lopsidedly caping her shoulders, appeared at the Prop Room door, as if she had been listening outside, and escorted Denise downstairs.

That left Burling and me to appraise each other like a pair of chess players unfamiliar with the other's style. Burling and his elder partners had taken on my parents as clients four years ago when Skipper broke with an Atlanta-based firm over some half-imagined malfeasance. Although Burling and I had met and spoken at holiday gatherings and recognized each other even at a distance, we had little in common beyond our generational proximity and our muzzy Southern heritage. Perhaps uncharitably, I saw him as a clumsy yuppie social climber, avaricious to the bone. He in turn undoubtedly regarded me as a guilt-ridden liberal mucking about in the psyches of disadvantaged children as a penance for my privileged upbringing.

Despite this latent distrust, we now tacitly agreed to get along. A truce, saving our energies for laying the dead to rest.

"Thanks for staying," he said. "She *does* need you now."

"She always has. At least my big brother Dapper can share the responsibility. One dummy or the other, eh?"

Burling shook his head impatiently. "You're too harsh on her. And on yourself. Quit analyzing everything. At least until Smittinger-Alewine has your father safely entombed."

"Safely entombed." I paced. "*Safely. En-tombed.* What does that mean, Burling? You entomb a living man, and he suffocates. You bury a dead man and he decomposes. No matter how much money you spend on the casket, the worms get in sooner or later. Or maybe your safe little ride to eternity gets an early unplanned detour. You remember a few years ago, down in Albany, when the Flint River broke its banks? It floated dozens of *safely* buried coffins merrily down its stream toward Florida. So, tell me, exactly how do you *safely* entomb someone?"

Burling let me rave. Then he said, "Define 'displacement' for me, Mr. Keats. I think they covered it in Psych 101."

I stopped pacing and looked at him. "Touché." My brain felt as if someone were trying to inflate it with a bicycle pump. I took a few breaths to calm myself down, just as I advised enraged or frightened schoolchildren to do. "That's three times," I said. "If I keep it up, I won't have a friend left. Forgive me"

"Forget it," Burling said.

Kelli returned from seeing Denise out. She had lavender-yellow grief bruises under her eyes. I understood but could not fully share her sorrow. Skipper had always treated her with more deference and tender-heartedness than he had shown me, the original human chip-block. Wrapped in her fringed serape, she sidled up, slid her arm around my waist, and leaned her head against me. Uncle Burling, as Kelli had called him earlier, fixated on her navel ring, but quickly roused to the impropriety of his gaze and brushed some imaginary lint from his suit.

"Where's LaRue?" Kelli said.

"She picked up Dapper and retreated to her bedroom," I said. "You should turn in too, kiddo."

"You guys haven't. What's going on?"

"Sit down." Burling made a bearlike swatting movement at the couch, as if on Skipper's demise he had inherited the role of host. We obeyed him, Kelli cuddling against me. Burling lowered his heavy rump to the edge of a delicate French chair and leaned toward us in his precariously overbalanced way.

"Let me explain what Smittinger-Alewine has proposed for a schedule. If you object, say so now. LaRue has heard this already and pretty much agreed to it all. But we can still make adjustments. I'd also like to lay out an unusual stipulation — an addendum to your father's will — which he made in private with Marc Alsogroom and me the day after New Year's."

I had once met Marc Alsogroom in a country-club setting. His knit Ralph Lauren shirt with its trademark emblem had prompted me to imagine the Columbus law firm of Voss, Alsogroom and Whickerbill as a team of overweight polo players.

Kelli said, "Shoot."

"A viewing Saturday night between seven and nine in the downstairs parlor — "

"A *viewing*?" I said. "Here? Don't sensible people usually hold them elsewhere, Burling? To preserve the home as a haven? To keep the curiosity-seekers and morbid crazies at bay?"

"Your father wanted a viewing. Here. Something like a traditional Irish wake. A vigil, with music and storytelling and booze in moderation. The three of you needn't worry about it. I'll handle the details."

"What about a casket?" Kelli said.

"On hand already. Skipper had us order it at our meeting in early January."

"Why? He always swore he was going to outlive us all. Did he know something about his own health he wasn't sharing with us?" I snugged Kelli up to me. Her heart hammered against my flank like a dulcimer.

Burling shifted uneasily. "I don't see anything out of the ordinary in such a sensible precaution. He turned sixty-seven only a few days later, Mr. Keats, and he probably wanted to spare his family as many trifling headaches as he could."

"Skipper rarely spared us anything, Burling. And given your efforts on our family's behalf, please call me Will. I get enough of that 'Mr. Keats' stuff at work."

"All right — Will. Anyway, for all I know your father may have had hints of his own vulnerability. Furthermore, he'd recently seen in a magazine feature a number of rather, ah, unique caskets that engaged his imagination. He clipped the article and marked the one he wanted for himself."

"A unique casket. Unique in what way?"

"Please. You'll see Saturday evening, of course. Now, as to the funeral. We have it scheduled for five o'clock Sunday evening in the largest chapel at the Smittinger-Alewine Mortuary. Florists will be contacted tomorrow. I'll consult all three of you on the choice of arrangements. The family mausoleum in Mountboro is already familiar to you."

Most interested parties here in the Southeast would have just enough time to arrive for the final service. Everyone — including me — could return home in plenty of time to catch a favorite Sunday evening TV show.

"No church involvement?"

Burling shifted uncomfortably. "Your parents' unconventional beliefs pretty much precluded it."

Kevin Keats had walked away from formal Catholic practice as an ambitious young ventriloquist busily playing supper clubs, wedding receptions, state fairs, horse shows, corporate barbecues — any gig he could grab. Life on the road had either disillusioned or cynically enlightened him. LaRue, meanwhile, whom he had met sharing a bill in Memphis, Tennessee, had come to her majority as an indifferent, if not quite apostate, Baptist. A perfunctory grace at meals had comprised almost the full extent of my religious upbringing. Only in their golden years had Skipper and LaRue evolved their idiosyncratic theology, a mishmash of New Age creeds and self-help maxims. I assumed Kelli had had to deflect a fair amount of half-hearted spiritual propaganda.

Luckily, she seemed to have succeeded.

As for me, I had a yawning hole where such things usually fit. Ordinarily I never felt the loss. But on a night like this, I almost wished for something to plug the metaphysical gap.

Burling said, "Entombment an hour after the funeral, in the family mausoleum next to Clayton and Cerell. And then it's all over."

"Strange, isn't it? A single weekend in which to wrap up and dump the sum total of a human being's life."

Kelli patted my knee. A dozen years separated us, and a potentially estranging gamut of distinctive experiences. "Come on, Will. This is life — life and death. This is the way it's done. You wouldn't want to laminate and shellac him and keep him around the house like Dapper or Simon, would you?" Her mild rebuke sounded to my ears more like a mother enlightening a child than a younger sister upbraiding her brother.

Tactfully, Burling ignored this exchange. "I have one final thing to tell you all. I'm counting on one or both of you to break this news to your mother, as I don't relish the task."

We waited, Kelli expectantly silent beside me. "Go on," I said. "Tell us."

Burling looked as if a judge had asked him to lower his pants in the courtroom. "Skipper wants . . . well, he wants Dapper O'Dell buried with him."

When my mind engaged its slipping gears once more, it offered up a single word: suttee. The Hindu custom of burning a man's widow on his funeral pyre.

Dapper had real market value. As a sentimental object, the figure conjured up a notable ventriloquist's career. As a piece of old-fashioned craftsmanship, it exuded collectibility. I had little doubt that the Bradley Museum, if not the Smithsonian, would gladly find Dapper a niche in its collection.

"Burling, we might as well cremate the whole lot of knotheads." I nodded at Simon Smallwood, Letitia Crone, and Davy Quackett. "We could throw Dapper on the bonfire, add a cord of seasoned pine, and give the citizens of Columbus the most expensive barbecue in their city's history."

Immune to sarcasm, Burling removed a photocopied document

from the deep interior pocket of his jacket. "Your Daddy's will, Will. Here's the clause." He pointed it out with a thumb like a cypress gnarl. "As you can see, it stipulates internment with the teakwood figure known as Dapper O'Dell."

I ignored the paper. "It sounds as if our father regarded himself as some sort of latter-day pharaoh. Maybe I shouldn't be surprised that a man who regretted missing out on the Golden Age of vaudeville would pull such a baggypants stunt."

Kelli dug her fingers into my knee, not to disable me but to warn me against slandering the dead. Or was she reacting to the eerie codicil in Skipper's will? I could not reliably say.

Burling, his spiel completed, advised us to get some sleep. Kelli, as she had done with Denise Shurett, escorted Burling down the stairs to the front door.

The only waking creature in the house, I circulated for a time through echoey rooms like an obsessive sleepwalker, turning off light after lamp after light, until the only illumination came from the Madonna in the bathroom and a few small baseboard night-lights. The nightlights' yellowing, thirty-year-old plastic shields, remnants of Dapper's faddish heyday, reproduced in ghastly miniature the dummy's features. And so, by deliberate caricature, those of my father as well.

◆ ◆ ◆

A troubling night. I slept naked in a canopied four-poster bed that as a boy I had regarded as a pirate galleon, a ship that I had unquestionably captained and that a score of cutthroat ghosts had crewed. Friday in the hours before dawn, the bed seemed only a bed, and much smaller than I remembered it, but it pitched and yawed as if a high wind and a barrage of turbulent combers swept ceaselessly through the room.

I awoke in darkness and put my feet on the the cold floor. Skipper and LaRue had had it tiled expressly because boys have numberless strategies for soiling both carpets and rugs.

A run of fragile, vaguely dissonant piano notes drifted up from the conservatory. *Rhapsody in Blue*? "Autumn Leaves"?

"Prisoner of Love"? They had all been among LaRue's favorites.

A sourceless roaring filled my ears, drowning out the notes. Without even considering my nakedness, I stole through Skipper's Keep, down the spiral staircase, and into the galleylike hall debouching on the conservatory, the xylophonic rattling of the piano keys beckoning me on. Outside the conservatory, hidden from any sidewalk passersby within the frame of the open doorway, I stopped.

LaRue herself had replaced her ghostly crinoline doppelgänger.

Her back to me, she sat in her kimono on the bench, summoning articulate trills and glissandos by the glow of a single white taper in a brass candlestick on the keyboard itself. Beside her, like a clueless music pupil, sat Dapper O'Dell. He no longer wore his corporal's uniform, but a swallowtailed tuxedo of spotless ivory. The music that my mother played washed over me as the imaginary combers upstairs had, but I still failed to identify it. Rachmaninoff? Ellington? Something of her own devising, revealing a talent never before apparent?

At a one-handed passage, LaRue gently lifted Dapper's miniature hands onto the keyboard. Together, they finished playing the mysterious piece.

LaRue bent to the level of Dapper's ears. "Bravissimo," she whispered, then kissed the dummy on the temple. Head still lowered, she angled her gaze upward, staring out through the glass roof at the stars. Like mother and child, tutor and student, young lovers, they rubbed cheeks, wood against flesh.

I returned to my canopied bed, which no longer rippled or bucked. I lay upon it wide-eyed until a scrim of pink showed in the eastern window and the goldfinches and mockingbirds began broadcasting from the sycamores.

CHAPTER 3

Almost everyone in Columbus — the greater Chattahoochee Valley — knew Skipper Keats. He had a local fame greater than that of any city politician, television newscaster, or entertainer. On the street, kids and adults alike hailed him affectionately.

His family and business partners and show-biz peers — now that was a different story.

Originally from Mountboro, thirty-five miles up State Highway 27, Kevin had grown up listening to radio programs and lurking on the fringes of gawking crowds at state fairs, where Edgar Bergen wannabes often took the stage with dummies so crude they resembled scaled-down department-store manikins or ill-sewn hand puppets.

Ventriloquism fascinated Skipper, and Mr. and Mrs. Clayton Keats — both past middle age when his mother Cerell bore him — indulged his preoccupation. They encouraged him to emulate his hero, Bergen, even scrimping self-sacrificially during the late Depression and the early years of World War II to pay a Mountboro cabinet maker to produce for Kevin a Charlie McCarthy clone: smaller, stiffer, and less handsomely dressed than its Platonic model. This first laquered protégé evolved through several models into the ultimate foil, Dapper O'Dell, this last figure an expensive Dennis Blitch production. Together, Skipper and Dapper entertained American troops during the Korean conflict. Postwar, between necessary but reviled money-making stints as a soft-drink salesman, Skipper sought tirelessly for his Big Break. But the levels of success he dreamed of eluded him frustratingly.

Skipper never quite made it nationally. He always hobbled one step behind the times. Whatever medium was hot was where Skipper was not. He fixated nostalgically on the ragged remnants of the comatose vaudeville circuit during a period when radio had all the action. By the time he shifted to radio-broadcast comedy, the juggernaut of television had overwhelmed that venue. Skipper harkened a little faster to the possibilities of this new medium. He and Dapper even managed one lackluster appearance in 1958 on the "Ed Sullivan Show": his one and only brush with nationwide exposure via the Tube. Skipper never tired of pointing out that Johnny Carson — or, more accurately, Carson's representative — had booked him and Dapper for a "Tonight Show" gig (a September Thursday in 1963, as I well recall from numerous recountings). But Skipper never made it out of the Green Room. Two other celebrity guests, big-name movie stars, had monopolized the program from midpoint to closing credits. Quivering with frustration backstage, Skipper had actually begun to cry — a glaring bit of unprofessionalism that had not endeared him to the Carson team.

And in that same year, of course, came my on-the-road birth, an event that Skipper would forever link to the slamming of all doors on his worldwide ambitions. LaRue's insistence on settling down with her new baby in a familiar and stable environment meant Skipper's exile from Hollywood. And despite a series of increasingly desperate long-distance inquiries — from both Skipper and his agent — he never got an invitation to return to the cherished late-night NBC spotlight. So from Day One of my life, my father had cast me as his sworn nemesis.

My birth year, of course, marked the actual nativity of what we all now call The Sixties. In the bright new glow of rock 'n' roll, of Pop Art and New Wave Cinema, of Mort Sahl and the youthful George Carlin, most ventriloquist acts had withered like vampires exposed to sunlight, instant anachronisms. Skipper Keats and his line of corn struck powerful show-biz impresarios as something out of a *March of Time* newsreel. Dapper O'Dell, in his stylized Richie Rich getups, resembled a Rover Boy at Yale, his mock-sophisticate speech evoking no actor more current than William Powell.

I had to credit Skipper with some initiative. Insofar as he could, he retooled his act. Like a Midwestern realtor trying to "get hip," he let his hair grow an inch or two. Although at the time Skipper was hardly older than I am now, he radiated the premature old-fogey aura so typical of his struggle-worn generation. Nonetheless, he forced himself to don some tasteful beads, open-collar shirts in psychedelic prints, and low-slung bell-bottoms with either flip-flops or huaraches. He dressed Dapper to match and early in each performance put explicit stress on his freshly ironic nickname, which now signified the "dapperness" of a foppish drug dealer. Skipper wanted to make sure that not even Timothy Leary or the Maharishi Mahesh Yogi could object to Dapper's street-creds. But of course both would have immediately seen through this sad and laughable sham.

Moreover, almost none of my father's intended new audiences — college students, the hungry i/Maxwell's Kansas City crowd, socially conscious young adults — fell for this contrived metamorphosis. And older enthusiasts, including potential fans from Skipper's native South and conservatives everywhere from the middle and lower-middle classes, actually despised the transformation. At a supper club in Mobile, Alabama, a heckler in a three-piece vanilla suit and white bucks literally tossed his oily Caesar salad at the pair, gashing Skipper's chin with the redwood bowl and raggedly adorning Dapper with romaine lettuce.

The duo retreated. Not underground in the manner of a Black Panther or a Weathermen bomber, but offstage, out of the spotlight (that small fraction of celebrity illumination they had ever claimed). Time to recuperate and rethink.

Then five, I had just started school, which offered a haven from my now house-bound father. Evenings, homework provided a welcome excuse to cloister myself in my room at the Keep.

LaRue persuaded Skipper to ditch the bohemian wardrobe, to return to the elegance of tuxedos, the bourgeois patriotism of uniforms and VFW caps. He would have to cede New York and Hollywood to the longhaired upstarts and drop down a rung on the ladder, deliberately marginalizing himself before others could do it to him. Once again he would have to rest content with play-ing second-tier but still respectable territories such as Atlanta, Miami, Birmingham, and lesser Georgia cities like Macon, Savannah, and Augusta. By lowering his expectations and return-ing earnestly to his roots, Skipper would refurbish his reputation, consolidate his audience, and boost his annual income.

The strategy worked. Throughout the 1970s, Skipper Keats and Dapper O'Dell headlined various convention banquets, sup-per-club shows, fund-raisers (primarily Democratic despite Dad's growing wealth and increasingly truculent conservatism), cruise-ship extravaganzas, upper-crust wedding receptions, and local television specials. Word got around that Skipper offered reliable, G-rated filler for any crowd more interested in their dinners than their on-stage divertissements. Bookings abounded.

Skipper invested in stock equities, real estate, automobile deal-erships, and a dance studio. Fort Benning called upon him at pre-dictable intervals to elevate the morale of young GIs or to amuse Central American military officers training at its controversial School of the Americas, where critics claimed the American instructors served up the protocols of torture and intimidation under the banal guise of self-determination. (Mouthpiece Dapper scoffed at these pinkos: "They accelerate through red lights, friends. No other color can make 'em go.")

So Dapper's handler and the handler's family fattened on the high-calorie, low-nutrition diet. National fame may have elud-ed the ventriliquixotic boy wonder from Mountboro, G.A., but a gracious accumulation of wealth did not. And the cordial advents of presidents Reagan and Bush did nothing to slow this amassing bounty.

In 1990, Skipper Keats joined with an old friend and business partner, a Christianized Indian named Satish Gupta, a transplant-ed native of Hyderabad, to buy a walk-up nightclub and bar in downtown Columbus. The district they invested in had grown shabby and disreputable with the defection of shoppers to Midtown Mall and the plusher and more extensive Peachtree Mall on the city's northeastern periphery. The renovation of an old river-side factory called the Ironworks as a convention center, the popu-

larity of productions at the Springer Opera House, and the continuing rehabilitation of homes in the historic district near the river
had all led Gupta and my father to conclude that a comedy club
downtown might not immediately founder — especially if Skipper
and his popular pals took the dais there at least once a month.
Skipper agreed. He and Gupta, both nuance-deaf paragons of bad
taste, promptly christened their club the Gag Reflex.

LaRue hated this name. To her, the phrase implied only chok-
ing, pain, and ignominy. Any standup who took the dais under
such an ill-omened banner would, she maintained, do so cringing
and primed for failure. Skipper countered that most real comedians worked best — most inventively — under pressure. They
would defiantly embrace the moniker LaRue hated, much as a
taunted cripple might come to flaunt his stump. And besides —
didn't she get the wonderful punny joke? As time passed, LaRue
relented. The club's prosperity won her over, for the dingy, slope-
floored hall on the second story of a nondescript building in an
evolving urban war zone proved a cash cow.

Skipper Keats and Dapper O'Dell held down the closing slots
on the third Thursday-through-Saturday block of each month.
Satish Gupta ran the club on a daily basis, with some help from
my father and a lot from Denise Shurett. Together, they booked
promising new comics and the occasional innovative jazz combo
to complete the weekly billings. Indeed, Skipper indulged in a lot
of undeserved self-congratulation for having caught remarkable
talents like Myra Doone, Tom R. Johnson, and Pablo Cabriales on
their ballistic ascents into the show-business stratosphere; he
regarded them as chip-blocks, at least as much as he did me. After
prating endlessly about how they owed their starts to him, he
would credit them and their talented but less famous cohorts with
playing a small part in the surprising success of the Gag Reflex.

On the other hand, he later regarded Cabriales as an ingrate,
muttering obscene curses against him for never tailoring an
episode of his Fox sitcom "In the Shade" for a compensatory
Keats and O'Dell appearance. "I'd've settled for a cameo," he
often complained to Shurett. "A ratings stud like Pablo could've
arranged it in a snap." Privately telling me this story at a

Thanksgiving dinner at the Keep, Denise had noted that a cameo made video sense only if the audience recognized the person in the cameo — a prerequisite that my father and his talking toothpick did not meet. Denise, naturally, never shared this observation with Skipper, who had died still extolling those protégés who manifested the proper gratitude and reviling Cabriales as a crummy opportunist. I took only meager solace from the fact that he had never included ethnic slurs in his attacks.

Had my father left this mortal stage a disappointed man? Yes and no. Even as the victim of a fatal blood-vessel explosion in his mind's engine-room, he must have heard the laughter of the crowd, felt its empathetic transformation into shock and solicitude. Slipping from his thronelike stool, he had surely pictured himself as the beloved dummy-sceptered monarch of his smoky kingdom, unjustly stricken down and spontaneously mourned. He had died stunned but fortunate: an esteemed native son.

In another sense, however, he had fallen enormously shy of his youthful ambitions. He had never attained the overarching wealth, the celebrity, or even the professional respect of his hero, the incomparable Edgar Bergen. And he had probably acknowledged the likelihood that he had failed not only because his act had seemed from the beginning a relic of the tawdry vaudevillian past, but also because ventriloquism itself — *belly-talking*, if you marched the term back to its Latin roots — had all the cachet of hillbilly hollering or watermelon-seed spitting. A refined soul like Bergen had given the enterprise virtually all the class it could bear, and Kevin Keats — despite his reputation as a tireless bootstrapper, and despite the money he had shrewdly amassed — would never qualify in his or anyone else's estimation as a true gentleman.

If these thoughts had not been uppermost in his mind at the exact moment of his stroke, they had certainly formed an abiding foundation layer of regret, a subbasement of his soul to which only my mother had the key.

CHAPTER 4

I pulled on yesterday's jeans and a college-era Bulldogs T-shirt from the bottom of my childhood dresser. It still fit, despite the intervening years.

Downstairs in the kitchen, Eula Cole, the longest-lasting of a series of maids and housekeepers, pecked me on the cheek and murmured condolences. Her agitation surprised me a little. Could any employee of my father's really have invested so much emotion in the old tyrant's well-being?

"Morning, Eula." I returned her kiss, my lips brushing her swarthy cheek, and put a hand on her shoulder.

Eula covered my hand with her own. "William, you must be hurting bad. Sit down. I'm going to pour you some coffee."

On the table, coffee cakes, doughnuts, Danish, and croissants rested either on company-best china platters or still in their aluminum baking pans. An entire baked turkey hobnobbed with several covered casserole dishes. These mostly homemade tokens of sympathy and comfort had apparently started arriving as soon as news of Skipper's demise had spread. Goodies would continue to pour in at least until the day after the entombment. Eula received, sorted, and set out these dishes. She also noted in a register the names of the givers.

Eula brought my coffee. "Mrs. Adcock stayed up all night to get that turkey done. Lord knows how she thawed it so fast. Might've even had to drive out to the all-night grocery to get a fresh one."

"Sent someone, you mean. And I seriously doubt she baked and basted that bird herself."

"You don't know she didn't, William. Besides, it makes no

never mind. Now, help yourself, but keep those arrangements looking tidy. I got to go help your mother." Eula wiped her hands on her apron and retreated.

Grief might annul the appetites of others, but my appetite raged. I devoured a prune Danish and a bear claw, and was gulping a second cup of coffee when the bimodal kitchen door swung inward.

Kelli padded in wearing denim cutoffs and a castoff tuxedo shirt of Skipper's. She had rolled its stiff buttonless cuffs up to her elbows and for the studs required in front had substituted three plastic-case safety pins: red, yellow, red. She drew herself a mug of Eula's high-test coffee and sat down across from me, the range of breakfast selections like an edible continent between us. Kelli snagged a croissant and bit deeply into it. I nodded. She nodded back. Outside, the birds in the peeling sycamores fussed as raucously as clowns: Skipper Keats had meant nothing to them.

I watched Kelli demolish the pastry. "Did you sleep?" I asked her crankily.

"Uh-huh. Like the dead." She crooked a smile that I couldn't quite read as either smart-alecky or apologetic. "Good thing too. Otherwise I'd've brooded all night. Or worse. Stumbled through a tangle of nightmares."

She didn't ask me if *I* had slept. To disguise my pique, I took another croissant and spread it with marmalade. "No school, eh?"

"Or for you either, right?"

"No. And I've got a lot of serious cases right now. I worry about one kid in particular. I've seen him three days running for a generalized school phobia and occasional panic attacks."

Kelli seemed interested. "What do you do for him?"

"Teach him deep-breathing exercises. Tell him to count to ten. Talk to him as if he matters."

Kelli considered this. "He'll get through today all right without you."

"Oh, yeah. Probably. But not painlessly. His teacher thinks he wimps out too easily and consequently treats him like a walking zero."

"What a bitch." Kelli took a slug of coffee. "Still and all, Will — we come first. A great performer — a great *man* — like

Skipper Keats needs you here today. And so does your family."

Something that Adrienne Owsley had once told me — about Buddha painfully deserting his family for the greater benefit of all mankind — popped into my head. Where exactly did *my* duty lie this morning? Not at all certain, I temporized.

"Thanks. I know I can always count on you and LaRue too. That train *should* run both ways."

Our first warm-fuzzy of the day, but a grudging one. Kelli still had Oompa-Loompas or one of my other jabs on her mind.

"What's bugging you, Will? Is it me? LaRue? It shouldn't be Daddy, after all. He's dead, remember?"

I thought about psychic ventriloquism from beyond the grave, greedy spirit possessing a living medium, and wondered if his death truly changed anything. "I don't want to start with you, Sis, but I can't sit here pretending that Skipper warrants the epithet 'great.'"

"Do it. Pretend. Just for today. Until we get him — "

" — safely in the crypt?"

"Yeah. Because you shouldn't have to pretend. Daddy deserved everything he earned — and more. With a break or two, he could've had his own TV show, or starred in movies, or — I don't know — hosted the Academy Awards."

"The summit of all human endeavor."

Kelli threw a scrap of crust at me. "Forget it, Will. Don't even talk to me."

I looked out the window. Squirrels on the lawn. A red-capped flicker on a neighbor's rain gutter, merrily drilling away. The ten thousand things, as Adrienne provocatively termed the phenomenal world.

"If someone had laid a red carpet out for Skipper leading all the way to the Show-Biz Hall of Fame, Kelli, he still would've tripped on it."

Kelli slapped her butter knife on the edge of the table. "And how do you know *that*, Mr. Bringdown?"

"Because I'm not blind. Our father had a derivative and mediocre talent and no imagination. A deadly combination." I did not look at Kelli as I said this, but I could feel her hanging on every word, listening with a fierce resentment. "He never did anything on stage, radio, or TV that someone else hadn't done before him — and usually a thousand times better."

"Will, I won't — "

"Dapper O'Dell rips off Charlie McCarthy so shamelessly that most people can't even tell them apart. I never mention to anyone anymore that Skipper is – *was* — my father. Either they say, 'Oh, Candice Bergen is your *sister*,' or 'Gee, whatever happened to Mortimer Snerd?' And they're not all old-timers on their way to the Alzheimer's ward either. Doesn't that tell you something about Skipper's fabled genius?"

"But he created Simon and Letitia and Davy Quackett too!"

"Believe me, you don't want to use them as evidence of Skipper's talents. I could list all the painfully obvious sources for each of them. They reveal his mediocrity even more than Dapper does."

Kelli composed herself. That she had not thrown anything else at me — scalding coffee, most likely — or stormed from the breakfast nook unsettled me. I looked more closely at her. An unhealthy flush had risen from her snowy throat into her cheeks.

"He had the best damn lip control of anyone in the business," she said implacably. "Even on the hard sounds. The Bs, the Ps, the Fs, the Ms. You *never* saw his lips move, did you?"

"No," I admitted.

"And he got better as he got older. He'd wear a sports shirt and you couldn't even see his Adam's apple bob."

Technicalities only a fellow vent or a hardcore fan would appreciate. But Kelli nonetheless spoke the truth. Astonishingly, Skipper's technique had improved with age. Even though he practiced less and less as the years rolled on, his stage presence and confidence with Dapper in particular seemed to grow, as if he had truly and not simply metaphorically forged a psychic link with this creature of teak and molded plastic. He might falter with Simon Smallwood and his other two figures (latecomers to his professional troupe and so to his affections), but he never did with Dapper. And those who candidly identified themselves as his fans usually did so because they liked Dapper and admired Skipper's work with him.

"I've seen clips of Bergen," Kelli said. "His lips flapped like laundry on an Oklahoma clothesline. Most of the time it looked like he and Charlie were chewing tar!"

I knew the man's history, as how could I not? "Radio ruined Bergen. As a beginner, he had better-than-average lip control. But over the airwaves, who can tell? It's almost an oxymoron: radio ventriloquism! He got lazy."

"And that never happened to Daddy!"

Kelli wanted this fact to count toward his elegiac assessment — his canonization? — as a show-biz great. I should have let the minor credit stand against all the man's debits, but the morning and my mood seemed ripe for truth-telling.

"Look at it this way. A singer can have masterful phraseology, better than Sinatra's in his heyday, and still fail the greatness test. Poor song selection. Wavering pitch. Spastic accompanying gestures. You name it. Anyway, Skipper had the vent's counterpart of all those failings, plus others. His exemplary lip control meant nothing against all that."

"Bull."

"You've seen the tapes of Skipper and Dapper from the late sixties. Remember his greying Beatles haircut and his hokey buckskin jackets? For a number of years there, he and Dapper looked like drugged-out mountain men, hippie-dippie badger trappers."

"Geez, Will, can't you give him credit for *anything*? He was trying to *adapt*. Maybe it didn't quite work — "

"It *bombed*. It also illustrated his total mediocrity. He never thought one step further than Fred Russell."

"Who?"

Clearly Skipper had not subjected Kelli to quite the same catechism as he had me. "English music-hall performer. First to put a floppy dummy on his lap. Skipper's patron saint. But my point is, Skipper's response to the sixties was utterly superficial."

Kelli folded her arms across her chest. "Okay, smartass — what would *you* have done?"

"First, kept my tuxedo as a kind of sardonic commentary on the whole shabby scene. Second, ditched Dapper. Third, taken advantage of new technology to replace him with animatronic figures. Maybe four characters who formed a rock band, all with their own distinctive looks and shaggy personalities. A hidden crew could've operated them, sort of like the Muppets, with Skipper in their midst, interacting as if they were real. He could have effectively tweaked them with hundreds of reactionary digs. Lord knows, the whole sacred-dropout, summer-of-love thing cried out for satire."

Kelli eyed me with interest, maybe even respect. "I never knew you'd given even a second's thought to the act, Will."

"I did. I have. Despite myself."

"Still, you've got the advantage over Daddy. Three decades of hindsight."

"I don't deny it."

"Something like that might've worked, though."

"Either my idea or another. Anything besides business as usual with cosmetics and Band-aids. But Skipper — our father — couldn't escape the tried-and-true. He lacked the imagination, he lacked the *genius*. So he reaped ridicule initially, and then the fruit of his tuck-tail return to a Golden Age vent style too exhausted even to die: a bland and comfortable life. In fact, he probably made more money than he had any right to expect. I don't dream that Skipper could have turned into the Vincent van Gogh of vents — but even Shari Lewis and Lamb Chop had more hipness and style than Keats and O'Dell."

"Lamb Chop sucks."

"No one would ever mistake her for Charlie McCarthy. Saddest of all, Skipper built his own cage. His self-imposed debt to Bergen — a debt he never quit paying — ensured he'd never go nationwide or gain even a quirky creative immortality."

"No greatness?"

"No greatness."

Kelli exhaled wearily. "Dead less than twenty-four hours, and we're already picking him apart. I really hate this entire conversation. Proud of yourself?" She stood, regarding me as if I had pulled a snub-nosed Luger on her.

"No. But I had to speak the truth, Kelli."

"What made you think I needed to hear it?" She left the breakfast room, the tail of Skipper's shirt hanging well down past her fanny, like an ambiguous white flag.

CHAPTER 5

he rest of Friday muzzed by in a blur of sympathy calls and fatiguing errands. I drove back to my place in Mountboro for a shower and a couple of changes of clothes. I had six messages on my answering machine. But only two mattered, both from Adrienne.

If the police ever went questing for suspects, employing an Identikit image of a generic sixth-grade teacher, they would never find Adrienne Owsley. Her willowy frame, blonde mane, and husky laugh would completely throw off any bloodhounds nosing around for sour and stern and hardened. Her students at Tocqueville Middle School in Speece County seemed to appreciate her atypical looks and grace. I knew I did, and so did Olivia, Adrienne's seven-year-old daughter. One who hadn't, however, was Byron Owsley, her ex, a six-foot-five ponytailed blacksmith and sometime metalworker.

Adrienne's sweet voice complemented her striking looks. "Will, I just heard about your father's death. They closed the newscast with it this morning on Georgia Public Radio. I met him only a couple of times, but his death still hurts. What I want to say — what I want you to remember — is that his death represents a change, not a departure. He still exists, Will."

I halted the tape. For Adrienne, every life event illuminated a sutra or posed a koanlike riddle. Her attitude and outlook simultaneously boggled and fascinated me.

I released the hold. "If you don't object — call if you do — I'll come to the funeral with you. I think I can get a sitter for Olivia. I can't make it to the wake though. Olivia has a violin lesson and

I promised to visit Annie Flegg at Holly Dover's" — an elderly friend in a nursing home in Tocqueville. "You could probably use me Saturday — you must have beaucoup to do — but please forgive me in advance. I can't disappoint either Annie or Olivia."

Adrienne's second message lasted less than ten seconds: Could she do anything for the surviving Keatses or bring anything in the way of food to Skipper's Keep on Sunday? I called immediately, but found only her machine at home.

After it beeped, I said, "Just yourself."

◆ ◆ ◆

The viewing seemed endless.

Beginning in full daylight and concluding under a purplish-pewter sky in which Comet Hale-Bopp sped away from Earth like a wick-flaring Molotov cocktail, the pared-down wake could have stood even more trimming. Or so I thought by the fifth hour and my fifth glass of Chardonnay. By then, faces had grown as blurry as the comet.

I believed I saw the lieutenant governor. A strong handshake and an odor of genteel toilet water. Also present were a celebrated party hostess, the managers of three different television stations, Columbus's own Mayor Williams (looking more distracted than sorrowful), several city councilors, four brokerage-firm executives, two generals, and the members of a crack Fort Benning drill team, smartly attired. Along with a host of more plebian Columbusites, many of whom I had last seen in my teens, they all filed respectfully past Skipper's casket.

And that casket: Burling had not exaggerated when he called it unique. In fact, it practically stole the show.

Skipper's corpse was reduced to playing second fiddle to a masterpiece of hallucinatory woodwork. Smittinger-Alewine employees had placed the casket in the parlor just off the central hall, where it dazzled everyone who confronted it. Crude but ingenious Haitian or Jamaican artisans had modified an expensive American coffin to resemble a scaled-down convertible stretch limo: chrome bumpers and hubcaps, a shiny enamel skin the color of elephant tusks.

Inside, lying on plush lavender cushions, Skipper faced properly forward, slightly tilted as if riding a bobsled. No seatbelt showed. Dapper O'Dell lay serenely cuddled in the crook of his right arm. Both figures wore white evening clothes with lavender shoes, cumberbunds, and ties. Their faces had woodenly identical features and a ghastly mortuary sheen.

Burling Whickerbill, as suave as his bearish self could look in a slimmingly dark suit, had reassured me early in the day that all was proceeding exactly as Skipper had wished. Smittinger-Alewine had kept the casket in storage since mid-February, and the human and puppet funeral suits had both undergone drycleaning specifically for this occasion.

I might have expected Kelli to succumb to teenage contrariness and applaud the tasteless casket. But multiple body piercings were no true indicator of her sensibilities. As soon as she saw it, she slipped her arm into mine and rolled her eyes. "I've never seen anything so horrible," she whispered. "And these people . . . all these people. They can't believe it either. I could *die*."

I whispered back, "Better not. We might give you the same treatment: a little red Corvette to haul your embarrassed soul to heaven."

"You wouldn't dare." Then, surprising me, she said, "But after seeing this, how can you say he lacked imagination?"

"You're mistaking vulgarity for wit, Sis."

"So. Not the sendoff a great man would plan? Not what he would rate?"

I nodded, not only to Kelli but also to a man with a plate of hors d'oeuvres coming down the reception line.

"Well, I love him anyway," she discreetly stage-whispered.

"Fine. You ought to."

"And if I cry, that's why." She tugged at her dress. "Although it might be because this damn tight bodice has pushed my Oompa-Loompa ring back to my spine!"

I chuckled. Then I ambled away to shake hands or to tender my cheek for consolatory kisses.

Meanwhile, LaRue sat across the hall in the first-floor library, accepting the repetitive solace of bridge partners, fellow Women's

Club members, and a few long-lost relations from Memphis. She would not look at her husband in the casket, or even the casket itself. She visibly seethed at Skipper's kidnapping of Dapper O'Dell into that monstrous vehicle and, via the unappeasable power of its silent engine, into a realm she could not visit until Death came calling again. She would never get Dapper back, just as she would never recover Skipper. And neither her own children nor Skipper's subsidiary dummies in the Prop Room upstairs could compensate for their loss. So she smiled, tightly, and sipped at white grape-juice, her repentant, post-Margarita-hangover beverage of choice.

Many of the mourners schmoozed incorrigibly, as if at a Friar's roast. They stood out from the locals as if the words "show biz" blazed across their brows in letters of flame.

Alan Papini, a third-rate vent from Atlanta, shuffled from foot to foot and daubed at his neck with a sweaty handkerchief. He had always envied Skipper's regional success. Myra Doone, Tom R. Johnson, and several other comedians who had once worked at the Gag Reflex formed a compact knot, their ill-at-ease spouses in tow. Officer Cobb — Jack Straywright, once "Cartoon Carnival's" telegenic hunk — had metamorphosed into a duffel-bellied octogenarian in moldy tweeds. Estelle Durand, a forty-fivish ex-Rockette with prominent neck cords and legs that began just under her acetate-strapped bust, had evidently forgiven Skipper for the bluster and bossiness that had accompanied his investment in her dance studio. Amy Fogarty, a twenty-something hostess at the Gag Reflex, had brought her slacker beau; his expression plainly said he'd rather be skateboarding. Dick Martin, one-time cohost of "Laugh-In," seemed intent on showing off his wife: a former Playmate of the Month, circa 1966. Her autographed photo in the Prop Room had fueled many of my adolescent fantasies, and it unnerved me to see how well she had maintained herself over the years.

Of course, the roster of entertainment-industry boys and girls also included Satish Gupta. To give him credit, the Gag Reflex's co-owner looked more sorrowful than businesslike in his three-piece ebony suit with a fey salmon stripe. His bleak Dravidian features seemed fated from birth to convey just this mournful attitude. His handsome Anglo wife, the former Sherri VanHouten of Green Island Hills, had not accompanied him. A woman my mother's age, similarly preserved and vibrant, she would have stood out even in this crowd.

A CD player in the parlor piped Tony Bennett numbers through a half-dozen hidden speakers in the downstairs rooms. The uniformed help from Blandford Catering circulated with canapés and cut-glass decanters of wine and tonic water. Frequently, Eula darted from the kitchen to supervise. I saw her press drinks on the purse-lipped Burling Whickerbill and his partners, Cleveland Voss and Marc Alsogroom, who huddled as if in court conference. The partners' attractive wives, at least twenty years apart in age, chatted distractedly with each other, probably because they knew hardly anyone else.

I wished that Adrienne had come. Despite my own small family's presence, I imagined that she had abandoned me to these sharks, clowns, and freeloaders. But Adrienne believed in modest amounts of hand-holding and in generous doses of charity. As if she had read my mind at a distance, I sympathetically registered her disappointment in me.

Burling approached. "Thanks for telling your mother." He nodded at the casket. "I don't know why, but I just couldn't."

"No balls." I smiled to soften the joke.

Hurt in any event, Burling grimaced. "Was it really my job? Skipper should have prepared you all. It was hardly fair to dump the task on an outsider."

"Skipper never believed in a just universe, Burling. Or else the universe's idea of justice never matched his. Otherwise, he would have died famous as well as rich."

"*Famous*? Look at this crowd! Denise tells me you've even had a lovely sympathy telegram from Candice Bergen."

"Yes. But she addressed it to Dapper."

Burling chuckled somberly. "My God, Will, what do you think Kevin wanted? A notoriety like Hitler's?"

"Mother Teresa's would have sufficed. He always wanted people to like him. But those who actually knew him found it difficult."

Peremptorily, Burling said, "My heartfelt condolences, Will."

"I accept, of course. On behalf of Keats Senior and Junior." I nodded toward the deceased. "Father-and-son funerals. What will they think of next?"

Burling grimaced again and withdrew.

Satish Gupta appeared almost on his heels. I had always liked the lugubrious, generally low-key Gupta. His bumbling course through life reminded me of that of a dodge'em car with a wonder-stricken child at its helm. If an inchoate panic occasionally shone in the headlamps of his eyes, he still managed to pilot himself to some attractive and profitable destinations. His ability to avoid damaging run-ins with Skipper, his partner, also testified to his dreamy, hassle-proof nature. That he had lured Sherri into the bonds of marriage, further underscored this strange man's ability to bemuse and charm. No one could have predicted that two such disparate people would ever marry, let alone remain together for decades. Still a looker at sixty, with a smile as bright and sudden as a photographer's flash, Mrs. Gupta exuded a romantic gaiety completely at odds with Satish's air of otherworldly abstraction.

Satish extended a hand to me. From beneath his cuff peeked a circlet of wooden prayer beads, the only outward sign of any religious connection he had ever displayed.

"Didn't Mrs. Gupta come this evening?" I said.

"No." He thought about the question a moment longer. "No."

"Not ill, I hope?"

Satish focused his attention over my shoulder, on Skipper and the vaguely smiling Dapper O'Dell. "Something like that."

"Is it serious?"

My solicitude startled him out of his reverie. "I don't believe so. A complete recovery is predicted."

Half drunk, I found Satish's formal brand of English full of charm. "Oh, really?"

"Yes, so I believe. By Monday or Tuesday, certainly she will have recovered. After the funeral, you know." He returned his gaze to the bodies lying in state.

"Death sort of sledgehammers her, I take it."

"How accurately you state the case. Sherri has always maintained a great fondness for your family. Your father's genius, his other qualities — all quite affecting. Their loss, I mean."

Genius. I had no stomach for another bloody dissection of Skipper's talent or lack thereof. I let Sherri VanHouten Gupta's opinion go. Her husband, meanwhile, strolled past me to the casket. I left my place in the receiving line and joined him.

Like a fastidious maid, Gupta reached into the casket to straighten the carnation on Skipper's lapel. His fingers lingered there. I could not tell if grief, bewilderment, or some dim Episcopalian epiphany motivated him. But even though his posture vaguely moved me, I still saw his reverent groping as an intrusion into Skipper's hard-won peace.

At length Gupta withdrew his touch. As he turned, he brushed a memorial wreath on a flimsy wire tripod. The wreath rocked, and he steadied it. When he saw the giver's card nestled in the arrangement's foliage, he yanked his hand away as if the flowers had burned him.

"This — this comes from the widow Sermak?"

I had taken no particular note of the flowers, assuming they all came from friends or distant family. The vaguely familiar Sermak name troubled me. I plucked the card from the extravagant display and read it aloud:

"*Evelyn Sermak.* I should know that name. Oh, yes, wasn't her husband Thaddeus Sermak?"

"Yes. Very much a factor in your father's life when you were only eight years old or so. Skipper and I had business dealings with him. Until he rather abruptly broke them off."

I had a dim picture now of a bluff, ruddy-faced figure, given to Bermuda shorts and loud sports shirts: a lumpish man with a sweet marshmallow center. During a certain period of my boyhood, he had visited Skipper's Keep two or three times a month.

"Whatever happened to Thaddeus anyway?"

"You know. You must know."

"If I ever knew," I said, "I've long since forgotten."

Sweat dotted Gupta's upper lip. "He killed himself. Most unnervingly. Now, please excuse me, Will. I have a slight indisposition."

Suddenly, I had no more interest in the tragedy of Thaddeus

Sermak, the stomach upset of an elderly man, or even my father's funeral. Feeling as if I myself had gone into the coffin, I let the Imp of the Perverse seize me. And so the assembled throng heard the muffled but forceful voice of Dapper O'Dell ring out:

"Hey, folks! Let me outta here!"

Gupta started as if someone had snapped a rubber band on the tip of his nose. Although Tony Bennett did not cease to croon "The Very Thought of You," everyone in the front hall and the parlor fell silent. Their massed attention turned to Gupta and me, the two mourners apparently nearest the voice.

Gupta pointed into the casket with a trembling finger. "Dapper spoke! Just as he did when Skipper so skillfully worked him!"

Incredibly, Dapper spoke again: *"Can the tributes, Satty pal, and yank me outta this overgrown Tonka toy! I ain't ready for the Big Variety Show upstairs. I still got a lotta living to do!"*

No one said a word. Even the background rattling of wine glasses and serving utensils from the kitchen ceased. Gupta looked imploringly at me. His eyebrows formed a bristly V over his black-button eyes.

"Blasphemy!" he finally said. "You make a horrible jest. Horrible!"

I had never seen Gupta so distraught. And instantly, albeit tardily, I regretted my impromptu homage to my late father's calling. He glared at me for a moment longer, then stalked away.

LaRue appeared from the library, but she stayed a good twenty feet away from the trestle supporting the casket.

"Never, Will. Never again."

Did she mean to forbid any repetition of my hoax, or simply to lament Skipper's death-stifled talent, or to deny the possibility of Dapper's animation? Genuinely chastened, I left the parlor.

◆ ◆ ◆

Alan Papini found me twenty minutes later in the kitchen, sitting at the breakfast bar with a saucer of barbecued sausage balls and a stout gin and tonic in a Barney Rubble jelly glass.

"Me, I attribute it to grief," he said.

I had no idea what he meant. I toasted him wordlessly with Mr. Rubble.

"Pulling that voice-throwing trick at your daddy's wake." He popped one of my sausage balls like a cherry, licked his fingers, and leaned toward me on his elbows. "Why should a guy show his grief just like everyone else? Let it come out however it wants to, I say. The real jokers weep and wail but don't feel a thing underneath."

"And you put my mother and sister in that category?"

"No, no, you've got me wrong." Papini pulled his head back a foot or so to observe me better. I thought he suspected in me a stage of drunkenness that had passed into cold-hearted sobriety and also a complete lack of remorse for my prank. Papini knew exactly how far he could push someone, a skill that had allowed him to reach middle age without suffering a crippling assault from an offended agent, manager, or rival.

Squat and pale, with a shock of hair that jagged across his forehead like a crow's wing, he reeked equally of servility and arrogance. *I may not pull down the big bucks your daddy did*, you could almost hear him saying, *but one day, baby, the Powerful Papini is gonna get what's due him!* Few people liked Papini. He went through support personnel faster than Ike Turner and James Brown put together. He had married and divorced four times, and no one ever blamed the wives.

Fortunately, Papini had one reliable boon companion: a gnomish dummy named Otto. A grotesque ripoff of the saintly Yoda of *Star Wars* fame, Otto specialized in belches, sneezes, prolonged flatulence, and horrified gulps. This repertoire of noises composed nearly Papini's entire gift for humor. Consequently, he worked a lot of truck-stop roadhouses, under-twelve birthday parties, and wardheeler-level political events. Generally, he made Otto represent the antagonist of choice: state cop, teacher, or rival politician. Skipper had always claimed that the awful pun Papini inevitably trotted out — "So, Otto, tell me: do you believe in Otto-eroticism?" — actually reflected his masturbatory relationship with his dummy.

"You have your daddy's talent," Papini said mollifyingly. "Not many guys can do the old muffled voice the way you did."

"Thanks. Skipper drilled it into me with the flat side of a hairbrush."

"'Course, it would've gone over better if you'd bumped the casket and dropped the lid, like. Gotta have what the marks see match what they hear, right? Take my shtick. Sometimes I bring a little fake fridge onstage for Otto to raid. He gets stuck in there, wiggling his butt, and I do these great muffled grunts and cries for help. You've seen it, right?"

"Oh, absolutely. Hilarious stuff." Papini had done his refrigerator bit at the Gag Reflex in '90, shortly after the club opened, and, according to Skipper, the raw recruits that night had gone bonkers over Otto.

"Wouldn't you like to resurrect your daddy's act, boy? Make Dapper come alive again?"

"What are you talking about?"

"Simple business sense. You inherited your old man's skills — I've seen that much. And the dummies rightfully belong to you. Surely you've thought about it before."

"Never."

"Oh, don't shuck me, son. Hell, you've got a ready-made audience! Just think of the billing. 'William Keats and Dapper O'Dell! Fresh from a Sold-Out Performance at the Springer Opera House and a Tour of the Major Gulf Coast Resorts!'"

"That's a mighty big marquee. Get real, Papini."

He studied me. "What's stuck in your craw, Will? You resent ventriloquism that much? You must practice now and again, to use it that fucking quick."

"I hate the sleazy lizards who make all vents look like immature con artists. And, sure, of course I practice."

"Terrific! How? Where? Just for friends? It ain't such a big leap to the stage."

"Papini, what do you really want?"

"Do you guys really plan to put Dapper in the ground with Skipper?"

"It's in the will. LaRue and Kelli and I have our hands tied."

"Man, what a waste! Dapper, he's a classic, a genuine Blitch. Don't you realize that Dennis Blitch made only a few dozen figures? And back in '85, a shed in Tennessee burned down with ten Blitches inside. Hell, you may as well bury a bag of money with your father."

"His dummy, Papini. His money. His decision."

"Couldn't you and LaRue get together and talk this over? If you and me can swing a deal — "

I set my drink down. "Say what?"

"I want to buy Dapper. I'll give you five thousand. Look, I've got my checkbook right here with me."

"He'd fetch twice that at an auction."

"Maybe. Maybe not. But he won't fetch a flattened red cent if you all close the lid on him and lower him six feet under."

Tony Bennett had given way to Abbey Lincoln. The bluesy lyrics of her "Hey, Lordy Mama" made infinitely more sense to me than did this conversation with Papini. Our talk of buying and selling a creature with a name and a past and a character made me suddenly feel like a slave trader.

As weary as I had ever felt, I said, "Why don't you talk to LaRue?"

"Hey, I already tried. She ran me off soon as I mentioned Dapper. Wouldn't even hear me out."

"Do you often try to transact business at people's funeral vigils?"

Papini grinned. "'Bout as often as you throw your voice into your daddy's casket, son."

"Papini?"

"Yeah?"

"Go easy, okay? I can't handle any more of this."

"Listen, I'll make you a deal on all of 'em. Simon, Letitia, that goddamn duck, Quacker or whatever you call 'im — "

I finished my drink. The only way to end this discussion was to rejoin the crowd. Sufficently fortified to mingle again, I stood up to go.

"Will, wait! Dapper — "

"Dapper, Dapper, Dapper! You sound like a teenaged girl with her first boyfriend. Don't you love Otto anymore?"

"Why, sure. Of course." Then, lowering his voice, Papini said, "But Otto's got no class."

CHAPTER 6

he next day at the Smittinger-Alewine chapel, I saw many of the people who had attended the informal wake at Skipper's Keep. LaRue, Kelli, and I — along with "Aunt" Denise and "Uncle" Burling — occupied special pews in a privacy niche near the altar and perpendicular to the rest of the seating. We had a bumper-on view of the stretch-limo casket — its convertible lid racked beneath the gurney — and a sidelong view of the clergyman who would conduct the services. An organ played popular secular music: "The Wind Beneath My Wings," "From a Distance," soundtrack excerpts from the film *Magic*. Mourners who had not come on Saturday, or who wanted a final meditative look, filed up one aisle past Skipper Keats and Dapper O'Dell, a team for eternity, and then back down the far aisle.

LaRue stared straight ahead, Kelli wept, and I felt little more than the gloved hand of Adrienne Owsley periodically squeezing my bare and icy one. Her daughter, Olivia, perched ramrod-straight to Adrienne's right, a tiara of cloth daisies on her head. The child's black patent-leather shoes and smocked white dress, along with her mother's navy-blue blouse and skirt, contrasted with the beige and black worn by many of the other attendees, who suggested a convocation of drab Dobermans.

Alan Papini paused beside the casket, touched his lips showily, and shook his head. Estelle Durand gracefully curtsied. Satish Gupta, wifeless again today, strode past as if propelled by an airport's moving sidewalk, scarcely even turning his head. Mayor Emory Williams stopped and, as reverently as possible, posed for a photograph.

The ventriloquist Ronn Lucas, carrying his trademark figure Buffalo Billy, halted to allow Billy a final decorous glance at his peer, then walked on with a peculiarly affecting dignity. Several other vents with their signature pals of plastic, wood, or cloth followed Lucas's example, again with blessedly more solemnity than one would have expected. Their gestures of respect made me feel something — loss or gratitude or confusion, or an unsettling mixture of all these emotions. Not even the appearance of a local comedian who had frequently ridiculed Skipper's various television ads diminished the impact of the parade of vents.

Next to bid farewell came Myra Doone, Maj. Gen. Hiram Householder, Mayor Bill Campbell of Atlanta, Mr. and Mrs. Ted Turner, and, propelling himself in his wheelchair, the junior senator from Georgia, Max Cleland. Cleland could not see into the casket but nonetheless paused and briefly inclined his head.

Adrienne favored me with a particularly intense squeeze. "You okay?"

"Yes. Because you're here."

The pastor, a distinguished-looking man of Skipper's age, did the obligatory prelims in a voice like the down on an electric blanket. Nondenominational comfort, New Testament assurance. His words had a rote quality that made my stomach clench, but his face shone with honest-to-God emotion, an unexpected radiance. My father's death had actually moved this man!

I relaxed a little when the pastor began talking about the laughter that Skipper had brought to so many, his countless humanitarian activities, the charities to which he had contributed without benefit of publicity. Like Kelli, this man believed — earnestly believed — that our father fell only a small step short of sainthood.

Myra Doone, an early headliner at the Gag Reflex and nowadays a regular on talk shows and the annual Comic Relief broadcast, delivered the principal eulogy. Myra had a body like an unselfconscious Egyptian belly dancer and a face like a conniving squirrel's. Onstage, her arms and hips always moved languidly, but her eyes would flash, her nose twitch, and her lips wriggle like galvanized eels. Today, she initially put a tourniquet on these mannerisms, but old habits prevailed as her talk progressed. However, the sincerity of her words disarmed sanctimonious nitpickers who otherwise would have found her ill-bred or profane.

Nor did she deploy only solemn phrases. As her tribute delved into Skipper's past stunts and classic choice bits, the chapel filled with laughter — hoots even. Handkerchiefs and facial tissues dabbed at tear-filled eyes and runny noses. Even LaRue ended up laughing, perhaps hardest of all, when Myra recounted Skipper's apocryphal insistence on bringing Dapper into their honeymoon bed. People applauded when Myra finished, and afterward everyone praised her honesty, wit, and good taste.

One her way back down to her front-row seat, Myra halted. "Anyone have anything to add?" she asked.

The invitation clearly surprised or daunted Skipper's mourners, me not the least. But then, tentatively, I raised my hand.

Myra saw me. "All right, Will. Come on up."

"Please, Will," Kelli said. "Let the others do the eulogizing. Don't make this harder on yourself than it already is."

Adrienne whispered, "Will, you don't have to do this. No one expects it."

"Oh, they expect it," Kelli countered. "But they can't know exactly what they're gonna get!"

I nodded solemnly at my sister, released Adrienne's hand, and climbed to the lectern. A black-and-beige peat bog of expectant faces undulated away from me, so many faces that my nerve almost failed. I gripped the edges of the lectern and leaned forward into the microphone, slugs of sweat already crawling their way down my flanks.

"You've all heard at one time or another what I want to say. But it still bears repeating, I think." I had everyone's attention, from Senator Cleland's to Eula Cole's, and now had only to keep it. "We all live dismayingly brief and unremarkable lives. In terms of either time or space, our lives scarcely even scrape the universe. A fading thumbprint on a cold windowpane has an equivalent duration and beauty, if you adopt God's viewpoint. Even so, no one with eyes or a heart can deny the importance of any single human life, however short."

The expressions of willing engagement on the faces of my listeners still held. So far so good. But I would have to hurry or risk losing them.

"I know you've heard this analogy before. Please hear it again: From one high window, out of absolute darkness, a colorful bird flies into a banquet hall. Below, the human guests feast and revel. In only a moment the bird wings out the far window, back into darkness. If any of the feasters notice, they spend no more than a few seconds considering the bird's plight. An exceptional person or two might try to guess what lies beyond the torch-lit gaiety of the banquet hall.

"A warm ocean, where we melt and mix with the Absolute, maybe. Or a city. Or an entire kingdom of angels and jaguars and radiant healing swords."

I glanced sidelong into the privacy niche. Kelli had slumped down coltishly; she had her face in her hands, her fingers splayed like claws. LaRue sat rigid and unamused. Adrienne, bless her, smiled at me. Out in the mass of mourners, a few people scowled or lapsed into chin-on-chest reverie. If nothing else, I thought distractedly, the novelty of Skipper Keats's son trying out his sophomoric allegorizing at a funeral should have entertained them.

Against my better judgment, I persisted: "And if the bird should fall dead within the hall? Some of the feasters might wrap its corpse in a napkin and surround it with gemstones. A poet might compose an ode in its honor. More than likely, no one would mention the mites in its feathers, or its birdy odor, or the sums of laundry that it had soiled."

Kelli had straightened, folding her arms tightly over her breasts. She may have expected the worst from me, but I hoped that the conclusion I had in mind would betray that expectation and possibly even cheer her.

"Guess what my father would have said about this turn of events, the inevitable human tendency to gloss over the worst? Any idea? Well, let me rephrase the question: What would *Dapper O'Dell* have said?"

The mourners, fascinated again and almost forgiving of my ramble, gaped cluelessly. Then came a female voice, half-disbelieving, half-scolding, with some of Dapper's legendary wiseguy scorn in it.

"*Would it kill you to smile?*"

Kelli stood clutching the pew, one hand self-supportively at her breastbone. Thank God she had played Abbott to my Costello!

"Right," I said. "The only proper response."

Spontaneously, en masse, the mourners applauded. I returned to my place between Kelli and Adrienne as this applause grew louder and more insistent, filling the chapel.

The pastor, resuming his place beside the casket, offered me a smile. Then, after his benediction, three Smittinger-Alewine employees came down front and quickly and neatly fitted the casket's top. LaRue wept, as she had early on Friday morning, and the organist, shielded from our view, played "Unchained Melody" as a recessional.

There were six pallbearers. Gupta, of course. Tom Johnson, Burling Whickerbill, Roger Durand (Estelle's husband), Marc Alsogroom, and, a surprise when first announced, Papini. With the help of the mortuary staff, they jockeyed the gurney out of the chapel and slid the embarrassing limousine casket into a long silver-grey hearse.

◆ ◆ ◆

Entombment occured approximately an hour later in the principal and oldest cemetery in Mountboro. Not unexpectedly, many of those who had attended the chapel service bade us Godspeed and left. Gratifyingly, many other folks joined our funeral procession north, past blossoming dogwoods, the ruins of wild azaleas, and the leafy runners of rejuvenating kudzu vines.

In Zalmon, more than halfway to the cemetery, a sudden change in a traffic light halted the family's limo at an intersection. The hearse drove on without us. A hill and a curve almost immediately eclipsed it from view.

"How come he's not pulling over?" Kelli asked.

It did seem odd. "Don't know, Sis."

By the time the light turned green, the hearse had smartly outdistanced us. We did not see it again until descending the steep

grade near the Crestview Tavern. By then, two other nonpartici-
pant vehicles had intervened. Our driver touched the gas more
determinedly and closed the gap between us and the strange cars,
both of which soon turned off. A mile south of Mountboro, the
hearse driver finally slowed to pick us up again. With due formality, the lengthy train of late-model cars, headlamps ablaze, passed
into town, turned right across the railroad tracks, and entered the
freshly mown grounds of the old Mountboro cemetery.

Shortly thereafter, we shelved Skipper like an old joke book.
He went into an upper-level cabinet in the ivy-filigreed mausoleum
between his parents, Clayton and Cerell Keats, and a great-uncle
and great-aunt, Spurgeon and Molly Keats. Eventually LaRue
would join Skipper in the same double-deep crypt. Kelli and I
rated a lower-level berth, should we ever choose to use it.

After the ceremony the pallbearers filed under the green awning
to offer condolences. Satish Gupta pecked LaRue on each cheek like
a grouse performing a courtship ritual. Tom Johnson, a black comedian who had once sung gospel, held LaRue's hands and, in a clear
baritone, carved out three chilling stanzas of "Amazing Grace."
Roger Durand whispered something to my mother. Her attorneys
embraced her. Papini shuffled up, started to speak, thought better of
it. His earlier tears had left dried salt trails on his cheeks.

Afterward, both Adrienne and my mother encouraged me to
return to Columbus to spend the night. Kelli, staring at the mausoleum, wept silently.

"No, that's all right. I'm a big boy, I don't mind spending the
night alone."

Actually, I wanted to spend all the intervening hours until morning with Adrienne, and Adrienne alone. But we had a long-stand-
ing agreement that I would not overnight at her place in
Tocqueville, out of respect for Olivia. Olivia deserved such regard,
but the arrangement was still, at times, both awkward and painful.

The cemetery had now virtually cleared. Dusk had crept in.
Soon, only the novel glare of the comet would light the polished
tombstones and the shabby nineteenth-century obelisks. Not far
from the mausoleum stood a headless stone angel.

Adrienne again encouraged me to go home with LaRue and

Kelli. I snapped something about needing nothing but a sandwich and ten hours of sleep, then apologized for my abruptness. LaRue and Kelli each hugged me goodbye, and the mortuary driver took them home in the boatlike Cadillac. Adrienne had driven her own car from the memorial service, not wanting to subject Olivia to our somber company in the limo.

A flicker in a sweetgum tree drilled through bark in search of insects. The scent of late verbena drifted by. Only some workers busy dismantling the awning remained to keep Adrienne, Olivia, and me company.

"Don't go in to work tomorrow," Adrienne said.

"Doesn't he have to make money?" asked Olivia.

"Not our Will, sweety. Money doesn't matter to him."

"I'm a holy man. I store up my treasures above."

Adrienne kissed me lightly. "I hope you haven't renounced all the attractions of this world."

"No chance of that, ma'am."

"Listen, Will, I mean it. Stay home. Take some time to — "

"To what? Recuperate? Pull myself together?"

"No. To fall apart. To grieve."

"No can do. Oakwood Elementary needs me. Only the stern hand of Captain William Keats keeps that ramshackle institution afloat. With its all-female crew, the place daily threatens to sink in a sea of PMS."

Adrienne waved her hand at the Smittinger-Alewine workers. "Should I give those guys another dead man to deal with?"

"Right. Kill me to keep me from suffering. There's a thought."

Bored with our banter, Olivia wandered away. She squatted next to an eroded gravestone, plucked a dandelion's yellow flower, and pressed it experimentally to the back of her hand.

"Treat yourself kindly, Will." Even as she spoke, Adrienne almost obsessively watched Olivia. "Take some time to meditate — "

I began to tighten up. "Work suits me better."

Realizing I was unswayable, Adrienne put her arms around me and gave me a soulful kiss. But even as we kissed, she manuevered to keep Olivia in view, as if afraid the grave would open and swallow her.

CHAPTER 7

My house lay less than four blocks from the cemetery. Alsogroom's wife had parked my Saturn in my driveway and then ridden to the entombment with her husband. As soon as Adrienne had driven off, I put my hands in my pockets and started to walk home.

By the iron gate, massive pecan trees dropped ragged curtains of shade. My eyes struggled to adjust to the shifting dimness. So I did not see a figure emerge from the lee of a time-blasted limestone angel, but instead felt a finger poke me unexpectedly in the lower back.

"Jesus!" I said.

"No, Will, just one of his cornpone footsoldiers."

I recognized the distinctive drawl of Hutchinson Payne, long the pastor of Mountboro's First Baptist Church. My heart throttled back down to a careening gallop.

"Are *you* trying to kill me too, Hutch?"

The rangy prelate chuckled. "Who else wants you dead?"

"Only my girlfriend. She seems to think death might give me some relief."

"Maybe. Maybe not."

I resumed walking. Hutchinson fell in beside me.

"Sorry about spooking you, Will. After your father's ceremony, I ambled over here to visit Lorette. Never stopped to think you might not see me."

Lorette, Hutch's first and only wife, had died about seven years ago of an arterial embolism. I had met her once or twice but barely remembered her. I estimated Hutch's age at little more than forty and wondered why he had never remarried. In a town as small as Mountboro, with a dearth of bachelors and an abundance of widows, no one could account for Hutch's extended eligibility without citing his devotion to Lorette's memory.

Despite my nearly unbroken record of weekly absences from either of Mountboro's two principal churches, on two or three occasions I had heard Hutch preach. No standard-issue homilies, his sermons glowed with the offbeat insights of a bucolic philosopher. In fact, he seemed less an authority figure than a fishing buddy. I hardly minded his company.

"Your father had a terrific talent, Will. It hurts to have lost him."

We were walking in the road proper. Mountboro has few sidewalks outside the business district. Hutch's church, a sprawling, brick-edged silhouette, lay just ahead of us, another squad of pecan trees and sweetgums standing sentinel around it.

"You were at the funeral too, weren't you? What did you think of my off-the-cuff eulogy? Was it too flip? Did I offend you or dishonor Skipper?"

"Hell, Will, I've heard worse lots of times from myself! You had something on your heart and you spoke it. A little humor's never amiss either. Even in the face of death. No, make that *especially* in the face of death."

We had stopped at a side door to Hutch's church. The sky straight ahead, above the oaks, elms, and sycamores, had begun to glow a medium-rare pink. An eighteen-wheeler growled by on Highway 27.

"Well, thanks, Hutch. I appreciate your faith."

"My faith in you, or in the Lord?"

"Both, I guess."

"Fair enough. Now let me ask you a question, Will. Do you think you'll be able to reach any peace with yourself, in the light of your father's death?"

"That's a tough one, Hutch. What if I answer you in a few months?"

He lifted a hand in a gesture of blessing. "Granted. As long as you don't forget you're carrying the question. Now, some advice.

Head straight home, take a warm bath, drink a hot toddy. And call me if you need to talk to someone."

Spontaneously, he stepped forward and hugged me. I hugged him back.

Then I walked on alone.

◆ ◆ ◆

The single-story house I rented from my parents for a nominal three hundred dollars a month loomed ahead. It had a lopsided screened-in wraparound porch, a drafty living room and three bedrooms up front, and an out-of-kilter kitchen and dining room on a step-down in the rear. Two large magnolia trees shaded the front walk. Whatever the season, they always dropped dismaying quantities of organic trash: waxy leaves, curling petals, prickly seed cones, crimson seeds. I could have spent an hour or two in the yard every day, raking up and disposing of all the debris. I loved those magnolias anyway, and the root-tangled plots around them, and the squirrel-plagued house that had for so many years sheltered my paternal grandparents.

Taking both Adrienne's and Hutch's advice, I made myself a gin and tonic, my first drink since my improvident binge at the wake. I took it into the study, a converted bedroom, and exhaled heavily. (My real bedroom was across the hall, the smallest and easiest to heat of the three rooms up front.) After briefly perusing my CD collection, I popped a disc into the player.

Gorecki's *Symphony No. 3* poured forth, the London Sinfonietta's recording. Dawn Upshaw's soprano, here the voice of universal bereavement, filled me with a bittersweet sense of lamentation. Skipper, who had tolerated only lounge jazz and forties-style crooners, would have scoffed at this highbrow self-indulgence. I toasted him anyway, only half sardonically, and lowered myself into a bargain-basement lounger.

As a kid in the Keep, I would often go downstairs to breakfast to find Skipper sitting at the table with Dapper O'Dell in his lap. This never struck me as peculiar. Skipper made his living — *our* living — with my wooden brother, who even *looked* more like my father than I did. How could I begrudge Dapper his place? Besides, without Dapper, who would I have talked to? While Skipper ate his poached eggs and white toast and drank his decaffeinated coffee onehandedly, Dapper pivoted this way and that on Skipper's left knee, kibitzing everything:

"Welcome to LaRue's Greasy Spoon, kid!" he would pipe on my sleepy arrival. "Hey, Eula, more java here for the boss! Say, boy, did I hear you still up and about at eleven? Good show, I guess. That Emma Peel is some babe, isn't she? But if you don't get your sleep, how will you grow? Or does Mrs. Peel help you grow, where we all know it counts?"

I blushed and fidgeted. But secretly, in a masochistic way, I enjoyed Dapper's bawdy talk. Any attention, however derisive, meant I existed. As I ate, Dapper cracked wise about my sleeping habits, my unfashionable clothes, my fondness for bad television, the alleged inadequacies of my developing body, the way LaRue coddled me, and the mental shortcomings I shared with the Scarecrow of Oz. While Skipper maintained a seemingly disinterested silence, his protégé tore me to pieces.

A smarter, more assertive kid would have refused to engage him, would have gone after Dapper's motivating force: Skipper, my father. But I always debated or talked with Dapper alone, holding delicately poised in my consciousness the paradoxical thesis that Dapper both did and did not speak for himself.

Gorecki's *Third* concluded, and I pushed a button to have it repeat. I finished my drink and ached transcendentally with the music. Listening to it again, I drifted off and slept dreamlessly until 2:17 A.M.

I awoke stiff and disoriented, night sweats drenching my body. A terrible fever ravened in me. I imagined murderers lurking outside my window. Panic rose in me like scalding chyle. The red light on the CD player still burned. I turned the box off and pushed against my lower abdomen with my hands. My breath ratcheted like a stripped transmission. If not my dreams, what else could have triggered this reaction?

Sit down again, I told myself. But somewhere else.

Turning on lights as I went — my mother's son — I stumbled

into the kitchen. I grabbed an ancient three-legged stool which Skipper had supposedly used in his first performance with Dapper in Mountboro, and perched on it directly under the high, insect-filled glass shade overhead. My right leg jounced like a dreaming hound's. A vision of Adrienne came suddenly to mind. With her stood an able professor from my undergraduate days, Stephen Bailey, the calmest teacher I had ever known, and a role model for my own interactions with kids.

Breathe, Adrienne and Professor Bailey told me. *Just watch your breaths come and go.*

Feet firmly planted on the linoleum, hands loose in my lap, I obeyed this advice and rode my breaths to a taut quietude. My panic ebbed, receding incrementally down the soiled beach of my mind. Then I clearly heard a different voice, as if someone had cruelly miked and amplified it:

Hey, get me outta here!

Dapper sounded frantic, stricken with real fear. It hit me then that my grief encompassed not only Skipper, but also the impertinent dummy that Skipper had taken "alive" into the tomb with him. From my birth until this very afternoon, Dapper had played the role of my resiliently spiteful older brother. A despicable little thorn of a sibling, but nonetheless a sibling to grieve over.

Hey, Will-yuuum, get me outta here!

Not *let*, but *get*. The choice of imperatives signified. I had to act, to do something resourceful and effective. Without considering the legality or propriety of what I planned, I realized that I had to return to the cemetery and rescue Dapper from his premature burial. My father had had no right to immure Dapper. The dummy still lived. He had just spoken to me.

Impulsively, I telephoned a friend of mine, J.W. Young, whom I hadn't seen in much too long. J.W. struck me as the only person in town who might fall in step with the crazy mission I had in mind.

He answered after seven rings. "If you've dialed a wrong number, don't tell me your name. Sure as God made little green apples I'll track you down and rip your lungs out. And if you're a misguided friend of mine who's dialed this number on lame brain purpose, God help you anyhow."

"J.W., it's Will Keats."

"Good Lord! William Bumble-ass Keats! I didn't think your homeroom teacher let you stay up this late. Do you know it's after two?"

"Yes."

"Then paint me green and call me Kermit. Obviously miracles will never cease. What can I do you for, buddy?"

"J.W., how would you like to help me rob a tomb?"

CHAPTER 8

J.W. Young, a bunch-muscled ex-Golden Gloves middleweight who in the ring had worn olive-drab shorts in tribute to his short-lived army career, stood just shy of six feet tall and had a broad handsome face with disheveled hair as dark and glossy as a Cherokee warrior's. His rascally blue eyes militated against the notion that any Native American blood traveled his veins, however, and despite or because of a truly cunning intellect, he enjoyed passing himself off as a dyed-in-the-cotton Good Ol' Boy. A year younger than me, he had an indulgent and pretty wife named — legally, I think — Babe; whatever the case, I had never heard J.W. call her by any other name.

At any point in time, J.W. held down four or five jobs simultaneously. He operated heavy construction equipment, pressure-washed fungus-blackened houses and their oil-stained driveways, trimmed trees, chainsawed firewood, and insulated attics. With the switch of a hat, he acted as carpenter, plumber, bricklayer, tile-setter, electrician, blacksmith, or roofer. He did all these jobs better than passably and in fact with finesse.

And, once upon a time, he had been the maintenance man and groundskeeper at the Mountboro Cemetery.

A brief silence at the other end of the line. Then J.W. said, "On a regular night, Will, no proposition would intrigue me more. But right now Babe and me are pretty much ready for the grave ourselves. We flew down to the Keys on Thursday and just got back around ten. I was lucky enough to pick up a sunburn that makes me look like a boiled crayfish and is giving me the shivers. Just managed to get to sleep, in fact."

J.W. had earned his pilot's license in his own craft, a well-maintained two-seater manufactured in the early 1950s. He and Babe frequently took spontaneous trips to the Gulf Coast, North Carolina, and other destinations around the compass. Assuming that he piloted the same way he drove — one-handed, mouth on fast-forward, wild to be wreckage forever — I had tactfully declined several invitations to accompany him in Babe's place on these wild-hair missions. Nor was I the only friend who had advised Babe, now pregnant with a potential J.W. Junior, to keep her feet firmly planted on the ground during her term. Modern medicine could work wonders, but equipping fetuses with miniature parachutes did not yet number among its achievements.

I heard J.W. take a drink of something. He smacked his lips gleefully, then belched. "Is this just any old tomb, Will, or a special one?"

I told him about my father's death and the clause that had taken Dapper along with Skipper on that eternal ride. "And now, J.W., Dapper wants out."

Another silence. "Will, I'm damn sorry you've lost your old man so unexpectedly. I can understand how such a happening might drive you 'round the bend. I just wish you had shared your total mental collapse with somebody else."

"J.W., Dapper wants — "

"Dapper don't *want* anything, you idiot! No more than a freakin' butcher block does!"

"He talked to me, J.W. Several times. He said, 'Hey, William, get me outta here.'"

"Ventriloquists' dummies always say that. They have to, it's written into their contracts."

I tried another angle. "Say it was only a dream. Don't dreams have meanings of their own? Do you want me just to ignore this? I thought you told me once I could count on your help."

A protracted, melodramatic sigh gusted over the wires into my ear. "Damn! That's right, appeal to my highly developed sense of ethics. Never mind that Babe's likely to kill me. Okay, you win. Let's crack that sucker!"

"Meet you there in fifteen minutes."

"Make it half an hour. I got to slather up with Noxema."

◆ ◆ ◆

The night air held a miasmic dampness and chill. I had walked to the cemetery, cautiously employing a hand-shaded flashlight to get me safely to the mausoleum. Standing now on the patiolike apron in front of the crypt, I shivered. Bedraggled floral arrangements — including the mysterious one sent by Mrs. Sermak, I assumed — exuded the vinegary smell of incipient decay.

I had expected J.W. to arrive stealthily, so I gawked like a yokel at the huffing, unlighted front-end loader that bounced into the cemetery. Behind its upraised bucket, J.W. flashed me a dim and ghostly grin.

"Luckily for you, Keats, I never throw away a key. The cemetery garage was locked up tight."

"Do we really need this monster?"

"You know what's involved here, Keats? Plain old muscle ain't gonna cut it. Now, first thing is, get those malodorous flowers out of my way."

I carried all the arrangements to one end of the stone apron, and J.W. edged his machine closer.

"Has the knothead in there called you again?"

"No."

"But you still want to get him out?"

"Yes."

Upon my reply, J.W. activated the headlamps, pinioning me in their glare and blinding me. Their brilliance seemed to mark a point of no return. I heard him leap down.

"Doing it this way ain't legal, my friend. But you knew that, right? Ordinarily, you get a disinternment permit signed by every petty little bureaucrat and his aunt and likewise a reinternment permit while you're at it."

"I don't have that kind of time."

"You changed from an underpaid counselor to a white-shoe lawyer maybe, son? We're only talking a day, tops."

"I need to go to work tomorrow, and Dapper wants out *now*. Besides, nobody needs to know about this but you and me."

"It's your funeral, Keats. In a manner of speaking. Anyway, I only ask one favor. When they haul you up in front of Judge Peddicord, try to keep my name out of it."

"Right."

J.W. leaned into the grumbling machine and hefted out a tool-box and sledgehammer. The toolbox rattled and clunked as J.W. set it down. Then he handed me the hammer.

"What's this for?" I inanely asked.

"We've got to get the inscription plate on your daddy's tomb off. That's the first step. I figured maybe you wouldn't want to make this look so much like an inside job. You smash the plate to pieces, it looks like some clumsy crook did it."

I realized now that I had failed to picture accurately the process of unearthing my father, had failed to picture it at all. In my feverish singlemindedness, I had leapt over all the grimy real-life scut work. I looked at the harshly lit granite panel with Skipper's birth and death dates on it. Already the latter date had fled into unrecapturable territory. The hammer slipped from my sweaty grip and clunked to the pavement. J.W. scooped it up and stowed it onboard the loader.

"Okay, that just makes it easier. More traceable, but easier."

"No," I said. "I've changed my mind — "

J.W. ignored me. He bent and rummaged in the toolbox, coming up with a device like a pronged screwdriver.

From the front of the vertical, eye-level plate protruded a bronze knob. J.W. inserted the pronged tool in notches inside this knob. With deft motions, he soon had the whole panel off. He set it down.

A stream of small, glittery objects rolled out of the crypt and bounced away. "BBs," J.W. said. "They throw a couple of hand-fuls in before the family gets here. Makes it easier to slide the coffin in. Okay now, Will — reach in and yank your daddy out."

"I . . . I can't."

"He ain't gonna bite."

"No, it's not that. I don't think I'm strong enough. Skipper weighed at least one-eighty, and the casket — "

"Hell, I'll bet back in high school you were always the last one up the rope. All right, but all this is gonna cost you something extra. You might have to take a little old plane ride with me."

J.W. reached in with both hands and pulled my father's car casket to the lip of the vault. Its movement made an ear-assaulting screaking-and-crunching sound. More BBs cascaded out.

"Watch your step, Keats. I don't want to have to haul two stiffs out of here."

"What next?"

J.W. yanked the casket a foot or so out of the vault. Again, that insupportable screaking. Satisfied, he remounted the front-end loader. Gunning it, he swung around ninety degrees and, with a dozen patient movements, eventually positioned the elevated scoop just below the casket, ready to receive its full weight.

"Pull it on out, Will. All the way."

Expecting the entire three-car Mountboro police force to descend upon us instantly, I delivered Skipper out of the crypt and into this world once more. Godawful metallic caterwauling accompanied his rebirth, as the BBs continued to spill.

When J.W. got his first good look at the customized coffin, he whistled. "Always did say your daddy had style, Will."

"So did Liberace. Can you lower the scoop without dropping the box?"

"Sure."

When the bucket reached the ground, the casket rested at knee level. Wishing this whole mad affair over, I impulsively pushed at the coffin's top. It wouldn't budge.

J.W. reappeared at my side. In his hands he held an assortment of odd devices.

"You won't get too far that way, Will. You need the right crank. Breaks the gasket seal and frees the lid. Now, I got cranks here for Batesville, York, Aurora, Toccoa lids, and a dozen others. But not necessarily for a Caddy or Lincoln Continental."

"Meaning what?"

"Either you force yourself to use the sledgehammer, or I fire up my chainsaw."

"Are you serious?"

"Mostly. But maybe we're jumping the gun — "

While I held my breath, J.W. tried various cranks. With the next-to-last one, he grunted appreciatively. "Batesville. Your daddy never settled for second-best."

There were two latches at either end of the miniature car. It took only seconds to break the casket seal.

A powerful odor of lilacs, shoe polish, and formaldehyde escaped. Both J.W. and I instinctively recoiled from it. Neither of us made a move to slide the lid off. As if stalling, J.W. began to instruct me in the finer points of entombment.

"We were damn lucky, son. If this weren't a Sunday, things would've been a sight harder."

"What do you mean?"

"The regular weekday help would've come in right after the words of comfort and bricked your daddy's coffin into place behind the inscription panel. Then they'd've sealed the brick barricade with caulk or cement. We'd've busted a gut just to get to the point we're at."

"So I got lucky?"

"Well, maybe lucky is the wrong word. Anyhow, William, it's your show from here on out." Stepping back from the casket, J.W. gestured me toward it.

I hesitated a moment and then, steeling myself, pushed the remarkably lightweight lid off the casket. The scent of formaldehyde assaulted me again, more powerfully than before, and Skipper's body had an eerily vampiric look. Both J.W. and I noticed immediately that Dapper had vanished from the crook of my father's arm.

"Damn!" said J.W. "Guess the little knothead decided not to wait for you. You sure he even started out on this trip?"

Like a dummy deprived of its handler, I could not say a word. Gripping the edge of the casket, I did manage a bewildered nod.

"Well, however the little Houdini escaped, we're not going to catch him standing here and gawping. Let's get busy."

Without speaking, we performed the whole crypt-robbing procedure in reverse. J.W. had even brought a small jar of BBs to replace those we had lost. They eased the coffin's reinsertion but still made so much noise that the vault seemed to contain a pack of joyless ghosts, who ranted mechanically as we strained and shoved.

CHAPTER 9

J.W. returned to Babe and I to the intermittent gnawing and scampering of my attic-pent squirrels. Their joist-chewing and insulation-strafing kept me awake, but I couldn't have slept anyway.

Someone had stolen my brother.

A person or persons unknown had liberated Dapper O'Dell from my father's posthumous embrace. Either that, or a highly exclusive Rapture, with bodily resurrection for wooden figures only, had whirled him onstage in vaudeville heaven.

So much for my extrasensory perceptions. I had psychically heard Dapper call out for release, or thought I had. But in fact the cunning chip-block had already escaped, although obviously not without help. Sometime between the closing of the casket at the Smittinger-Alewine chapel and the arrival of my father's hearse in the Mountboro cemetery, someone had snatched Dapper. A dummynapping. Did that even qualify as a crime?

Absolutely. Theft, and not the petty sort either. The world contained only so many bona fide Dennis Blitch ventriloquist's figures, each one of which had Stradivarius status among devotees. Given that Blitch himself had died in the 1960s and that many of his figures had gone into museums or the private sacristies of wealthy collectors, Dapper O'Dell probably represented the most famously valuable Blitch manikin at large. And now, regrettably, Dapper's ritual entombment had so addled at least one collector that he or she had pulled off a pretty slick heist.

Until twenty minutes before dawn, I ran permutations of motives and suspects through my sleep-deprived brain, hoping that one pairing would produce the culprit. Almost everyone I knew loomed as a suspect. Burling Whickerbill and his associates. Denise Shurett. Satish Gupta. Myra Doone. Pablo Cabriales. Dr. Sammons. Alan Papini. Estelle Durand. Could I even exclude LaRue? She had taken Dapper to bed with her as a surrogate for her dead husband, and she treasured each of his other dummies, albeit none so much as she did Dapper. Still, I didn't think she would disregard my father's final wishes simply to spare one expensive puppet from a bizarre entombment. On the other hand, ever since Kelli's birth, LaRue had grown torturously more mysterious to me.

Beyond friends and family lurked other menacing figures. Greedy collectors. Crazed fans (for in the mid-1970s a small organization of devotees had spontaneously assembled around Skipper, the Dapper O'Dell International Fan Club; I believed that now they even sponsored a Web page devoted to my father). Money-hungry GIs from Fort Benning. And those were the *likely* culprits. Some small chance existed that I could not even imagine the identity of the real perpetrator.

I finally abandoned the whole effort for want of hard information and hit the shower for a wake-up jolt. Then, wearing nothing but flip-flops, I shaved my chapfallen face. My complexion resembled a smoked marbled ham. By chance, I assembled an outfit boasting two matching socks and a tie that didn't clash too loudly with its accompanying shirt.

No one at Oakwood really expected me to come in, but I had kids to see, paperwork to file, a DFACS worker to contact. Duty called, in tones simultaneously affording irritation, accomplishment, and anodyne.

I climbed into my Saturn to drive the seventeen bucolic miles north into Speece County. Preoccupied with thoughts of death and theft, I failed to enjoy the usual sights: skittish deer, strutting flocks of wild turkeys, spiderwebbed azaleas, updraft-riding hawks, dozens of well-kept farmsteads. The fog in the pine copses duplicated that in my mind. Only one new thought emerged lucidly from the murk: perhaps no premeditated theft but some sort of logistical mix-up had occured, the fault of

Smittinger-Alewine. Unlikely, but I entertained the possibility long enough to picture Dapper sprawled safely on a divan in one of the funeral home's lounges.

Slowing for a stop sign, I remembered, as if kinetically, the most puzzling aspect of yesterday's cortege: after the red light in Zalmon, that brief period of separation between the hearse and the other vehicles in our procession.

Clearly, the abduction *must* have taken place in that convenient interval. Someone in the hearse had removed Dapper and passed him to a confederate at roadside. Or else the driver had acted alone, hiding Dapper under a seat until, once back in Columbus, he could remove the figure unseen. Both variants looked tenuous and crazy, of course. The first demanded a long concatenation of perfectly timed events, while the second required an untutored driver not only to reckon the value of a hunk of shaped wood but also to risk his job to kidnap it. But what other options existed?

Assuming that one of the versions of this scenario obtained, I next had to ask what the thief or thieves intended to do with Dapper. Fence him? Call LaRue for ransom? Start their own ventriloquistic careers in Gambia or Finland, where Dapper would pass unrecognized? And should I go to the police with my tale and various theories? How could I, without implicating J.W. in the midnight grave-robbing? For the moment, I decided against contacting the authorities.

I wheeled into the school's parking lot and absentmindedly overlapped two adjoining spaces. In every way exhausted, I wondered if I had erred in coming to work. But all doubts blew away when I entered the reassuringly familiar school.

In a waxed-floor corridor flanked by coat lockers and bulletin boards from which hung crayon drawings and photocopied announcements, I nearly bumped into Mrs. Lapierre exiting her office. A big but well-proportioned woman of fifty, our principal wore an ankle-length black-and-white-check skirt and a sweater vest featuring appliqué school buses.

"William!" Having gracefully avoided colliding with me, she pulled me to her in a consoling hug. "You came in!"

Semismothered, I did not point out that she had stated the obvious. "Actually, I had to."

Mrs. Lapierre clucked solicitously. "No, no, this simply won't do. I've a good mind to send you straight home."

I tried to make light of her concern. "Budget crunch, right? The system always dumps its counselors first."

Mrs. Lapierre pushed me out to arm's length. "Why do you say that, William? Have you heard rumors?"

My antennae instantly extended. "No. What rumors are out there to hear?"

She studied me appraisingly, then abruptly changed tacks. "I'm very sorry about your father, William. The loss of such a talent diminishes us all. Douglas" — Mr. Lapierre, her husband — "was heartbroken. He loved Skipper and never understood why the networks refused to give him his own show."

"Skipper could have talked Mr. Lapierre's ear off on that topic. A good thing they never met."

"I'm glad your sense of humor's still intact. But do you really think you belong here today?"

"I'd do myself no favors taking the day off. I have a daunting backlog of referrals and lots of stuff to do."

Stuff to do. The phrase revealed nothing of the true extent of my obligations.

Last week I had met with six emotionally at-risk children in a divorce group. I could have easily rounded up eighteen more for three additional groups. I had reported two instances of physical abuse to the Department of Family and Children Services: a blistered earlobe and a welt-covered lower back. Neither injury had jibed with the kids' affectless, monosyllabic explanations. What else had I struggled with last week? The same recurring menu of mundane tragedies and horrors to which the eleven other elementary school counselors in Speece County — all female, all but one or two dedicated and proficent — had likewise partially hardened themselves.

"I admire your dedication, William. But if I or anyone else on staff can help, let us know. And if you feel you need to leave early, leave."

"Thanks."

She hugged me again, patting my shoulder blade with one hand and my cheek with the other. Counselee instead of counselor, I felt awkward and kiddish myself. As diplomatically as possible, I disengaged and strode away.

In my office — a cinderblock cubicle that was a converted mop closet still redolent of ammonia and Endust — I braced for my first referral with a cup of black coffee from the teacher's lounge. A timid knock announced his arrival.

Shawndrell Tompkins, a second-grader, took a tentative seat in the scoop-shaped plastic chair I had snugged up next to my own. For two weeks after his grandfather's death in March, Shawndrell had stopped talking. He had also reduced his daily food intake to a bowl or two of sugar-coated cereal. Outside school, the grandfather had focused Shawndrell's life. Together they had gone fishing, built fruitbox go-carts and bluebird houses, and even watched Saturday morning cartoons.

"How you doing, Shawndrell?"

He shrugged and wistfully turned his gaze to the inverted cardboard puppet theater atop my filing cabinets. Inside that box, several soft-body puppets — a penguin, a raccoon, a ferret, a tiger, and an ugly genderless humanoid creature — called powerfully to him. This troupe — Paloma, Rocky, Frederica, Jack, and Windy — plainly interested him more than I did. His rump inched forward on the chair, causing its rear legs to rise. I steadied the chair's back.

"Think you might like to talk to me today, Shawndrell?"

The boy pointed at the theater. "Frederica. Okay?"

I fetched Frederica down and handed her to him. Shawndrell put his hand inside the sleeve of the ferret puppet, gestured extravagantly with her, and said through clamped lips in a high-pitched unnatural voice, "Windy! Come out and play, Windy!"

I dug out Windy, the sexless humanoid, and prepared to assume the irascible persona of that felt-and-leather monster. I donned the creature, turned it to face Frederica, and growled in Windy's characteristically grouchy way:

"Who woke me up! I don't want to see anybody!"

Shawndrell made Frederica bump Windy. "Come on, Windy! You gotta see people sooner or later!"

"Who says, huh? Why can't I just hide in my box? Not see anyone! Not talk to anyone!"

"You can't, Windy. Nobody'll leave you alone. Besides, who'd you play with? You can't play tag alone. Or Power Rangers."

"Hey, I never thought of that. Suppose we ask Mr. Keats about it? What do you say, Mr. Keats?"

In my normal voice, I said, "I think Shawndrell's right on target. In fact, if Frederica and Windy went off to play together, he and I could probably have a real nice talk."

Miraculously, Shawndrell consented. When he removed the ferret from his hand, I doffed Windy and returned both characters to the theater.

"So how you doing, Shawndrell?"

"Goooood." A smile split his thin face. He touched the hand with which I had animated Windy. "How *you* doing?"

The reversal of my question moved me. "I've seen better days, Shawndrell. You know, something has happened that makes me understand even better how you felt when your granddaddy died."

"Sad."

I nodded. "Sad and confused. Like you were lost in a strange neighborhood far from home."

Shawndrell cocked his head. With more shrewdness than I had anticipated, eliding the final consonant of my surname after the fashion of many of his classmates, he said, "Somebody up and die on you, Mr. Kee?"

Why lie to the kid? In the closed ecosphere of the school, news of my loss would quickly make the rounds anyway. "My father died last Thursday night."

Shawndrell squinted at me, then looked away and pounded his knees like a jazz drummer keeping time. Abruptly, he stopped. "Can I go get somethin' and come right back?"

"Sure."

At the door he paused. "Wait right here, Mr. Kee. Don' go no place."

I repressed a smile. Shawndrell darted out. Technically, he had no business unaccompanied in the hall. But his classroom was only two doors down, and I expected his teacher, Miss Friend, to extend her blessing once she understood Shawndrell's errand. Indeed, only a moment later he popped back in, carrying what I had suspected he had gone to fetch: his memory box. He held the foil-wrapped shoebox — thoughtfully constructed, decorated, and filled — as if it were a saint's relic.

I often had kids construct and stock these small portable shrines. Invariably, they opened many doors. Last week, for instance, when Shawndrell had compared his to Mitzy Eggling's, both had benefited, pulling out and examining coat buttons, military insignia, automobile keys, worry stones, matchbooks, fishing lures, torn postcards, a tobacco pouch, a foreign stamp, a bracelet of pop-top pulls, a packet of photos, an engraved pair of fingernail clippers. Now Mitzy and Shawndrell rarely passed in the halls without nodding or speaking to each other.

"You need to make one of these," Shawndrell said.

"Probably so."

"What would you put in?"

"I'd have to think about that."

"Well, just pick somethin' your daddy really loved."

I refrained from telling Shawndrell that the material object my father had most loved had already gone into one memory box, so to speak, and later bewilderingly escaped.

The day trudged on like a lame horse. At noon I walked down to the front office and asked Irene Nix, Mrs. Lapierre's secretary, if I could have access to an outside line and a little privacy. Customarily Miss Nix, an apple-cheeked, gossipy bachelorette, mounted formidable opposition to any out-of-the-ordinary request. Today, almost comically eager to help a mourning colleague, she speedily agreed.

I placed a long-distance call to the Smittinger-Alewine mortuary. A woman answered. I asked if she would divulge the name of the employee who had driven the hearse for the Keats funeral. She countered by asking my name and a few verifiable particulars. Once I had passed her test, she wondered aloud if I had any complaints.

"Oh, no," I said. "I just want to thank him tangibly. In the hustle, I forgot — "

She went huffy. "Every person who works for us gets an adequate salary, Mr. Keats. We forbid gratuities."

"Well, then, could I at least shake his hand and thank him face to face? It was a longish drive, and he conducted himself professionally."

She sounded startled, as if competence were the last charge she had ever expected anyone to level against the man. "Oh, *really*?"

I brought in the heavy artillery. "My mother concurs in this, ma'am. We'd both like to express our gratitude."

"Do you want to speak to him now? I can easily summon him to the phone."

"No, please. I'm calling from work, and my break's almost over. Couldn't you just tell me his name so that I can contact him at a less hectic time?"

She did not reply. I thought I had blown it, but she must have been consulting either her memory or her employee file. "Lawrence Budge. His friends call him Larry."

I expelled a breath that I had unwittingly swallowed and held. "Thank you. Thank you very much."

She gave me Budge's home telephone number, and I hung up. A satisfaction out of all proportion to my accomplishment filled me. I had taken a positive step in Dapper's pursuit, however tentative and clumsy. My success so elated me, in fact, that I remained upbeat and gracious even when, upon opening the door, I had to catch the eavesdropping Miss Nix to keep her from tumbling ignominiously to the floor.

God bless her if she could make more sense out of this inscrutable mishmash than I could.

CHAPTER 10

Only one Lawrence Budge appeared in my home copy of the Columbus phone book. I wrote down his address, and only then noted the blinking light on my message machine.

Adrienne's voice spilled out like honey: "Will, why don't you come to supper with me and Olivia? Fried chicken and red-cabbage coleslaw. Afterwards, some cutthroat Scrabble and an exclusive fifty-fifth viewing of *The Lion King*. I'll even give you a break on the dishes. Let me know."

Had I misplaced my priorities? Adrienne's invitation to spend a peaceful evening with her could not at the moment compete with my fixation on tracking down and buttonholing a more than likely harmless stranger. I could not imagine recounting my midnight adventure with J.W. to Adrienne, or explaining why I had an urgent craving to visit the driver of my father's hearse. I did not return her call.

The thirty-five-mile drive to Columbus passed as quickly as a low-flying cloud across the face of the sun. During the ride, I dredged up every recoverable detail of my brief interaction with Budge. What I remembered of the man suggested an old-fashioned certified public accountant rather than an amoral thug. Moreover, his address placed him in a sedate mixed-race neighborhood: tidy brick houses, well-pruned boxwoods, and lawnside banks of primroses, thrift, and ivy. I pictured a man who lived quietly, even clandestinely, and who considered the renting of an R-rated video a wanton debauch.

A little before five I entered Budge's eastside neighborhood, between Buena Vista and St. Mary's Roads, and cruised it looking for his number. The houses had deteriorated noticeably from my last trip through: missing shingles, dangling rain gutters, flaking paint. Even the lawns had gone too long unwatered and uncut; owing to the random deaths of their grassroots, some featured bizarre discolored fairy rings and crop circles.

Had Budge even left work yet? I found his house — a low-roofed blond-brick crackerbox with a chainlink fence around a treeless front yard — and parked a little beyond it. I stared at his desiccated checkerboard of lawn and at his picture window where late afternoon sundogs winked and spun. My hands grew clammy on the wheel: Budge's house reminded me of some sort of woebegone fortification on a Maginot line of the psyche. Did I really want to emerge from my trench and storm it?

No car occupied the driveway. The house boasted a garage, but its corrugated door and windowless walls told me nothing of what lurked inside. I pondered my options. Leave the car and saunter up and down like a misplaced boulevardier? Continue to sit like a cop on stakeout? Beep my horn like an overanxious teenager picking up his date?

At that moment, a hand drew back the curtain on the picture window, and just as quickly released the emerald drapery so that it again shielded the interior. Budge — or someone — had been watching from within. He had to have seen me. And judging by his refusal to show himself, the watcher had no wish to greet me, whether he recognized me or not.

I flew out of my car and leapt over Budge's waist-high fence, fleetingly snagging my trouser cuff on a loose barb, but recovering quickly and transitioning into a purposeful stride. Halfway to the house, I sensed rather than saw the door opening. A thick-shouldered Labrador retriever barrelled through the ever-widening gap, all blackness, crypt-deep bark, and electrically erect mane. The dog plunged down the steps on an implacable search-and-destroy mission.

Panic could have undone me. You never run from an angry or a territorial dog. So, instead, I tucked my hands nonthreateningly into my armpits and uttered a few presumably soothing noises, cooing and chirping like a demented parakeet.

The Lab halted a yard away, skinning his lips back from sharp stained teeth, his tongue lolling as if to taste the air. I told him what a good fella he was, squatted on my haunches, and slowly extended the back of my left hand. My refusal to turn tail and flee, along with my sweet talk, visibly settled him down. He kept barking, but less wrathfully. The ambiguous motions of his hindquarters I interpreted as a prelude to tail-wagging rather than as preparation for an all-out attack

Budge, leash in hand, appeared on his porch. "Orcus! Orcus, hush!"

"Can you calm your dog down please, Mr. Budge?"

Budge squinted. "Don't know as I want to. Why'd you jump my fence?"

"I'd like to talk to you."

"Pretty badly too. Well, you don't look like a burglar, I guess. Orcus, sit!"

The dog obediently dropped his butt. Budge stepped down and sidled warily toward us. Only when he had snapped the leash to Orcus's choke collar did I relax and stand up.

"Thanks. Ordinarily, I like dogs, but not enough to offer myself as their next can of Alpo."

"Hell, Orcus never bit a soul." Budge winked. "'Least not so as to leave *too* bad a scar. You wanted to say something to me?"

"Mr. Budge, you drove my father to the Mountboro cemetery yesterday evening. I wanted to thank you."

Now I had time and presence of mind to note Budge's appearance. He wore tan slacks and a green banlon shirt. An oily abundance of old-fashioned tonic slicked down his thinning amber hair. Square and nondescript, his face reminded me of the blunt handle of a much-used tool. I sensed immediately that he had no family other than Orcus, no hobby other than Orcus, and in the sense that the dog signified death and fate, no god other than Orcus. In jumping his fence, I had badly frightened Budge. He had released Orcus as his weapon of first, last, and only resort.

"Why didn't you call or go by the funeral home?"

"I did telephone. That's how I got your name. But the woman

I spoke to led me to believe that we couldn't have a frank discussion there. I had in mind a little gift."

"Oh." Budge smile wanly. "Would you like to come in?"

"Yes, I would. If Orcus doesn't mind?"

"'Course not. He does what I tell him. But I'll pen him out back if he bothers you that much."

"Thanks. If you don't mind."

Budge waved me inside. I remained in a shabby parlor while he escorted Orcus deeper into the house. I heard a screen door creak open and then slam shut. Orcus, I assumed, now had the freedom of his familiar run.

Budge's house smelled of excited dog, wintergreen air freshener, and recently burnt toast. A fake-leather lounger with a floor-to-ceiling pole-lamp beside it wore an open copy of *People* magazine on one torn arm and a dirty T-shirt on the other. A grease-stained and empty pizza box jutted up from a waste-basket. Obviously, I had guessed correctly about Larry Budge's lack of family.

Budge returned. He stood facing me, a little nerdishly, a little disdainfully, in his oppressive living room.

"Sorry about your loved one," he said dutifully.

"Loved *ones*," I said.

"What?"

"We buried two bodies yesterday. My father's and my brother's."

"I don't follow. I drove just one box to Mountboro. Are you pulling my leg?"

"Not at all, Mr. Budge. Everyone at your workplace must have hooted over the news since Friday: Skipper Keats taking his dummy into the crypt with him."

"Oh, sure! And you're calling the dummy your brother — that's pretty rich. I never thought of it that way, but it makes a funny sort of sense, I suppose. Say, you care for a drink?"

Was Budge deliberately changing the subject, or just being clumsily gracious? "No thanks. Let's get back to Dapper. He's gone missing. The coffin held him when they loaded it into your vehicle. He's not in it now." I hoped Budge wouldn't ask me how I knew. Luckily, he didn't.

"What are you saying? You think I took the dummy? Cracked the box in the hearse and then sealed it again? That's nuts!"

"I'm afraid that's exactly what I suspect, Mr. Budge. I'd appreciate it if you told me what prompted you to do it."

"Listen, I drive hearses, I don't — "

I raised my fisted hand, neither threateningly nor nonthreateningly, and peeled fingers up from it to illustrate my points. "Fact: Dapper lay safely in the casket when you started your drive. Fact: No one but you got close to the box unsupervised between the chapel and the cemetery. Fact: Dapper's fled. I can reach no other conclusion, Mr. Budge, except that you took him."

Budge's eyes cut hurriedly away from my raised partial fist. He pocketed his own hands, as if they might independently move to choke me. "I gotta have a drink."

"It's your place, sir. Help yourself. I'll wait right here." If Budge had fenced his backyard to contain Orcus, he couldn't easily run out on me that way.

Budge left and returned with a pony of orange juice, spiked I suspected with something more potent. His voice contained less chagrin and nervousness, as if in the interval he had decided on a tactic. "Okay, suppose someone did make off with the dummy? What's the hook? Why would they bother?"

"Mr. Budge, I already asked you that. Although I do have a couple of ideas of my own, I wouldn't mind hearing yours."

He licked his pouty lips. "I guess the dummy's valuable, huh?"

"Yes, it is."

"Like how valuable?"

"Why do you ask, Mr. Budge? Do you think whoever hired you to take Dapper took advantage of you?"

"Who said anybody hired me to boost it?"

I wanted to maintain my cool, but anger rose in me like mercury in a thermometer. "Almost everything about you, Mr. Budge, from that twitch at your temple to the way you're chugging your drink. And now that I've talked to you, I have to wonder if you possess either the brains or the initiative to plot the theft of a pencil from a blind man."

"Hey, that's a cheap shot! You think it was easy — "

"Pardon me? Was what easy?"

Budge knuckled sweat from his brow. "I'm gonna sit down. You too."

We sat. Budge leaned forward and addressed me, seemingly off topic.

"In the service I worked in the motor pool, drove the brass hats everywhere. When I got out, all I wanted was to be some rich guy's chauffeur. But no rich guys were standing in line waiting to offer me a job. So where'd I end up? Smittinger-goddamn-Alewine, trundling stiffs around for only a little more dough than I could make dishing out fast food. How you suppose that made me feel?"

"As if you could earn the respect and riches you deserved by violating someone's grave?"

"Oh, the hell with you! Why should I expect you or anyone else to understand?"

"Mr. Budge, please put your resentments aside for a moment and cooperate. Who paid you to steal Dapper? And why?"

Budge stood. "If you think I took your precious daddy's god-damn toy, why don't you have a look around? Go ahead. I won't even ask you for a warrant. Turn the whole place upside down for all I care."

His offer startled me. "You don't really want me to do that."

Confidence filled Budge to pompous dimensions. "Sure I do. What have I got to hide? Go right ahead, Mr. Dummy's Brother."

Did Budge have the cleverness to make an offer that could snare him, all the while betting that I would refuse to take it? I doubted it; the logic was too sophisticated, the potential outcome too risky. If he genuinely wanted me to inspect the premises, then Dapper unquestionably resided nowhere within his house or the surrounding five blocks.

"I can tell that I won't find him here, Mr. Budge. But I still believe you took him. Why not tell me who put you up to it?"

To this point in our conversation, Budge had vacillated between clumsy denial of and smirking pride in his theft, as if the heist qualified as the high point of his shabby life. Until now, though, he had never had the gumption to admit it outright. Now he swayed toward affirmation: "Guess."

I shot the first arrow from my quiver of suspects. "How about a hack ventriloquist from Atlanta named Alan Papini?"

Budge visibly recoiled, as if my bolt had hit its target.

"How much, Mr. Budge?"

"A thousand." His mouth slumped clownishly at the corners.

"A *thousand*!" I blurted. Then I calmed myself. "Mr. Budge, I'd've paid you that much to buy the lonely Mr. Papini three or four inflatable girlfriends."

"I never thought — "

"Please, Mr. Budge, when did you hand Dapper over to him? Where did Papini take him?"

"Last night." He thought for a moment. "Back to Atlanta, I guess."

I moved to leave. "Enjoy your sad little windfall, Mr. Budge. Lay in a few Kansas City steaks and a supply of Chivas Regal. Buy Orcus a squeak toy or twenty, and toss him a steak now and then."

"What are you talking about?"

"A man of your ambition and accomplishment, a man who earned a thousand dollars for pilfering a valuable relic, deserves something other than cold pizza now and then. So does his faithful dog, who's probably his last friend. Thanks for talking to me."

As I drove away, I saw Budge peering out the window again in the gap made by the lifted curtain. He looked like a paraffin dummy in a cheap wax museum of grifters and failed suicides. A sad man, a sad life, a sad accomplice in an oppressive and predatory scheme.

CHAPTER 11

Back in my car, shaking more from a weariness born of my sleepless night than from the interview with Budge, I was surprised to find the evening's weather turning nasty. A storm had begun brewing while I dredged information from Budge, and now a downpour seemed imminent.

As I headed toward Skipper's Keep, the tumult struck: wind and extravagant sloshings of rain, lightning and laggard thunder. My wipers metronomed to the storm's dark music. Sirens and car alarms went off, traffic lights waltzed, and cataracts of spray attended every creeping vehicle. At the eastern end of Wynnton Road, I saw a Georgia Power truck already parked next to a transformer pole and one helmeted worker struggling aloft. Columbus Square Mall, a failing enterprise ever since the advent of Peachtree Mall to the north, now looked utterly dead, its signs blanked. I drove through Midtown Plaza to Hilton Avenue, where most of the shops and residences still had power, although wind-flung paper, trash cans, and broken foliage littered the yards and driveways.

Skipper's Keep had escaped any falling limbs or electrical interruptions. But in the driveway, a vehicle I didn't recognize: a sporty red Nissan plastered with leaves and glazed with rainwater. A visitor, but who?

Eula answered my knock and let me in. She looked tired, no doubt from round-the-clock attendence on my mother. Eula's normal schedule — arrival at 7:00 A.M., departure around 6:00 P.M. — had fallen victim to the chaos surrounding Skipper's death. Sleeping over on an emergency basis in the room reserved during my boyhood for live-in employees, Eula had shouldered duties both common and unusual, running interference with merchants and friends, phone-callers and visitors, as well as keeping up with her standard cooking and cleaning duties.

"That car out front?" I said.

"Young man named Ryan Malley. Showed up about half an hour ago. You remember him."

"I do?"

"Wanted to write a book about your daddy."

I groaned. *That* Ryan Malley.

Over a year ago, after I received a telephoned warning from Burling Whickerbill about guarding Skipper's privacy from newsy snoops, Malley had materialized on my doorstep in Mountboro with a tape recorder, a camera, and an ingratiating aw-shucks facade repellent to me from the moment he opened his mouth. That he had dared intrude on LaRue and Kelli the day after Skipper's funeral appalled me. Did Malley imagine that Skipper's oft-stated distaste for the press — for Malley in particular and confessional divulgences in general — had evaporated so soon? That the Keatses would now welcome him as a comforter?

"Where is he?"

"Parlor. You want I should announce you?"

"Please don't, Eula. I think I'll just barge manfully on in."

She smiled faintly and drifted away. I moved toward the parlor, grateful that LaRue had not invited Malley to the Prop Room where Dapper's siblings silently sat, a peanut gallery of remorse.

Malley occupied the front edge of the sofa, Kelli beside him. Wearing a handsome black pantsuit, LaRue perched opposite them on an upholstered desk chair. Seeing me, Ryan Malley rose with a look of commingled pleasure and expectation on his callow soap-opera-hero's face. Although cut around his temples in a fade, his hair above his ears bloomed into a pomaded shag. Under a tanned forehead his huge blue eyes reminded me of a street vendor's: an oversoulful corn-dog salesman's, say. Without bothering to rise, LaRue made unnecessary introductions.

"Good to see you again, Willy. Your father's sudden death — "

"Forgive me, Mr. Malley, but I've never liked that nickname, and I'd appreciate it if you don't call me by it. As for the *pro forma* expression of sympathy, I've heard so many lately that a respectful silence would come as a blessing."

Malley lowered his outstretched hand and sat back down. "Right. Sometimes we do better just offering the bereaved our sympathetic presence." Kelli, her hands on her knees, admired Malley's profile wistfully from her perch next to him. "I wanted to attend the funeral," he nattered on, "but just couldn't get here on time. An interesting assignment on the Georgia coast to cover."

"Please don't fret it," I said. "Skipper would have wanted you at the funeral only if you'd left your reporter's instincts in Atlanta. And he probably wouldn't have wanted you here tonight at all."

"Will!" my mother and my sister chimed.

I could see that stale courtesy outweighed a bracing veracity here but could not quite bring myself to surrender without a parting sally:

"But why respect the wishes of the dead? Nothing legally enforceable about them. Just a matter of ethics and faith."

Incredibly weary, I snagged a second desk chair and straddled it backwards, gunslinger at a fashionable soiree. I guessed Malley's age at only twenty-five or so, but he had already toiled at least five years for the *Atlanta Journal-Constitution*, including a collegiate internship. He had won several regional press awards for his reporting and now hoped to add the writing and publishing of full-fledged books to his curriculum vitae.

Without really meaning to, I had upset the balance of amiability in the parlor, and no one knew what to say. Why had LaRue consented to entertain this print-media vampire? Kelli had her adolescent hormones as an excuse, but the same did not apply to LaRue. I could not conceive of Malley as her type. And LaRue knew well that Skipper had already denied Malley access to his life and career.

Courtesy failed me, because I could not help suspecting Malley of ulterior motives, opportunism run amok. "Can I get you anything? Box of tissues? A black armband? Copy of the will?"

"No more of that, please," LaRue said evenly.

I looked at her. "Pardon my confusion. I just don't know what role Mr. Malley thinks he's playing tonight. We don't count him as a family friend. He's never had any professional connection to Skipper. You no longer even subscribe to the newspaper he works for, or I could assume he's come to check on your level of satisfaction with its delivery schedule." I turned to Malley. "Would your journalistic principles permit you to divulge exactly why you've showed up tonight?"

"He still wants to write a book about daddy," Kelli said. "And he'll probably do it whether we help him or not. So why shouldn't we help him, Will? To make it the best book possible, for Skipper's sake?"

"Excuse me, Mr. Malley, but I'd call that a subtle form of blackmail."

Malley finally flushed. "I came here this evening simply to inform your family of my plans. I want to do the right thing by you all, not sneak around. I'm *serious* about this project. Two years of research, if you'd like to see my notes, and a letter of commitment from an Atlanta publisher. They believe we can profitably market your father's biography here in the Southeast. We might even go national, as a specialty item.

"Sure, I'd benefit immeasurably from your help. But if you can't see your way clear to assist, at least I've told you my plans. And I should also tell you that this book will not in the slightest resemble your standard celebrity exposé. I have in mind a lively study of a unique show-business tradition, with a clear and flattering focus on Skipper Keat's underappreciated talent."

"And he has a great title for the book," Kelli said.

"Tentative title," Malley said.

"Let's run it up the flagpole then," I said, making exaggerated "gimme" gestures at him.

"Okay," he said. "*Would It Kill You to Smile?*"

◆ ◆ ◆

Ryan Malley left with LaRue's promise that she would call him with a firm yes or no within the week, and Kelli accompanied

him out to his car with an umbrella. Meanwhile I followed
LaRue into the conservatory. The glass-walled room housing the
expensive baby grand offered her a solace virtually independent
of Skipper's achievements. She sat on the bench and rested her
fingertips on the keys, but did not play.

"In the week after Skipper's funeral, you shouldn't even have
to think about Malley's proposal, LaRue, much less make a bind-
ing decision."

"Life goes on."

"Then at least consult with Burling or Cleveland Voss."

LaRue laughed sharply. "My lawyer-distrustful son actually
wants me to consult the family attorneys?"

"In this case, yes."

LaRue lifted a hand to her temple. "I barely slept last night.
You?"

How could I tell her that disentombing the paterfamilias's casket and then brooding about Dapper's theft had prevented me
from getting my usual untroubled seven-hour complement? She'd
either have me committed or raise some kind of official hue and
cry that would send Papini — and my wooden sibling — fleeing
to the ends of the earth.

"Not much," I said guardedly.

Kelli returned, adopting a faintly guilty stance in the doorway.
Her cheeks burned now, as Malley's had earlier. With both
women present, I pressed on.

"What else did Malley want?"

"Permission to take a photo of Dapper," Kelli said.

I laughed. "No chance of that. Why didn't you just offer him
one of the old glossies?"

"He already has those," Kelli said. "He wanted something
unique, something fresh. He planned to pose Dapper on a chair
at the cemetery, looking at Skipper's crypt. He thought it would
make a great dustjacket."

"Tasteful, too. Thank God Skipper took Dapper with him."

Kelli said, "You just resent someone other than yourself acting
to preserve daddy's legacy. Especially a young hotshot like
Malley. Someone with real grit."

I swallowed a retort. LaRue had begun playing unlinked sequences of notes, clumsily, softly.

"I assume you told Malley of Dapper's fate. Did he ask to substitute one of Skipper's other figures? Did you take him to see them? Did he want to borrow them?"

"Of course not," Kelli said. "Any fan who knew daddy's act would recognize Simon or Letitia or Davy as second-best. They'd wonder, Where's Dapper? And then the cemetery photo wouldn't work."

"Why don't we just disinter Dapper and hand him over to the persistent Mr. Malley? Why consider Skipper's wishes at all?"

LaRue's hands froze. "It hurts to say this, Will, but maybe Satish's accusation of blasphemy rings true."

"Mother, I'm defending my father's right to protect his legacy, not insulting his memory. How can you say I'm blaspheming against him?"

Kelli interrupted before LaRue and I could get into the topic any deeper. "Why all this concern about the other dummies?"

"I just want to know if he mentioned them or not."

"Only to say they wouldn't work in place of Dapper in his cemetery shot."

The rain had slackened to a virtually noiseless drizzle, but a crooked candelabrum of lightning manifested suddenly in the conservatory's skylight, and a following rumble of thunder shook the glass walls around us. "That doesn't mean he still wouldn't have designs on the other chip-blocks," I said, ignoring the thunder.

"Designs?" said LaRue. "What kind of designs? You're not suggesting that Mr. Malley intends to rob us?"

Kelli crossed her arms over her midriff — an outsized Collective Soul T-shirt covered her faux-barbarian navel ring — and glared at me. "That's crazy! He'd never do such a thing!"

"Still, I want you all to keep your doors and windows securely locked."

"Someone's almost always here," said LaRue. "Especially since Eula's been sleeping over. How could anyone get past us?"

"Much more easily than you imagine." A sudden apprehension

took me. "In fact, under cover of this storm, with all of us in this one room — "

LaRue looked over her shoulder at me. "Oh, come on, Will."

"Kelli, do me a favor and run up to the Prop Room to check on Simon and company."

"Humor him," LaRue said, and Kelli, rolling her eyes, turned to do my bidding. As soon as she had left, LaRue began to weep.

"I miss him," she told me or the fading storm in an anguished feline croon. "I miss him I miss him I miss him. . . ."

"Of course you do. Miss him as hard and long as you have to. Let it run."

She obeyed me easily, and I approached her from behind to place my hands on her shoulders and to brush her hair with my lips.

"*You* don't miss him," she whispered. "You compared his corpse to a dead bird's. You spoke of death's stench, Will. You said not one kind or generous word about the man who gave you life and sustained it."

"I think you misread me, Mama."

"No. You denied his life any substance."

To a certain extent, I supposed, I had. Skipper Keats had spent his life belly-talking and playing with freakishly articulated dolls. He had placed Dapper O'Dell above his flesh-and-blood son and lived almost exclusively for the approbation of strangers. I wanted to say that of course the life of such a man lacked real substance, but LaRue's tears prevented me.

Kelli came running breathlessly back into the conservatory. "They're gone! You had it figured right, Will!"

"*What?*" I lifted my hands from LaRue's shoulders and strode past Kelli into the polished hall leading to the staircase. Kelli followed.

"Yes, the Grinch must have visited! Piles of ashes have replaced all the dummies! And the culprit left a note! 'So you dared laugh at my invention of the heat ray! You fools!'"

I stopped dead. Kelli began to chortle, a quiet titter at first, then uproarious guffaws that left her cheeks tomato-red. I returned to her baffled.

"Kelli, don't do this."

"Oh, come on." With difficulty she stopped guffawing. "You've been such a stuffed shirt lately, big brother. Your balloon needs popping." She donned an expression of almost self-parodying solemnity. "But you'll never know if I'm joking unless you go see for yourself."

I could not dispute this. So I jogged down the hall and up the stairs and sauntered anxiously into the Prop Room.

The whole sad wooden cast of my father's tragicomedy — save Dapper of course — sat peacefully in a row on a Victorian chesterfield. Kelli had lied. Or, to put it more charitably, she had played a belated April Fool's prank on me. I rapped the slack-jawed Simon Smallwood on his yokelish head, straightened the pince-nez on Letitia Crone's pointed nose, and picked up Davy Quackett.

With my hand in his back, I made Davy say, *"You know, William Keats, you ain't quite the detective you quack yourself up to be."*

CHAPTER 12

Despite the late hour, I drove home to Mountboro because it put me almost forty minutes closer to Atlanta, and because I still intended to work tomorrow. LaRue had asked me to stay, of course. Even Kelli had asked me to stay, her way of apologizing for her prank. The two Keats women in Skipper's Keep still loved me, it seemed, although who could fathom why? Had they known of my ghoulish grave-robbing proclivities, would they have pled with me so fervently to remain? Probably, if only to kick my sorry butt and force all the details from me.

A second message from Adrienne on my home machine: "Sorry you couldn't get by this evening, but hope you at least dropped in on LaRue and Kelli, and gave them my best too." Olivia's voice piped, "Goodnight, Mister Will. Don't let the bedbugs fight." Adrienne corrected, "Bite." "I know that," said Olivia, "but sometimes I like to say it different." Adrienne sighed maternally and continued: "How about an informal fast-food supper tomorrow, Will? Call me as late as ten-thirty tonight. Otherwise I hope to hear from you sometime on Tuesday."

At that moment the digital clock in my den flashed 10:47. Given Adrienne's usual quick descent into sleep, snugged even at this season under a smothering drift of her late grandmother's quilts, I decided to postpone my call.

I needed to see Alan Papini. The sooner the better. I had no guarantee that Budge, upon my departure, had not called Papini to warn him of my pursuit. But I was counting on Budge's guilty silence, his fear of what Papini might do if he determined in his frustration and paranoia that Budge had double-crossed him. Wheels within wheels. Or, Russian-style, dolls within dolls. And what if Papini, safely in possession of Dapper, had simply caught an overseas flight at Hartsfield International?

Would that matter? Did it matter that a three-dimensional carven image of my father as a young man might have flown to Tahiti or Tanzania? That a block of painted wood no longer lay as ballast in Skipper's coffin? On one level — the practical, the legal, the utilitarian — it scarcely mattered at all. But something within me balked at that level's imperatives. I could not simply let Dapper go like a duffel of old magazines or a castoff suit. Blood loyalty and a bond of spirit demanded that I track Dapper down.

Pursuing Dapper was beginning to look like a full-time job. Too bad I already had one at Oakwood Elementary, where even my briefest absence could deprive students and staff members alike of valuable help. I needed a private detective. Unfortunately, PIs seldom work for free. And until I came into my full inheritance, I could not realistically afford to hire one.

So I would continue to blunder my own way through.

◆ ◆ ◆

Ten minutes after my alarm went off on Tuesday morning, the telephone rang. I heard it just before stepping into the shower and padded naked into my study to answer it.

Without greeting, Adrienne's voice said, "For God's sake, Will, put some clothes on."

Her clairvoyant joke made me shiver. I felt pinned in some voyeur's binoculars. Was paranoia my lot, now that I had earlier suspected almost everyone of complicity in Dapper's theft?

"I'd rather just cover my birthday suit with yours."

My glibness concealed nothing. Adrienne had an uncanny ability to read volumes into silences and inflections. The whole timbre of her voice changed.

"You didn't return my call. You must have gotten in awfully late last night."

"Yes. The situation's turned — well, tricky. I'd really like to go out with you and Olivia this evening, but I don't know if I can."

"Tell me about it."

"I want to. I'm counting on your insights for help. But not over the phone. It's too important for that."

Adrienne said, "It's another woman, isn't it? You picked her up last night, and she's there with you now."

It took me a moment to realize she was joking. "Shhh," I said. "She'll hear you. It's Mrs. Lapierre. I've had this fetish for principals ever since fourth grade."

Adrienne laughed. "Call me when you work it out of your system, Will. I love you, quirks and all."

"And I love you — madly, ceaselessly, quirkily."

After she hung up, I pictured her preparing breakfast and helping Olivia select her clothes for school. My imaginings had the reassuring but unrealizable normality of a Norman Rockwell painting.

The first child I saw in my broom-closet office on Tuesday morning, little Talulah Grimes, had an unusually husky speaking voice, a regular Carol Channing growl. The school nurse, Resa Murawski, and I both suspected some kind of alien growths — throat nodules, hopefully noncancerous. The circulating district speech therapist concurred. A free examination by a nose-and-throat specialist would settle the question. Resa had sent a permission slip home with the girl, asking Talulah to have her mother sign and return it. Weeks later, no slip. Frustrated, Resa had sent Talulah to my office for a gentle grilling.

Back in October, I had reported to DFACS — as law required — a suspicious welt behind Talulah's ear and a shiner like a cluster of Concord grapes. In an interview after the filing, her mother had expressed surly contempt. She had told me face to face that I was a skunk and a scoundrel. Why, Talool often hurt herself outdoors, the child played so wild. I had grossly flattered Mrs. Grimes for her keen perceptiveness and active involvement in Talulah's welfare. But surely she could understand that we teachers, administrators, and counselors had both the parents' and the child's well-being at heart. Our own superiors demanded close attention to anything out of the ordinary. And so forth and so on. With these standard but heartfelt rhetorical tactics I had calmed Mrs. Grimes, who had left my office a dubious ally . . . at least until my next report.

The daughter resembled her mother the way a puppy in your lap conjures up a yard-staked pitbull. Talulah had spiky red hair and a nose like a mushroom cap. When she came in, she asked to hold Jack, the tiger puppet, and hopped him around during her entire stay.

"Your mama hasn't signed that permission form yet, Talool."

"She won't," growled Talool, her voice so deep and animalish that it suited Jack almost perfectly.

"Why won't she?"

"Says my voice is fine. Ain't no noodle stuck there."

"That's nodule, kid. Like a bump or a cyst. Have you ever seen anybody with a cyst? Would you want one in your throat?"

"Yuck!"

"Can I phone your mama, Talool?"

"Sure. But she might not like you to."

Mrs. Grimes answered on the seventh ring. I explained a situation that I knew she already fully understood.

"I won't sign another shred of paper for you busybodies."

"Not even a field-trip permission, Mrs. Grimes?"

"Well, maybe — but not no doctor's slip!"

"Mrs. Grimes, haven't you noticed Talulah's voice getting deeper, thicker? Just since February — "

"No! It's not true. She just does it to get attention. It makes people laugh, to hear a kid talk so. Who you think knows her better? Her own mama or some damn long-nosed stranger!"

And she slammed her distant handset down.

I cradled my own phone gently and turned back to Talulah. She waggled the fiery-eyed Jack at me.

"'Spect she told you off, huh? Does that mean I got to go back to class now? Couldn't me and Jack play a few more minutes?"

As there seemed little else I could do for Talulah, I granted her wish.

At lunch I told Resa what had happened. We sat in her office in a rickety mobile unit, eating a fine-tasting sandwich of turkey, cranberry sauce, and provolone on sourdough bread. Its deliciousness I judged first-hand, because she shared half with me. Around chews, I detailed how I wanted to fix Mrs. Grimes's wagon.

"We drive out there after school, before Talool gets home on the bus. You, me, Mrs. Lapierre, Mrs. Iselin. Maybe even a DFACS worker. Hell, we'll look like the Publisher's Clearing House Prize Patrol! When Mrs. Grimes comes to the door, we'll hand her a banner-sized certificate that we ran off on the school computer. 'Congratulations!' we'll tell her. 'You're the grand-prize winner in our Stupidest Parent in the County Contest!' One of us will tape the whole embarrasing visit with a videocamera. Then Mrs. Lapierre announces that the tape will run on the six o'clock news. That should do it."

An implacably serene forty, Resa popped the last crust of her sandwich into her mouth, then turned her almost automatic handbrushing into deliberately scornful applause. But she neither laughed nor smiled. "I know how you feel, Will. But what would such humiliating hoopla accomplish?"

"*I'd* feel a hell of a lot better."

"Briefly. But you know that in the long run it would only make your job harder."

"Come on, Resa. Grant me my little fantasy at least until we have to punch back in."

"Okay. Hmmm, let's see. What if I settle a Burger King crown on her ditzy head when you hand her the banner?"

We carried on in this vein for another frustration-relieving ten minutes or so, and then Resa padded out into the corridor to resume her daily battles with head lice, ringworm, impetigo, broken arms, and preadolescent body odors.

◆ ◆ ◆

After the last bus left that day, Mrs. Lapierre gathered everyone in the lunchroom for a staff meeting. She stood at a lectern on the shallow stage to address us, her glasses down at the end of her nose and her expression grimly resolute.

"Speece County will have a serious budget shortfall next year," she began.

Dawn Creedon, a long-term fifth-grade teacher sitting next to me at a wobbly front-row table, spoke out distinctly but not belligerently: "Tell us something we don't already know, Donna."

"All right. You probably don't know that the shortfall will result from a change in the way the DMV collects tag fees."

Dawn said, "Is this a 'good news, bad news' joke? We all get free tags next year, but the school system goes bankrupt."

"Hardly. The DMV is switching to staggered collections, based on driver birthdates. The money will come in surges, not all at once. So the Board of Education won't have all its funds upfront, at the start of the fiscal year, to pay contractors or to purchase supplies and equipment. Efforts to secure contingency funding from various state agencies and commercial enterprises have failed. Hence, the crunch."

Several rows back, Miss Friend whispered, "Time to update the old résumé."

Mrs. Lapierre dropped the full bomb. "Each school in the county has to cut a minimum of fifty thousand dollars from its budget. No exceptions. Now, I can't do this alone. Rather, I *could* do it alone, but I'd rather get some input from all of you. I want each person here to submit some money-saving measures to me. Things we can implement practically, if not totally painlessly. Otherwise, I'll have to do some straight across-the-board chopping. And that will cripple us."

The meeting ran longer and touched on other topics. But no one paid total heed to these discussions, and I sat there obsessing anxiously about the budget issue. On paper, the neatest and fastest way to reduce any budget is to eliminate a salaried position or two. And, where I was concerned, it wasn't altogether a matter of "last in, first out," but rather "least credentialed gets the boot." I had no teaching certificate. I could not automatically fill a classroom slot that opened up through the inevitable process of teacher attrition. Moreover, I lacked the four consecutive years of employment in the Speece County system that would have granted me tenure. (Admittedly, Miss Friend, Mrs. Tarken, and Mrs. Holcrow crewed that same boat with me, but they all had those good-as-gold certificates.) I would have three consecutive years in June, but that crucial last year stood almost as far off as the moon.

During the meeting Mrs. Lapierre never once met my gaze. But whether to interpret this as pity for my already-sealed fate or a kind desire not to spook me unnecessarily, I had no idea.

Calling from the front office afterwards, I left a message on Adrienne's answering machine: "Can't do dinner tonight, but really wish I could. Have an errand in Atlanta. Will explain later. Love you. Bye."

Only half an hour afterwards, heading north in my Saturn on I-185 to Atlanta, did it occur to me that she might well reply to my facile "Will explain later" with an equivocal, punning "Adrienne listen later. Maybe."

CHAPTER 13

Alan Papini, a bachelor again, lived in the Edelweiss, a moderately ritzy apartment complex on Lennox Road. I had written down the street and number of the café-au-lait-colored stuccoed fortress from Skipper's address book during my last visit to the Keep. When I turned into the vehicle-crowded parking area, I half expected a Beefeater or a papal Swiss Guard to appear and grill me about my intentions. But I drove on through without even seeing the usual elderly rent-a-cop.

Papini lived on the third floor of the fortress, the side farthest from the road. I climbed the interior steps, past two chained bicycles and the unmistakable odor of grilling pork ribs, to Papini's door. When I knocked, a young woman in a pair of pleated tan shorts and a magenta halter came out of the adjacent apartment carrying a lowball glass. She swirled the amber liquid in it, took a fastidious sip, and squinted at me nearsightedly.

"Looking for Alan?"

"Yep. I'm from the collection agency. Time to repossess his soul. Fortunately, we expect to find it completely unused."

Papini's svelte neighbor wrinkled her nose in distaste. "You show-biz types can't answer a simple question without making a joke, can you?" She made as if to retreat into her apartment.

"Wait a minute, please. I apologize. Unfortunately, Papini always manages to snake about a mile up my craw."

I was wagering that Papini irritated her as strongly as he did me. Given his habitual crudity and male chauvinism, I figured my chances much better than even.

The woman grinned. "He has that effect on almost everyone,

doesn't he? Well, in that case, you're forgiven." She switched her drink to her left hand and extended the other. "Joy Frazer."

"Will Keats. Do you know if Papini's home now?"

"He's not. He has a show tonight."

"Of course. Did he say where?"

"Giotto's Galley. He insisted on putting me on the guest list, even though I told him a dozen times I wouldn't come. I made that mistake once already."

"What happened?"

"As soon as he spotted me in the audience, he and Otto launched into a string of vulgar sexual innuendos about a woman of my exact description."

I cringed. "How do I get to Giotto's?"

"Drive up Lennox to Peachtree and hang a right. Another block or two, and the neon will knock your eyes out. If I were you, though, I'd eat somewhere else. The way their chef treats food, he should be locked up without parole."

"Thanks. Thanks for your help."

"No problem. If you plan to sit through Alan's show, you'll need all the help you can get." She raised her glass in a mock toast and withdrew smiling into her book-lined apartment.

The drive to Giotto's Galley took less than ten minutes; in fact, when I turned my car over to the openly scornful valet, my watch read only 7:15. I intended neither to eat the burnt offerings nor to listen to Papini's coarse patter. I hoped to close with my target, deploy all available firepower, and get out quickly with Dapper and the truth.

The Galley already had a noisy crowd of diners, Atlantans intent on getting their full-night's worth of fun. But their giddily preoccupied faces astonished me less than did the Galley's interior. Five levels of Disneyfied simulation of a pirate's caravel: rigging lines, fish nets, belaying pins, anchors, and even three or four cross-sectioned wall-mounted dinghies. The waitresses wore white buccaneer shirts, jag-hemmed black miniskirts, knee-high boots, and crimson bandanas. The light suffusing the nightmarish place came either from net-wrapped candle bowls or glowing red "portholes." Glass-topped ship's wheels balanced on capstans formed the tables.

A hostess approached. "Ahoy, matey! 'Baccy, or no 'baccy?"

The lighting had already given me a headache. I felt disoriented and oppressed. But in this distress I plainly had no comrades: the diners clinked their silverware like Errol Flynn and Douglas Fairbanks engaging in a jolly swordfight. "I'm afraid I don't see . . ."

The pirate's doxy frowned, as if I had willfully spoiled her game. "Smoking or nonsmoking?"

"Oh, neither, really. I'm a friend of Mr. Papini's, and I need to see him before the show."

"Has he put you on his guest list?"

I hesitated only a moment. "Yes, of course. Joey Frazer."

She dug out a clipboard and consulted it. "I have a 'Joy Frazer' here."

I exuded charm and amusement. "An obvious mistake. Do I look like someone named 'Joy' to you?"

She smiled. "Of course not. Welcome to Giotto's Galley, Mr. Frazer. Your comp pass entitles you to a free cup of grog, but the cost of any selections from our Treasure Map you incur yourself."

"I don't even want the drink. I just need to talk to Alan. In fact, what I have to discuss might qualify as an emergency."

The hostess lost her grin. "Impossible, Mr. Frazer. Mr. Papini forbids us to permit anyone to disturb him before a show — for *any* reason. It breaks his concentration." She spoke with deep respect, as if Papini's talent rivaled Itzhak Perlman's. "And Mr. Haggard, the owner, would hold me responsible if tonight's show suffers as a result."

I had met an impenetrable wall. Apparently, for the sin of supposing myself a detective, I would have to sit through Papini's act. "Mr. Haggard owns the Gallery? What happened to Giotto?"

The hostess smiled. "Oh, there never was a Giotto. Mr. Haggard just thought it sounded classy."

"It fits your place perfectly."

"Thank you!"

I let her conduct me upstairs to what obviously ranked as a choice seat. Papini must have *really* wanted to get into Joy

Frazer's pants. Directly across the cavernous interior from me, a walnut-colored piano occupied a foredeck-*cum*-stage. A vent's stool stood beside the instrument. As I sat, a tuxedo-clad male pianist appeared and began to play: "Sea Cruise," of course.

The waiter brought me my grog, a watery bourbon on the rocks. I settled in for the inevitable. Two purchased drinks, later, the pianist rose, bowed, accepted some desultory applause, and exited the stage. Next appeared the man who surely owned this aqueous inferno. Haggard wore a black turtleneck, a black jacket, and whitish twill slacks. He took a mike from its stand, meanwhile radiating pride in his tacky emporium and its low-rent headliners.

"I know the chef will kill me for saying this, folks, but we now present a tastier ham than anything that ever came out of the kitchens of Giotto's Galley! If you can bear to set your silverware down, put your hands together for Alan Papini and Otto von Troll!"

Papini strolled onto the stage past Haggard, carrying his ugly soft-figure puppet. He sat down heavily on the stool that Haggard spun toward him and waited for the audience's rather vague applause to die down.

"Say good evening to everyone, Otto."

"Good evening, lesbians and genitals."

"My, my," Papini chided, "I hope that was only a slip of the tongue, little man." Turning to the audience: "You'll have to excuse Otto, folks. Just before coming onstage, he had a wee too much Downy fabric softener in his prune juice."

"Wait one darn minute, Pappy! You were hitting the sauce pretty hard there too."

"Heh-heh, he means the chef's famous hollandaise, of course — don't you, Otto?" Papini made a threatening fist that everyone could easily see but which we were supposed to imagine he meant to conceal. He got a few laughs.

I myself gaped in amazement. A minute and a half without a fart, a burp, or a vomit joke. What had come over Alan Papini? Maybe simply having Dapper in his possession had inspired him to delete the most obnoxious crudities from his act. Meanwhile, plate scrapings and silverware clinkings continued to provide the humdrum soundtrack for his reconstituted act.

"Now, Otto, let's tell the folks about our new friend."

Otto sniffed. "He's *your* new friend, Pappy, not mine. He looks like a stuck-up nellyboy to me."

"Otto, I'm appalled! What if we have some sensitive members of the gay persuasion out in our crowd? Don't you imagine they'll take offense at your choice of words?"

"Why should they? Do I take offense at their choice of lipsticks or clothes?"

Here manifested the old Papini I had dreaded from the start. He got his predictably nasty laughs all right, for a small portion of the Galley's customers hooted like apes. But this derisive barrage washed over me without effect as I realized where Papini planned to go, down a path that probably I alone could guess. Unable to resist any temptation for longer than three seconds, Papini intended to debut the reconfigured Dapper in his act tonight, practically in Skipper's backyard.

"Now, now, Otto," said Papini, "Please don't talk about Randy that way. He's new in town and needs a friend. Why, you two can have a barrel of fun!"

"With Randy, I'll most likely end up *in* the barrel or *over* it!"

"Well, Otto, Randy's coming onstage after the intermission, and I want the two of you to play together nicely."

"Pappy, maybe Randy can just play with himself!"

I couldn't let Papini introduce Dapper as his own character. Not even Skipper's many deficencies as both ventriloquist and man merited such a posthumous humiliation. So when Papini concluded his provocative opening dialogue and departed the stage, I pushed back my chair and trotted down the stairs to the main floor.

With a twenty-dollar bill I could ill afford to squander, I persuaded the skeptical hostess to carry a message backstage to Papini: "J. Frazer" had seen his new act and wanted to talk to him. Even so, I couldn't count on the lustful Papini's welcoming J. Frazer backstage before the end of intermission. Crude and stupid as he generally showed himself, he never missed or delayed a professional entrance. So ten seconds after the hostess disappeared through a door marked EMPLOYEES ONLY, I slipped through it too.

A dim corridor of battleship-grey cinderblocks led me behind the largest dining area to an abrupt dogleg studded with dusty two-by-fours. I trotted quickly down this aisle. At length, a dark-gray door broke the monotony of the painted cinderblocks. The hostess had disappeared a second time, but I assumed she had delivered my note and departed by another exit. Facing the door — it had DRESSING ROOM stencilled on it in broken yellow letters — I raised a hand to knock, thought better of it, and bulled on in.

Papini sat before a mirror at a cosmetic-cluttered table, a designer paper plate of congealing french fries at his elbow. Otto perched almost alertly in his red-velvet-lined carrying case on a nearby chair. I saw no sign of Dapper at all.

Papini jumped to his feet with surprising agility but quickly recognized me and exclaimed, "William! What the hell are you doing here?"

"I want Dapper back, Alan."

Relieved that I was neither a marshal with a subpoena nor an aggrieved husband, Papini dropped back into his canvas chair. He leaned back and cocked his head at me. "Well, sure, who wouldn't? But it's a little too late to cry over spilled beer now — especially when you did all the spilling, despite my advice and goodwill."

"I know you've got Dapper, Alan. Just give him to me, and we'll forget the whole moronic affair."

A shadow of genuine puzzlement flickered over his face. "Do you mean to say the little treasure's not in its chest anymore? Now, how could that be?" Speculatively, Papini rubbed a smear of makeup alongside his nose. "And how could you know? Did a sudden change of heart turn you into a graverobber, boy?"

I watched the cream on his nose glisten unnaturally. "Never mind how I know. The fact is, Dapper has disappeared. And here's another fact for you, Alan. You paid Lawrence Budge a thousand dollars to boost Dapper before the entombment."

"Budge? Who the Christ — oh, the hearse driver."

"Come off it, Alan. Otto could lie more convincingly."

"Cross my heart and hope to fry, Will, Budge is jerking your chain. Sure, I approached him. Anything's worth a shot, right? I talked to him at the funeral home before the ceremony in the chapel. Made him an offer, but he turned me down, colder than a penguin's prick."

"So how did Dapper go missing?"

"Oh, Budge probably stole him all right — just not for me. I put the idea in his head, and he cleverly went freelance, the two-timing wanker."

Papini's lack of guilt or remorse, the absence of any nervous reaction, had me baffled. Was I to believe him, or the opportunistic Larry Budge?

"Then why all that onstage patter about a new puppet? You had to have meant Dapper, right?"

Papini laughed so heartily that a terrific chill snaked down my spine. "Randy ain't Dapper, Will. He's one of my old figures rigged up new. Figured I'd ride a few miles on all this gay propaganda in the news nowadays."

"Could I see him?"

Papini got up and retrieved a second dummy case. In it sprawled a muscled-up mannikin dressed like the leather-clad character in the Village People. The wind of elation that had briefly filled my sails modulated into a sour mistral of disappointment.

"You want to search this place?" Papini said with justifiable cruelty. "Come home with me after the show, and you can look around there too. We'll share a couple of beers, have us a few companionable laughs. Talk about old times and Skipper's glory days."

Papini's happy-go-lucky innocence depressed me. My primary accusation had boomeranged stunningly. "Thanks anyhow, Alan, but I don't need to search. And I'll take a rain check on the beers. Besides, I've got to work tomorrow."

"And I go on in five minutes. So that's a wrap then." Papini saw me to the door. "Drive safe, Will. Sorry to burst your bubble. Let me know if you ever catch the little Gingerbread Man."

In the corridor I turned and extended my hand. Surprised, Papini grasped it warily.

Out in the Galley, the pianist had resumed playing: "Sea of Love."

◆ ◆ ◆

Near midnight, I looped into Tocqueville and crept past Adrienne's place on Coster Circle, a street of renovated mill houses not far from the hospital. Adrienne always kept a light on in the bathroom for Olivia, but nothing else about the house suggested a waking presence. Idling my Saturn at curbside, I stared at the shadowy figure of a small stone Buddha in a niche between two hydrangea bushes and briefly considered leaving a note on Adrienne's windshield. But in the end the gesture appeared too self-serving and impersonal, like posting a message about your stalled car for a traffic cop.

Twenty minutes later I lay in my bed in Mountboro, listening to a squirrel gnawing at the fume-emitting foam insulation in my attic. I could hardly remember what a good night's sleep felt like.

CHAPTER 14

At 6:30 A.M., I telephoned Adrienne. After my cheery hello, she plunged for the jugular."What's going on, Will? What could possibly take you up to Atlanta on a Tuesday evening?"

In the background, Olivia clinked her spoon on a bowl as she tunelessly scatted along with a Whitney Houston number on the radio. An image of the Buddha nestled among their hydrangeas smote me. More time than strictly considerate must have passed, for Adrienne suddenly said, "*Will!*"

Startled, I said, "Still here," and told her everything that I had kept from her since Skipper's funeral.

"Report this to the police," Adrienne said. "They get paid to do what you're knocking yourself out to do. And they've got the experience and contacts you don't have."

"Dapper's disappearance won't rank high on the police blotter. No APBs, no countywide search. They'll probably call it a prank, not grand theft or kidnapping. They might devote a few grudging hours to the investigation. And what will they say about my own illegal despoiling of Skipper's grave? They'll probably bust *me*. Would you wait for me till I got out of the pen? Knit me sweaters and visit me every week?"

Adrienne actually laughed. "Oh, Will, give it a rest. As Skipper's son, you had every right."

"Maybe, maybe not. But I still don't want to involve the police. Not yet, anyway. Maybe after I do a little more snooping of my own."

After an ambiguous pause, Adrienne said, "Byron's picking up

Olivia this afternoon. I'll be footloose and fancy-free for a few hours anyway. What say I drive down to the Will Keats homestead after school?"

"I'll see if I can pencil you in. Hmmm, Mrs. Lapierre has cancelled her appointment. Sure, come on down."

"You're quite the romantic."

"More so in person."

"That's what I'm counting on."

Her kiss over the wires provided a promissary note on the real thing.

◆ ◆ ◆

I saw Shawndrell Tompkins, Talulah Grimes, and several other children that day; did a guidance lesson in our fourth-grade classrooms on inappropriate social behaviors; arranged two overdue parent conferences; and made a referral to DFACS of suspected sexual abuse involving a male second-grader. I used Paloma, the penguin character, in my guidance lesson, throwing my voice into a supply cabinet, a desk drawer, and a book bag.

After school, Adrienne met me at my house. She wore a long red rayon dress with a smocked bodice and large blue and orange flowers in a repeating pattern, and looked like sunshine on parade. I led her inside and kissed her hungrily. She spread the fingers of one hand on my chest and held me back.

"Feel like shaving first?"

"Me or you? I don't mind hairy legs."

She rubbed my jaw. "This barbed wire, mister."

"Sure. But only if I find you naked in bed afterwards."

"Sounds fair."

I shaved in less than three minutes. Adrienne had undressed in fewer. She sat cross-legged on the downturned covers, sleek as Greek marble. We kissed again for a long time, then strove to erase the sorrow of the preceding days with some unselfconscious and joyful lovemaking.

Dinner consisted of two cold Rolling Rocks, ham and Swiss

sandwiches laced with hot mustard on black rye, all of which we consumed in careless crumb-scattering fashion in bed. When we had licked the last tasty oils from our fingers — she mine and I hers — Adrienne said, "What now?"

"I'd like to track down Lawrence Budge for a second round of dummy-dummy-who's-got-the-dummy."

"Fine. But only if I get to tag along."

"Part of my master plan from the beginning."

Adrienne drove. In Columbus we stopped at the Smittinger-Alewine Funeral Home, and she went inside to ask if Budge were available. She returned almost immediately, wearing a look that mixed bewilderment and pique.

"The biddy at the desk says he never reported for work today. Calls to his house go unanswered."

My stomach did a queasy roll. "He's run."

"Should we go over there and make sure?"

"Absolutely."

Ten minutes later, we cruised into Budge's shabby neighborhood and parked in front of his ugly blond-brick bunker of a house. He had left the door on his garage rolled up, and no vehicle occupied the interior.

"Shit!" I said.

"Easy. We already suspected he'd run."

"It's not that. I never thought to search his garage. Dapper was probably sitting in there all the time."

"Maybe. Maybe not. By the time you visited him, he could have already handed Dapper over to the real mastermind."

"Let's check it out anyway."

We walked up the long drive and entered the cement coolness of the garage. A stack of uncut molding lay against the rear wall. A greasy rubber trash pail stood beside a gasoline-powered lawnmower missing one wheel and its handle. A bundle of tabloids awaited recycling. Other than these items, the musty-smelling grotto held nothing whatever.

I led Adrienne out of the garage and up to the house's front door. No one answered my knock. The emerald drapes on the picture window did not twitch, and no frantic barking erupted in response to my pounding fist.

"What now?" Adrienne said.

"Let's try around back."

I banged on the kitchen door even harder than I had on the front, to the same disspiriting effect. "Time for a little B and E."

"Wow. You ex-cons have such a colorful vocabulary."

I rattled the knob, then kicked the bottom of the splotchily stained hollow-core door. Something splintered, and the door swung inward. A smell at once like rancid grease and spoiled vegetables washed over us. Pinching my nose, I told Adrienne to wait for me outside. She had no objection. I took out my pocket handkerchief and, holding it to my mouth and nostrils, stepped inside.

Someone had stripped the place. Furniture and clothes, foodstuffs and trinkets, all gone. Even the familiar scents of dog had vanished, giving way to a suety miasma of early decay. The rooms echoed like squalid caverns.

In the basement, I found Orcus. The dog lay curled in a blue plastic wading pool, now collapsed around him like the petals of a cheap artificial flower. Cartoonish sea horses and octopi decorated those petals, and the heat of the past forty-eight hours had begun to ravage the dog's corpse. Reluctantly, I knelt by the dead Labrador. Lifting his massive head, I spotted a small red hole at the base of his skull. An exit wound gaped beneath the lower jaw. Most of Orcus's blood had puddled in the folds of the deflated wading pool.

I let go of Orcus and stood. Lawrence Budge had shot his innocent if rambunctious god. What fears had driven him to deicide? And how could I have failed to recognize his instability? At some point in our interview, my hard-earned counseling skills should have kicked in. Useless remorse. Budge had pulled the trigger, not I.

I rejoined Adrienne out back. She was sitting in a glider in an ivy-covered bower, but I remained standing, taking in grateful breaths of untainted air. I told her what I'd found.

"What a monster. He could have so easily walked away."

"Twisted logic on his part, Adrienne. He probably saw the murder as an act of compassion."

"That word doesn't even apply here. Budge clearly has no conception of its meaning."

I trudged to the house next door and knocked. A squat, timid-looking woman in a nondescript beige duster opened the door and stared at me vacantly.

"Do you know Lawrence Budge? Or have any idea where I could find him?"

The woman's tone verged on hostility. "A man in a gray and white pickup truck came to his house yesterday and took away a lot of his belongings. Three trips. Then Budge drove off too. Is he in trouble? Are you the police?"

"No, ma'am. Just an acquaintance of your neighbor's."

She relaxed a little. "Sure looks like he's gone for good."

"What kind of truck was it?"

"I don't recall exactly. A Chevy maybe? Or a Japanese model? Goodness, they all look alike nowadays."

"Did you happen to notice Budge or his friend carrying off a lifelike male doll dressed in a suit? It belongs to me."

"No sir. But they toted off plenty of boxes."

"Any chance you remember the truck's license number?"

"Never even thought to pay heed to such a thing."

I sighed. Further leads seemed unlikely to drop from this stubbornly unobservant woman. My irritation made me brusque: "Lawrence Budge killed his dog. It's stinking up his basement right now. After a while, the smell's going to hit your house too. Would you mind telephoning the police or the health department?"

She lifted her chin almost militantly. "Why, sure. I'll do it now. It's only right."

On that note of civic responsibility, we parted.

◆ ◆ ◆

Adrienne drove us back to I-185 by way of Buena Vista Road. Fort Benning traffic galloped and banged around us: freeway white noise with occasional percussion. Neither of us spoke until we had taken the Box Road exit.

"So what now?" Adrienne said. "Some cat burglary? A bank

job? A carjacking? Can I be the gunsel with the gat?"

"I believe the traditional role for a woman of your physical assets is moll. But for now just carry us unobtrusively back to Smittinger-Alewine."

"You think Budge's pickup-driving buddy might work there?"

"Worth a shot."

Somebody loved us. A gray and white Dodge Dakota pickup occupied an employee slot behind the mortuary. By parking out front earlier, we had missed it. Earlier, of course, it would not have signified.

Seeking out the gorgon receptionist did not appeal to me. So I left Adrienne in the car and walked straight to the cupola-surmounted hearse barn. There, a skinny fellow in a polka-dot shirt and khaki pants was skating a chamois over the hood of a Lincoln. He looked several years younger than Budge and as amiable as a Springer spaniel. He wore his British-style chauffeur's cap backwards.

"Excuse me. Do you know the owner of that Dakota pickup?"

"Hope so. That's me. Ben Gregory. And you?"

"Will Keats."

He furrowed his brow. "We helped bury your father the other day, right? Any problems?"

"Not really. I'm looking for Lawrence Budge."

The question did not unsettle him. "Larry's a gone guy. Took off for someplace that starts with a C." Gregory scratched the nape of his neck. "Canada. California. Colorado, maybe. Said he'd come into some money and wanted to quit the stiff-stacking business. No disrespect, you understand. That's just how we talk amongst ourselves."

"You helped him move?"

"You might say that. He gave me most of his stuff and lit out with just two suitcases."

"Did he offer you his dog too?"

"Say, how'd you know? Yeah, he wanted me to take Orcus, and I would have except for my wife. Paula sneezes up a storm if any furry critter comes within half a mile of her."

"Budge didn't leave you a ventriloquist's dummy, did he?"

"Like the one your daddy had buried with him? Nosir. Just

books and plates and furniture and so on."

Adrienne appeared in the doorway, her face in shadow but her hair aglow and her flowered dress Kodachrome-vivid. Gregory's eyes widened.

"Did you see anyone talking to Mr. Budge before the Keats funeral?" she asked.

"Mr. Alewine. He always goes over the route with the drivers one last time beforehand."

"Anyone else?"

That itch drew Gregory's hand back up to his neck. "Why, yessum. Two or three of the mourners. They came up at different times before things got going really good."

"What were their names?"

"Can't rightly say. I never knew 'em."

Adrienne rephrased the question. "Were any of the people who approached Budge among the pallbearers?"

Gregory brightened. "Why, sure. All of them. A big, tall, straw-headed fella. An older, foreign-looking guy with dark skin. And someone sort of familiar, maybe a show-business type—a stocky little dude."

Burling Whickerbill, Satish Gupta, and of course Alan Papini. A regular convention had surrounded Budge.

Adrienne gave Gregory a drop-dead smile. "You've narrowed our investigation a lot. Thanks for keeping such a keen eye out."

Gregory almost permitted himself a spaniel-like wiggle. "Glad to help, ma'am. You too, mister."

We returned to the car and drove off.

"I'll send you my bill through the mail," Adrienne said. "Hundred dollars a day, plus expenses. And believe me, I can really put away the Wild Turkey, kiddo."

I had no attention to spare for a retort. I knew Papini's story. His apparent involvement had seemed an inevitable consequence of his greed and his envy. But Whickerbill and Gupta? What could have motivated them to seek out Budge?

As if reading my thoughts, Adrienne said, "Time to pay a couple more strategic visits, eh, Sherlock?"

CHAPTER 15

drienne insisted that we drive by to see LaRue and Kelli. Her ex, Byron Owsley, expected Adrienne to meet him in the food court of the Tocqueville Mall at 8:30 P.M. to pick up Olivia. This agreed-upon rendezvous meant that we could spend only about forty minutes visiting my family. Keeping Byron waiting did not constitute an option. Irritably punctilious, he had a low tolerance for what he perceived as the slackness of others.

"If we visit the Keep," I said, "we forfeit more playtime at my house."

"And if we don't, your bad karma hits a new high."

"My guardian angel. But don't forget to come down to earth once in a while."

Adrienne smiled at me sidelong. "Oh, the lotus always grows out of the mud," she said cryptically, then chauffered me to Skipper's Keep.

Once there, we saw Burling Whickerbill's great-white-hunter Jeep Cherokee in the driveway, its front bumper pinning Kelli's Monte Carlo Z34 against the garage. The attorney who never slept. Did the Keats finances or the Keats females hold his interest tonight? Adrienne parked on the street, and we walked to the front door holding hands.

Before I could use my copy of the house key to let us in, Adrienne said, "Are you going to tell LaRue everything? She might prefer handling the whole affair her way."

"I seriously doubt it."

"Aren't you patronizing her?"

"No. LaRue relishes others' taking control. It frees her to mope and swoon."

"Don't you want her to break that pattern? To assert her independence now that Skipper's dead?"

"Not possible. I've had thirty-four years to assess her personal dynamics, and you haven't had even one. Trust me. LaRue will not suddenly jump up and take charge if she hears about Dapper's theft. And even if I *was* going to tell her, now is not the time." I cocked a thumb at Burling's Jeep, then inserted my key in the front door. Surprisingly, it did not engage, as no one had bothered to turn the lock.

As I pushed the door inward, the usual chime sounded in the foyer: the opening notes of the theme from Zeffirelli's *Romeo and Juliet*. Still, no one showed. Eula must have earned some time off. Lights blazed, as on the night of Skipper's death, but the house felt either unwisely rented out or mothballed and plastic-draped.

"LaRue! Kelli! Burling!" I guided Adrienne down the hall toward the conservatory, but a breeze in a cross-corridor stopped me with the enticing odor of charcoal and grilling meat.

LaRue appeared in the opening at the end of this corridor. Elegant in black pants and a long-sleeved white blouse, a stem of red zinfandel in hand, she said, "I *thought* I heard someone. You're just in time for dinner."

Adrienne closed the gap between us and LaRue. She embraced my mother gingerly, wary of the wine glass, and they brushed cheeks. "We can't stay, Miss LaRue. We just popped in to see how you and Kelli were faring."

Less diplomatic, I said, "Mother, haven't you ever heard of home invasion?"

LaRue responded to Adrienne first. "Burling brought lots of chicken for the grill, and tons of deli goodies. You *have* to stay." She looked then to me. "Home invasion? What a crude term. You've been watching too much true-crime television, Will."

"It happens," I insisted, vaguely aware that I had recently ridden this same hobbyhorse. "Especially when your front door's unlocked. Masked thugs break in, tie up the whole family, then strip the house."

LaRue waved her glass airily. "How tiresome, and what a lot of work. If only they asked pretty please first — "

"Don't make light of this, LaRue. It could easily happen here."

LaRue intuited that the real sources of my unease lay elsewhere. "Will, what's the trouble? Talk to me."

I sagged from the exertions of the day. "Later. It's not really something you can help with."

"Perhaps not, dear." LaRue brightened. "Anyway, I insist on the two of you sitting down with us. Both of you look peaked. A meal will do you a world of good."

"If we do, we'll have to leave right after." Adrienne explained about Olivia and the appointment with her ex.

LaRue said, "We won't keep you a minute longer than you want to stay. Now, follow me." Wearily, besieged by both hunger and conscience, I fell in with the two women as they headed outside. LaRue continued to chatter: "Burling spent the afternoon here discussing insurance benefits, Social Security, and what-not. Then he insisted on firing up the grill and cooking for us. Doesn't it smell heavenly? He has so many talents."

"Like a high-school variety show," I muttered as we stepped onto the patio in the tenuous dusk. Fortunately for my karmic debt, the chef did not hear me.

In seersucker trousers and rolled-up shirt sleeves, Burling stood at the elaborate brazier, wielding a bottle of sauce and a pair of blackened tongs. His eyes glistened with smoke-primed tears, lending him an ursine melancholy. Despite the fearsome crackling of the chicken and the occasional burst of grease-fed flames, Burling did manage to glance our way.

"'Lo, Will. 'Lo, Miss Owsley. Hope you all'll join us." A bluish-yellow flare shot up alarmingly, and Burling backed away like a bear from a hive of agitated bees.

"I guess we're going to," I said, with as much graciousness as I could muster.

As LaRue poured Adrienne a half glass of zinfandel and Burling tiptoed around the brazier, poking at the searing meat, I wandered deeper into the yard. Twilight had drifted under the Japanese maples, black oaks, and sycamores, and I struggled to collect my thoughts. Where was Kelli? Her obvious infatuation with Malley still troubled me. Could she possibly conceive of him as some sort of Skipper-substitute, a fit object for the affections she could no longer lavish on our father?

I wandered farther from the patio. The back yard at Skipper's Keep had more height than depth, progressing upward within its confined space via slopes and landscaped terraces. On the lowest terrace, a series of plaster bird baths. On the next, a modest vegetable garden. On the highest, a pet cemetery and an expensive Italian sun dial. But trees grew on every level, and I climbed past an algae-stained bird bath to the tallest sycamore.

In this sycamore's ragged foliage, Skipper had built — with the help of an obliging neighborhood handyman — an impressive tree fort. He had built it for me, perhaps as a substitute for the swimming pool that he would not allow on the premises, ostensibly for fear of accidents and lawsuits, but more probably as a sensible acknowledgment of his own inability to swim. In any case, I had loved that tree fort more than any other of his distinctive gifts, and for a month or two after its completion he had actually made time to play with me in it, without hauling Dapper along. We had camped in it together, played cards, plotted future father-and-son adventures in Kenya or the Yukon, and told each other flamboyant stories. Then Skipper had ventured out on several out-of-state gigs in a row, which not only interrupted but absolutely disposed of these idylls. Fortunately, the hideaway itself had provided a kind of consolation.

I caught the old rope ladder in my hand and reminiscently twisted it. Time and rough weather had severed two of the rungs. A rotted floorboard above my head hung down like a wooden tongue. An empty bird's nest perched where two joists met.

LaRue's voice dispelled my cloud of nostalgia. "Will, it's almost time to eat!"

I returned to the patio. LaRue and Adrienne had gone into the sunroom to set the tile-topped table there. Burling forked cooked chicken onto a platter. He then placed the last three raw breasts on the grill and nudged them impatiently with his tongs. Over his shoulder, I said, "Does the name Lawrence Budge mean anything to you?"

Burling flinched and recovered. "Famous canary breeder, I believe?" He grinned at me lopsidedly.

"Lawrence Budge drove Skipper's hearse, Burling."

"Oh, really? Is he a friend of yours, Will?"

"No. But I happened to visit his house this afternoon anyway. It's empty. Budge has skipped town."

Burling reoriented himself to stare me in the eye. A look of genuine puzzlement overspread his features. "This must mean something, Will, but I confess I can't imagine what."

Either the man had the acting talents of Olivier, or he truly knew nothing of why I might take an interest in Budge. With no pick to unlock this mystery, I decided to assume — for now — his innocence.

"It's something that might become apparent later perhaps. Meanwhile, just forget it."

Burling shrugged and returned his gaze to the grill. "Whatever you say, Will. Here." He handed me the plate of cooked chicken. "Take this in, please. I'll come along as soon as the rest are done."

After barging inside and setting the platter down, I repositioned and straddled one of the ladder-back chairs at the table. A basket of wheat rolls and several opened cartons of deli fare — slaw, potato salad, cold rainbow tortellini — had appeared as appetizing side dishes. LaRue was laying silverware as Adrienne extracted ice cubes from an insulated bucket and placed them in big plastic cups.

"Kelli," I said. "Where's Kelli, LaRue?"

"She had a sort of date."

"With whom? She's not seeing anyone I've heard tell of."

LaRue dropped a fork, which rang on the tiles of the table. "She went with Ryan."

"Ryan Malley?"

"Yes."

"Good Lord, LaRue, how could you let *Malley* take her out? He just wants to pick her brains. Dig up dirt on our family."

"You're maligning him, Will. He asked Kelli out very politely, and in my presence. He said he found her — very interesting."

"As a source, not as a person. Kelli's a great kid, but she's just that — only a kid. Malley has Pulitzer Prizes and book advances on the brain, not innocent romance. Where — exactly — did they go?"

"I . . . the Bradley Library, I think."

Standing, I said, "I'm going after them."

Adrienne, who had just edged around me, levered me back down into the chair. "Hey, Lone Ranger, sit down. Kelli's not with the Boston Strangler, you know. You've never interfered with her dates before. Why start now?"

Reluctantly, I subsided. Despite my suspicions that Malley would beguile and misuse my sister, I could hardly hang at her elbow every minute. Adrienne smiled reassuringly, and with the weary resolution of a good son, I even reversed my position on the chair, prompting a complementary smile from my mother.

Burling entered with the last charred spoils of the grill, and LaRue offered a peculiar free-form blessing — something about flesh nourishing flesh, spirit feeding spirit, and our fortified souls communing with our beloved dead. Burling, after fetching a six-pack of Pete's Wicked Summer Brew from the kitchen fridge, spun a long waggish story about the reactions of some of the Smittinger-Alewine employees at Skipper's funeral to the ventriloquists who had actually brought their trademark figures along: a female ostrich, a Viking in a brass helmet, a Mexican mouse. Even I could not help laughing.

As I sipped my second beer, Adrienne daubed at her lips and leaned toward me. "Will, we've got to go. Byron will try to score custody points against me if I'm even a minute late."

I did not want to leave until I knew that Ryan Malley had returned Kelli safely. Surprisingly, Burling showed himself sensitive to my dilemma. He offered to drive me back to Mountboro once Kelli had come in.

Having consented, I walked Adrienne to her car. In the darkness of the driveway, we kissed. I opened the driver's door for her, and she slipped inside.

Closing it, she said, "Can't accuse you of failing to show a girl an interesting time, Will. An abandoned house, a murdered dog, a hearse-waxing, and a cookout, all on the same date."

"Dancing and drinks next time, kiddo — just you, me, and the moonlight."

"Like any good PI, I've got my tape recorder running, you realize."

I placed my hand over my heart. "My word is my bond."

I watched her car's taillights until they disappeared, then went back inside.

Upon my return, LaRue and Burling fell silent. Sipping her iced-tea or gnawing meditatively on a chicken breast, my mother disdained further conversation. She had fallen into a fragile but impenetrable reverie. Burling and I exchanged a sympathetic glance and then discussed sports in a desultory manner. A tedious half-hour or so later, footsteps sounded from the front of the house.

Kelli's voice: "Hello! We're home!"

When she and Ryan Malley actually appeared, my sister looked schoolgirlish in denim shorts and a lavender shirt, her hair in a braid. Malley looked collegiate in khakis and a navy-blue jacket. LaRue sprang up, kissed Kelli, and escorted Malley to a place at the table, a corner spot where he settled like a favorite nephew. Kelli pulled up a chair beside him and quickly secured him a piece of chicken.

"What did you all do at the Bradley?" I asked Malley without preamble.

Spooning slaw and salad onto his plate, he replied without even looking up: "We used the microfiche readers. I wanted to check out some issues of the *Columbus Ledger-Enquirer* from the seventies."

"Research on Skipper?"

"Partly. But I also had some personal matters to track."

LaRue asked if Malley had family in Columbus.

"Not anymore." He smiled at her and took a mouthful of food.

Kelli said, "In case anyone cares, *I* checked out a couple of books for my history paper."

The conversation turned to other issues. I tried to overcome my strange irritation with Malley enough to join in. For someone purportedly hip and cosmopolitan, he had dismal table manners, ripping wolfishly at his chicken and speaking as he chewed. Moreover, he had opinions or information to share about almost everything, from Third World politics to haute cuisine to Hollywood film scores. Forty boorish minutes after Adrienne's departure, he finally thanked LaRue and Burling for feeding him, and stood to leave. With an oddly effecting punctilio, he bowed to both LaRue and Kelli.

Burling said, "Guess I'll be going too. C'mon, Will." He pushed back from the table.

"Wait a minute." Malley looked at me. "Do you need a ride home? I'm driving to Atlanta. Let me drop you off in Mountboro. Then Mr. Whickerbill won't have to go out of his way."

Burling smiled, relieved that the long nocturnal roundtrip would devolve on someone else. "That okay with you, Will?"

A chance to ride with Malley perversely appealed to me. What peculiar illuminations might light my journey home?

"Sure," I said.

Malley gestured toward the hall, and together we went through the house and outside to his low-slung black rodent of a sports car.

CHAPTER 16

Malley kept a cluttered car. On the floor below the front seat, research materials — xeroxes and cassettes — composted with candy wrappers, soda cans, stained credit-card receipts, and even some crumpled grocery coupons. I got in gingerly to avoid scuffing up the mess any more than I had to. On the backseat rested a laptop computer, a gape-mouthed satchel, several issues of the *Sandman* comic book, three or four paper-backs, a stack of manila folders, and a few different baseball caps. The smell of the interior blended WD-40, Stetson cologne, and rancid french fries.

Malley pulled out into traffic with a gear-grinding disregard for safety. I kept my mouth shut, though, and so did he, driving capably for a silent quarter-hour. In the sheen of oncoming lights and roadside signage, his profile betrayed nothing but focus and forebearance. As we approached the city's northern outskirts, I turned toward him.

"Appreciate the ride."

"No sweat."

Two Gary Cooper wannabes, struggling to give away as little as possible of either our feelings or our knowledge. To hell with that. I jacked up the volume:

"But I *don't* appreciate your recruiting Kelli into your self-serving biographical project. Clearly you've charmed her, but she's impressionable because she's underage. Don't forget that. "

Malley registered no discomfort. "Actually, Kelli's very mature for sixteen. She's helping voluntarily. All my cards are faceup, Mr. Keats. Most of them, anyhow. And yours?"

"I don't regard this matter as a hand of poker, Malley. So let me make it clear that if you hurt Kelli in any fashion, you'll answer to me."

"Understood."

In the cruising RX-7 we cleared the final strip of businesses on Hamilton Road and plunged headlong into the tree-bracketed darkness of Highway 27. The road had narrowed, and the headlamps' beams shot out before us like an insect's fragile feelers. Malley's profile had become a hatchet-shaped silhouette.

"You don't know who I am, do you?" He spoke to the windshield, without inflection.

The question's strangeness hung between us. Did Malley intend to reveal his role as thief, the purloiner of Dapper? "Not in any real sense, I suppose. Do you?"

Malley laughed bitterly "I'm the *only* one who does. Take your mother, for instance. *She* should know. But she doesn't."

"You're leaving me way behind here, Malley."

A grin split the cutout's edge. "Suppose I told you that you and I spent a night together in that tree fort in your backyard?"

"In another life, maybe."

Now Malley seemed positively playful, like a kitten toying with a grasshopper. "No, no, this life, the only one we've got. I'm quite certain of it."

"If you're not jerking me around, this happened a long time ago."

"Oh, yes, indeed. Jimmy Carter newly elected, me about five. Sound familiar yet?"

"You're claiming we met over twenty years ago?"

"Absolutely."

"And you spent the night in my tree fort with me?"

"Right again."

"None of this clicks for me, Malley."

He chuckled, then portentously intoned, "The Flaming Lobster of Doom," whereupon the entire fled memory snapped into place like a jackpot clicking on a slot machine. I felt myself flush crimson, something of a parboiled lobster myself.

Skipper often scheduled four-day weekends out of town. Home

could rarely compete with the allure of the road and of far-flung audiences. The summer of my fourteenth year had held more than its share of Skipper's absences, but I may have missed Dapper more than I did him: no playmate for Will. On one of these hot, interminable Fridays, a woman friend of LaRue's showed up at the house with a wide-eyed little boy skittishly in tow. LaRue immediately designated me his keeper so that she and her visitor could chat. The kid's name was Ryan, after the actor Ryan O'Neal, then a popular icon; the woman with him was not his mother, but a close relative with a surname different from the boy's.

I took the quiet, big-eyed kid out back. My tree house — with its scratchy rope ladder, shingled sides, and screened windows — beckoned us. A gift from my father, that fort elicited immoderate pride in me, but once we had scrambled up, Ryan proved properly appreciative, exploring every nook and feature, marveling at the solid-state portable TV, its battery as big as two volumes of my Grolier encyclopedia. Ryan could not read yet, but he already enjoyed theater, spectacle, performance. So as Skipper's hammy scion, I took all the parts of a *Daredevil* comic, and easily wrested from him an earnest round of applause for my efforts. Later, thirsty and hungry, we clambered down.

Inside, the woman who had brought Ryan wore a summer-afternoon glow all too familiar to me. LaRue always sported a similar aura after several fragrant bourbons. Spotting Ryan, the woman told him it was time to go. He crossed his arms and braced his feet like a miniature Superman. "Don't wanna."

Boozily indulgent, the woman said. "Well, what *do* you want to do?"

"Stay here with Will. Sleep in his fort."

The woman chided him for manufacturing this invitation, but LaRue stepped in, affirming that I loved to sleep in the tree fort and that I would gladly welcome Ryan as an overnight guest. Her first clause rang true — I did enjoy camping in my lofty sanctuary — but the second outraged me. Another teenager I might have tolerated in that consecrated place, but LaRue had unilaterally extended my involuntary servitude as a *babysitter*, and I seethed with resentment. Neither adult took any notice, and in less than a minute they had arranged the munchkin's sleepover.

Back up in the fort that evening, Ryan and I watched television and engaged each other in cutthroat games of Battleship, Yahtze, and Uno. In fact, *I* was the cutthroat and handily won every game. Ryan surrendered sweetly every time and just as sweetly begged for another chance. It was well after eleven before I could convince him to put on his pajamas and stretch out on the built-in sleeping bench across from mine.

"You know, Ryan," I said conspiratorially, "not many kids your age do very well when the monsters finally show up here at the Keep. I'm sure you'll do fine, though."

He clutched his blankets tightly. "M-monsters? What monsters?"

Inspired, I spoke matter-of-factly rather than flamboyantly. "Giant lobsters from Saturn. They glow like fiery demons."

Ryan squinted skeptically. "Unh-unh." A feeble protest.

"Yes, Ryan, it's true. And you know what they like to do?"

He propped himself up on one elbow, his big eyes now as gratifyingly large as hubcaps. "What?"

"They especially enjoy peeling people's faces off."

Ryan said, "No, they don't."

"Believe what you like, but I'm only telling you the truth."

After an additional flustering exchange, Ryan fell asleep.

Using a flashlight I stole down the rope ladder and into the house. In the kitchen I found the water-filled Coleman cooler containing the three sluggishly stirring lobsters that LaRue had purchased for Skipper's triumphant return on Sunday. I squatted beside the cooler, took a deep breath, and quickly withdrew the biggest of the claw-banded monsters. Then I returned to the fort and struggled one-handed up the rope ladder.

Ryan snored slightly. After setting the feeble lobster on the floor, I found a stubby candle and a pack of matches on the shelf above the television. I lit the wick, dripped wax onto the lobster's thoracic segment, and cemented the glowing candle in the wax. Equally deliberately, I released the lobster's claws. My final ingenuity was to boost myself through a trapdoor in the ceiling, where I could lie on the flat roof and look back down on my stagecraft. I awakened Ryan by sharply and repeatedly calling his name. At length he sat up and stared uncomprehendingly at the crawling harbinger of doom.

As Skipper had taught me, I threw my voice.

"Rye-eye-an, I am the leader of the lobsters from Saturn. Although you do not believe in us, we have come for your face. We intend to rip off your nose and ears and claw out your eyes."

Ryan grew as rigid as a crowbar as his eyes fixed on the advancing alien death. His mouth opened, and although I feared that a scream would bring parental intervention and thwart my full revenge, only choked burblings emerged.

"Rye-eye-an, prepare to surrender your lips."

The kid's paralysis broke, he leapt up and virtually tumbled from the fort. Apparently, screaming like a banshee, he managed to get down the rope without killing himself.

Hurriedly, I scrambled down from the roof, snuffed the candle and removed it from the lobster's back, popping its wax base too off the innocent creature. Then I snatched up the lobster and followed Ryan. As he stood screaming and banging on the glass of the sunroom, I entered the kitchen by another door and restored the lobster to its Coleman cooler. Then, angling around as if coming from the fort, I joined Ryan.

LaRue and Ryan's guardian had already found him, and Ryan clung to our visitor's legs. LaRue put a hand on my shoulder and squeezed it punitively. "William Keats, just what happened here?"

"I guess he had a nightmare. I tried to help him, but he wouldn't let me."

Too distraught to dispute this, Ryan wailed, "I want to go ho-o-o-o-ome!" Nothing any of us tried calmed him in the least, and eventually both he and the woman had to leave, presumably so that Ryan's parents could deal with him.

At the time, I had not regretted frightening Ryan. I regretted only that no one else had witnessed the minor extravaganza that had sent him caterwauling into the house. That no one had applauded my ingenuity or remarked on the effectiveness of the deceptive distant voice that Skipper had taught me, less through patience and praise than through badgering and rebuke. I wished that Skipper could have seen and heard. He would have appreciated the show. He might even have arranged to tell me so, if only through the equivocal agency of Dapper O'Dell:

"*What vocal pandemonium. I'm proud of you, knothead. Maybe we're siblings after all.*"

◆ ◆ ◆

"That was *you?*" I said in Ryan Malley's cluttered Mazda. "You were the annoying brat I sicced the flaming lobster on?"

"The same, Mr. Keats. It took me a year to go to sleep at nights without the lights on. And another six or seven to realize what a truly barbarous trick you'd played on me."

I shook my head. Today I made my living counseling children, many of whom shared the shapeless dread that I had once purposely inflicted on Ryan Malley. The irony did not escape me, and in the concealing dark of the car's interior I flushed again.

My victim, grown, drove us into the southern precincts of Mountboro, a strip of restaurants and filling stations, a lone video outlet or liquor store for variation. I had no recollection at all of the past eight miles of our journey.

"Would you like to know why my aunt brought me over that day?"

The shoulder harness suddenly felt constricting. "Sure. But — do you know where I live?"

"Of course. The house where Skipper grew up, with Clayton and Cerell Keats."

"Let's talk there."

"Why not?"

In less than five minutes, then, we sat at my kitchen table, jelly glasses of apple juice and a steaming bag of microwaved popcorn between us, as if unconsciously replicating that overnight camp out. Malley studied the room — from the nearly antique gas stove to the turret-surmounted refrigerator — as if assimilating it for future description. For a moment, the weird reality of my living in Skipper's childhood home struck me forcefully.

"Do you remember anything at all about the woman who brought me to the Keep?" Malley abruptly asked.

"Only that she and LaRue got mildly blitzed on Wild Turkey."

"You never even knew her name, did you?"

"No."

"What if I told you she was Evelyn Sermak?"

I considered this datum as Malley, juggling a handful of popcorn to cool it, peered intently at me. The story of the Sermaks had tangled roots, and I failed to understand how Ryan had sprung from them.

Evelyn Sermak was the wife — by then actually the widow — of Thaddeus Sermak, who during a streak of arcane bad luck in 1970 had commited suicide. Him I now remembered surprisingly well — my memory jogged by Satish Gupta at Skipper's wake — despite my being not quite eight at the time of Sermak's death. Sermak had joined forces with both Skipper and Satish Gupta in the late sixties to finance a mail-order business predicated on various ventriloquial and show-business products: cheap Dapper O'Dell replicas, Letitia Crone Halloween supplies, comedy recordings, autographed photos, how-to booklets, and the like. Sermak had total management responsibility for this arm of the Keats empire, although he had to report directly to Gupta. Sermak died spectacularly in that year, shooting himself in the head while perched on a parapet on the Dillingham Street bridge between Columbus and Phenix City, then plunging into the Chattahoochee River before at least a dozen astonished witnesses. Upon his death, secrets spilled from containment like sour milk from a tipped bottle: Sermak had been cooking the books, diverting sizable sums for his own use, failing to fill orders, kicking back to cut-rate supply houses that dealt in shoddy merchandise. Other personal failings surfaced only as tremulous whispers unfit for the ears of youth.

As for Evelyn Sermak, these days she lived in Florida, as I knew from the address on the expensive floral tribute she had sent to Skipper's wake. Now a pointed question led Malley to reveal that she had resided there even during the period when she visited the Keep with young Ryan. She had never remarried, but supported herself as a trainer and groom at a major horse farm west of

Ocala, having turned a girlhood hobby into a life-saving career after her husband's death.

"Okay," I said. "Just how are you connected with the Sermaks?"

"Officially, she's my aunt. My father Brendan's sister."

"Only officially?"

"That's right. I'm really her son by birth. She gave me up to her older brother and his childless wife, Anna. They raised me, but Evelyn Sermak is my biological mother."

My head spun. "Thaddeus can't be your father, though. He died too soon."

"Right. Guess who my father is."

"How should I know? Anyone might claim that honor."

"If my dad were just anyone, I wouldn't be sitting here."

I felt queasy then, and my hands grew clammy as two peeled potatoes. "You don't intend to imply . . ." I couldn't finish.

"I don't mean to imply anything; I'll say it flat out. My biological father was Skipper Keats. Evelyn told me on my twenty-first birthday, and she had no reason to lie."

I stood up, splashed the rest of my apple juice into the sink, and pulled two bottles of Dos Equis beer from the refrigerator. I rapidly uncapped them and set one down in front of Ryan Malley with a bang that rattled his jelly glass and propelled a half dozen jacks of popcorn out of their scorched bag. A peculiar sort of laugh escaped me.

"Well, I'll be damned."

"No sooner than our father," Malley said.

I nodded at the Dos Equis in front of him. "Despite the dubious ethics of our father's intimate consolation of the widow Sermak, I guess this late-breaking news calls for a toast."

"Sorry. I've still got a ninety-minute drive home."

"You're not Skipper's son if you refuse a drink." I sat down and took a hearty swig from my own beer.

"A man's son doesn't take after him in every way."

"God, I hope not." I sipped more temperately. "Why'd Evelyn bring you to the Keep that day?"

"She planned to disclose my parentage and hauled me along

as evidence. She thought it past time that the truth come out."

"What stopped her from telling LaRue?"

"Pity, I think. LaRue greeted her warmly, hugged her, gave her a drink or twelve. As they drank, LaRue explained how much she missed Skipper during his absences and how faithfully she awaited his homecomings. They laughed and joked with each other, and Evelyn eventually determined that she could not hurt LaRue, that she could not in good conscience betray her betrayer."

"Obviously, Evelyn Sermak qualifies for sainthood."

"I think so."

I finished my beer and seized Malley's untasted one. We took turns plunging our hands into the popcorn bag, until only unopened BB-like kernels remained. A quaint but companionable silence had fallen between us. Suddenly, though, I laughed uproariously.

Malley said, "What is it?"

"I thought you had the hots for my sister, Kelli. But she's *our* sister, and that puts the kibosh on that scenario."

Malley blushed vividly. "I thought the unlikelihood of any such desires became obvious once I revealed my paternity."

"Well, of course. But Kelli's still in the dark, and I think she's more than a little smitten."

"Oh, I doubt that."

"Afraid so. So I'd appreciate it if you stayed away from both her and the Keep until we can figure out a way to break the news to LaRue."

Ryan Malley — Ryan Sermak Malley Keats? — stared at the backs of his hands and then looked at me with raw adolescent bemusement in his eyes. "You said 'we.' Does this mean you might help me with my project?"

"That damned buttinsky book of yours? Hell, why not, bro'? Let's air *all* of Skipper's dirty laundry."

"I've told you — "

"One last thing," I cut in. "You didn't pay the driver of Skipper's hearse to steal Dapper O'Dell for you, did you?"

"God, no!" The look on Malley's face exculpated him far more eloquently than any more elaborate verbal denial.

Although he pressed for the basis of my question, I would not explain myself. Eventually, I walked him out to his car as if we had known of our relationship for years. As he motored off, the eighteen-wheelers and logging trucks on Highway 27 prowled up and down the road like huge nocturnal reptiles.

CHAPTER 17

I could not sleep. A host of different issues gnawed at me: Skipper's death; my mother's tenuous grip on reality; the revelation that Kelli and I had a half brother, Ryan Malley; Kelli's apparent infatuation with this surprise sibling; the theft of Dapper O'Dell; the disappearance of Lawrence Budge; the assassination of the Labrador retriever, Orcus; Shawndrell Tompkin's grief for his beloved grandfather; the refusal of Talulah Grimes's mother to take the girl to a doctor; the likelihood that I'd lose my job; and the niggling suspicion that Adrienne Owsley might eventually come to prefer someone with a more conventional set of problems. Suddenly a quick and painless suicide ceased to strike me as an ignominious way to attain relief.

I thought about Thaddeus Sermak looking down into the coffee-colored Chattahoochee with gun in hand. Sermak had planned a fail-safe self-destruction: blow his brains out and then smash into the distant drowning pool. How many issues had Sermak been mentally juggling on that concrete bridge rail? Simply how to handle his recently discovered profit-skimming at Keats & O'Dell Enterprises? His inability to father a child with Evelyn Sermak, even though they had both publicly placed the blame for their infertility as a couple on her? The symptoms of diabetes and ulcerative colitis that Sermak's doctor had uncovered during his last physical? Or possibly his daily failure to reconcile his own uncouth appearance — apelike arms, permanent flush, gloriously tacky shirts — with the urbane or debonair looks of his business partners, Keats and Gupta? Additionally, rumors that Sermak gambled, drank, and popped pills had long run rampant.

Whatever the issue or issues, the conundrum of his place in the world had become too much for Sermak, and he had deliberately taken his exit from it. At least he had never learned of Skipper's adultery with his widow or the birth of a son he could never father.

When Georgia Public Radio blared from my clock radio at 6:00 A.M., I realized that I had dozed in tiny squalls. I silenced the radio and staggered into the bathroom. Under the shower, I sorted through the points that my fragmentary sleep had clarified for me:

1. Lawrence Budge had more to hide than the theft of a dummy.
2. Ryan Malley would eventually want some of Skipper's estate.
3. I needed to make an appointment with Satish Gupta, last of the three suspects to have approached Budge prior to the funeral cortege.
4. Adrienne loved me too much to let matters outside my control, however bizarre, influence her affections.
5. And within the next two weeks or so the Speece County Board of Education would very likely give me the sack.

Point No. 5 left a rueful grin on my lips all the way into work.

◆ ◆ ◆

Nora Friend sent Shawndrell Tompkins to me from her first-grade class. He came in carrying the memory box honoring his grandfather. I opened a desk drawer and removed a bite-sized candy bar from the bag of Butterfingers I kept there.

"Have a treat, Shawndrell."

"Mama says I can't eat no candy until after we has lunch."

"'Any' candy. 'Have' lunch."

Shawndrell eyed the candy hungrily. "Right."

"Well, suppose you save it in here till then." I tucked the bar into his shirt pocket, and he rewarded me with a smile. "What brings you in today, Shawndrell?"

Shawndrell dragged his plastic chair around the desk next to my padded caster chair. "I got a new problem, Mr. Kee." As if to fortify himself for a battle, he fished the Butterfinger out of his pocket, unwrapped it, and slipped it into his mouth. It crunched audibly. Still chewing, he said, "I seed him last night, Mr. Kee."

"Who? Your paw-paw?"

Shawndrell nodded. Narrowing his eyes, he gripped his own elbows and began almost imperceptibly to rock in place.

"You *dreamed* you saw him. Is that it?"

"Couldn't'a been no dream, 'cause I wasn't sleeping. I was crying on my bed, thinking how we usta go fishing together. That's when I seed him. Everything just like regular. He had his ol' boots on. He had his pole. He had his cap. Only thing strange, he was floating up near the ceiling."

"Up near the ceiling? What could he have been fishing for there? Was he fishing for you?"

Shawndrell nodded. "That's so. He told me hisself. 'Grab hold of the line, Shawndrell,' he said. I tried, but I couldn't. Then he started to float up through the roof. 'Paw-paw, stop!' I hollered. But he didn't hear me, or maybe he couldn't control hisself. Anyhow, he disappeared." Shawndrell stopped rocking but released the remainder of his breath like a leaky tire.

I put my hand on his knee. "That had to be a dream, Shawndrell. But it was also your paw-paw's spirit visiting you because he still cares. He just can't stay, that's all. Dreams like that are strong and real, but not quite strong enough to bring back to our world someone who's passed. Still, your paw-paw came to visit and left you a lovely midnight gift."

Shawndrell looked at me forthrightly. "I don't want him to do it again, Mr. Kee. He *scare* me, scare me and make me sad. I didn't get me no sleep, him coming like that."

"Maybe you needed the visit more than the sleep. Try to think about that."

Shawndrell made no reply, but I hoped that he would revolve the idea in his mind and perhaps see that the distressing strangeness of his dream was counterbalanced by its mysterious beauty.

I concluded our session by doing several miniature puzzles with the boy. He left after giving me his permission to discuss the whole incident with his mother. I would call her from Mountboro later that evening, when she had arrived home from work.

◆ ◆ ◆

Because I did not have bus duty that afternoon or a parent conference, I got away a little early and drove directly to Tocqueville Middle School to see Adrienne. A secretary whose name I could never remember advised me to go to the media center — the *library* my generation had called such rooms — to await Adrienne amidst the computers, the racks of VHS tapes, and the bedraggled books. Once there, I spotted that morning's *Columbus Ledger-Enquirer* folded over a bamboo rod. I took it from its rack and sat at a stumpy table idly turning pages. An item in the local section snagged my wandering eye.

DOG FOUND SHOT IN VACANT
COLUMBUS RESIDENCE

Yesterday evening Maudine Weyrich came upon the dead body of her neighbor's dog in an abandoned rental property at 65 Millar Street.

Concerned that her neighbor, Lawrence J. Budge — last seen departing his residence with two suitcases but without his dog — had left his pet unattended, Mrs. Weyrich chose to investigate.

Finding the rear door of Budge's home ajar with its lock damaged, she entered. Eventually she came upon the dog in the basement, dead in a plastic children's swimming pool. It had been shot in the back of the head, execution-style.

Mrs. Weyrich immediately called the police. The authorities learned that Budge, 45, had been employed by Smittinger-Alewine Mortuary Services as a hearse driver. However, he had not reported to work for several days.

Budge was renting the house from Chat-Val Realty, Inc., a local firm principally owned by well-known businessman Satish Gupta. . . .

Adrienne put her hand on my shoulder. She wore flats, a simple pink and brown dress, and a snow-white sweater. I liked looking up at her exposed throat and the backlit gold of her hair. Carrying a sailcloth beach bag full of textbooks and student papers, she was ready to go home.

"Did you successfully defend your sister's virtue last night?"

"Better than you ever defended yours."

"Oh, I can protect myself just fine. But against a pussycat, how much defense do you need?" She tousled my hair.

"What ever happened to 'tiger'?"

"You've got to earn your stripes."

I creased the paper to highlight the article and held it up to her. "Here, read this."

Adrienne did so. "Maudine was kind enough not to mention us, I see."

"Thank God. I hope the police don't go taking prints from that backdoor."

Adrienne dropped the paper to the table and frowned. "That's exactly why I advised you against doing all this on your own. Go to the Columbus police and tell them about Dapper's theft. So far only a dog has died. But if anything bad happens to a person, you'll regret it for the rest of your life."

I rested my head against her hip. "If I haven't found anything out by Saturday, I'll tell the police. You have my word."

Sighing, Adrienne said, "If that's the maximum compromise I can hope to extract, okay. You seem to love this amateur sleuthing too much to give it up."

"Not exactly. It's just — I feel a personal obligation, okay? And I *am* finding things out. For instance, last night I uncovered a new member of my family."

"Made of teak and plastic, I presume."

"No, flesh and blood. His name is Ryan Malley." I explained the Evelyn Sermak connection and recounted with some long-delayed pleasure and some equally belated embarrassment my fiendish adolescent ingenuity on the Night of the Flaming Lobster.

"Neat, Will. And curious too. But I don't see how that discovery gets you any closer to Dapper."

"I have a feeling Ryan's parentage does somehow tie in. I can't say exactly how yet, but I sense that Skipper's old lusts do matter."

"So what do you plan for this evening? Dinner with Olivia and me, or a visit to Gupta?"

"The latter, if I'm going to finish this investigation before Saturday."

Adrienne, pulling away, took a long stride toward the door. Then she stopped and looked back: "Why don't you just telephone the stuffy old coot?"

"And miss the chance to look him in the eye when I ask him if he paid Budge to steal Dapper?"

"You really do enjoy playing Sam Spade, don't you?"

"Adrienne, you can't just — "

In a rare display of sustained annoyance, she said, "This is a merry-go-round discussion, Will. The same lame wooden creatures keep coming into view."

I gave her a smile of unalloyed admiration. In fact, I wanted to take her into my arms and simply hold her for two or three quiet minutes.

As if reading my mind, she shook her head and said, "Good luck, Will, but I can't pretend to endorse all this. Call me when you get home, and don't mind the time. Olivia can sleep through a four-alarm fire next door, and I won't fall asleep till I hear from you."

She walked fluidly away, with a trace of anger still visible in her carriage, and I dismissed any hope of a consoling embrace. Probably just as well. Media center personnel never relish hosting the sort of interactive educational exhibition I had in mind.

CHAPTER 18

Back down to Columbus, this time to the swank residential estates near Lake Oliver and the sprawling fairways of Green Island Hills Country Club. Satish and Sherri VanHouten Gupta lived on a wooded cul-de-sac with a ravishing view of the lake. Their house and grounds dwarfed those of my parents. And Skipper, having denominated his small castle with the generic appellation "Keep," soon realized that Gupta had also bested him titularly, for Gupta had chosen to call his estate "Golconda," after an ancient Indian kingdom. I had visited Golconda before, of course, but each sight of it momentarily stopped my breath. This afternoon I halted at the base of the dogwood-colonized hill that it dominated to marvel again at what this driven immigrant from Andhra Pradesh had accomplished.

Centered on its lush billiard-table lawn, Golconda rose above the fringing pines and the dogwoods like the extravagant castle of a rajah. On the model of the Charminar, famous landmark in the center of Hyderabad, the house boasted an open arch giving access to an interior courtyard where visitors could park their cars on a raked gravel oval amidst climbing vines and sinuous marble statues. Ersatz minarets grew from the corner abutments, higher than the nearby trees. The structure's façade mixed natural-toned wood, polished plaster, and pastel tiles. Potted topiary shrubbery on three different balcony levels shared the literal spotlights with rotatable wind scoops of colorful sturdy fabrics modeled on the picturesque breeze funnels of Pakistan.

Looking at such prodigality from afar, I pictured costumed theme park employees wandering the grounds, selling Indian food and trinkets, and wondered why anything-for-a-buck Gupta had stopped short of such self-exploitation. I shifted my car into gear and drove upslope. Entering the actual grounds through a wrought-iron gateway, I noted the inactive fairy lights strung among the trees. On public holidays and personal anniversaries, Gupta would — with as much glee as he seemed capable of exhibiting — command the well-maintained displays to come ablaze. Hundreds of thousands of lights shone like fireflies in the woods or dripped like icicles from the minarets. The perimeter of every arch galloped with chasers. LaRue's best efforts notwith-standing, Skipper's Keep on the night of my father's death had shed less than a hundredth of the wattage.

"I burn my lights as a gift to Jesus," Gupta liked to say. "As a gift to America." America — in the form of hundreds of local inhabitants — responded in kind, driving into the hills to ogle. The bumper-to-bumper traffic enraged the neighbors, and during these exhibitions Gupta and his wife had to use a private lakeside road to enter Golconda, thus avoiding the shouting matches and fisticuffs that ensued among the frazzled spectators, one or two intolerant homeowners, and occasionally some unsuspecting motorists.

I pulled up behind a restored '57 Cadillac in the parking atri-um and ascended a flight of front steps that could have accomo-dated a parade of elephants. I knocked on a nailhead-studded door the size of a flatcar, using a knocker shaped like a multi-armed female Hindu deity. Each time the goddess thudded against the wood, a gong reverberated inside.

At length, a young woman appeared. She wore a sari-like tan-gerine and gold garment and had a vivid caste mark on her fore-head. I had never met her before, but she said, "Welcome, Mr. Keats," and ushered me into the living room, an airy expanse with a cathedral ceiling.

This room harbored leather-spined books and odd displays of exotic musical instruments, from trombones to sitars to African drums. A suit or two of Moghul armor stood like vigilant sen-tries. Movable brass posts linked by wide strands of red ribbon cordoned off the extensive parquet floorspace into irregular aisles and boxes, an innovation since my last visit. Either Gupta planned a formal exhibition for selected friends, or he had indeed begun running tours.

Before I could speak, the sari-clad woman placed her hands together prayerfully, bowed, and silently vanished. Then I heard footsteps, and Gupta's wife, Sherri, entered through the farthest archway. Like a bipedal lab animal, she navigated briskly through the ribbon maze until she stood before me.

"William." She stretched out both hands, obligating me to clasp them. A disconcerting fever radiated from her skin.

I could hardly remember the last time I had seen Sherri Gupta — perhaps three and a half years ago, when I had received my counseling degree and the Guptas had dropped by to congratulate me. She still looked good, but sadder and frailer. A directed gust from one of the wind funnels would undoubtedly bowl her over.

She wore a long-sleeved dove-colored shirt and knee-length white linen shorts. Artful platinum streaks concealed the emerging gray in her once dark hair, and a gold choker snaked about her neck. Subtle makeup softened the crow's-feet at her eyes and lip corners. Her open-toed sandals disclosed that she had painted her nails a garish Urban Decay shade of purple more popular among young women of Kelli's age.

"Have you forgiven me yet?" She released my hands.

Startled, I said, "For what?"

"Missing both the viewing and Sunday's funeral services."

"Of course. Satish said you were indisposed. He seemed quite concerned."

Sherri waved away her husband's alleged solicitude. "Do I look well now?" She showed me a gaunt but still finely chiseled profile.

"You and LaRue just get better looking every day."

She tapped my chest. "Skipper had a similar penchant for shameless flattery. I always loved it. But you didn't stop by just to see me, did you?"

"Actually, I wanted to speak to Satish."

The pupils in her violet eyes dilated alarmingly. "Of course. Satish. Why do you want to see him?"

"Can we sit down? This takes some explaining."

"Very well. Follow me." She led me onto the ribbon-divided floor.

"You folks planning to install tellers' cages in here?"

"Very funny. I've simply cordoned off the areas that Satish favors. That way, he doesn't violate my territory, and I don't violate his."

Despite myself, I gawped. "Oh. Do you do this in every room?"

"Certainly not. Only in the ones I care about. And that does *not* include Satish's bedroom. We sleep separately — in fact, on opposite sides of the mansion and on different floors. That's been our arrangement for years."

"Sherri, I had no idea things had gotten so bad between you."

"Bad? Have you ever seen *Who's Afraid of Virgina Woolf?*"

"Did the two of you ever discuss counseling?"

She laid a hand on my cheek. "Are you offering your services, William?"

"I really only work with kids, Sherri."

"What makes you think Satish and I don't qualify?"

We reached a backless settee with a red-velvet seat. Sherri dropped down and patted the cushion beside her. "All right. Explain this mysterious business you have to see Satish about."

"After Skipper's funeral," I said, sitting, "we discovered that someone had stolen a family heirloom."

Sherri cocked her head. "Oh, really. What?"

"Forgive me, Sherri, but I'd rather not say until I talk to Satish."

"You can't believe I'd pass the information along to *him*?"

I spread my hands. "Not really, but — "

She laughed. "I interrupted your story. Please tell me the rest. Or at least the parts you don't mind divulging."

I shifted position and resumed. "Evidence concerning the theft points to the driver of the hearse. I confronted the man, but he lied to me. When I discovered the lie, I returned to his house, but he had moved out — hurriedly and messily."

Sherri tapped my knee. "Why don't you call the police?"

"A young woman I know keeps asking me the same thing."

"Sounds like an intelligent girl. The very worst sort of rival."

She laid her hand on her breast in self-mocking coquetry. "But it's good to know that the impetuousness of youth has chased you into the private-detective business."

"Tell Adrienne that."

"Is she your girlfriend? I hope we never meet. In any case, I don't see where Satish plays a part in your story."

"The hearse driver rented his place from your husband's realty company. I thought maybe Satish might know his whereabouts."

"I've often accused Satish of anal-retentive behavior, but I doubt that even he has the forwarding address of a former tenant at his fingertips."

"Do you mind if I ask him myself?"

"Of course not. But he's not here. It's Thursday night."

"Right." Just as I had failed to forecast that Alan Papini might have a show on a Tuesday night, so I had forgotten Gupta's diligence in overseeing the Gag Reflex from Thursday through Sunday, its most profitable times. Then I had another thought. "Satish is keeping the club open the week after Skipper's funeral?"

"You expected him to close up for a week out of respect for your father's memory?"

Apparently, I had.

Sherri traced the line of my jaw with a fingernail. "The show must go on, you know."

"I'd like to know why."

"You already do. You just won't admit it to yourself. Under the guise of staging a memorial tribute to Skipper, Satish figures he'll rake in a bundle. He has all the sensitivity of a warthog."

"If you hate him — and it certainly sounds as if you do — why do you go on living with him?"

With a gesture like a gameshow hostess's, Sherri indicated this room, and by extension all of Golconda. "Look at this place. If I've chosen to remain in this vulgar Taj Mahal, believe me, it's only to reap every last material perk I've earned."

"I do believe you."

But Sherri Gupta scarcely heard me. "Until we took to our separate rooms, I shared the man's bed for better than thirty years. I indulged his grandiose business schemes — listened with forced appreciation, even gave him some smart advice. I sweet-talked and coddled him through setbacks. I won't let him discard me without securing every last penny — every last trinket and furnishing — that's rightfully mine."

"Does Satish have plans to discard you?"

The question refocused her. "No. I don't think so. If anything, the opposite. He'd like nothing better than to keep me caged here, in virtual purdah."

"Sherri, I see recrimination ribbons here" — I nodded at the swagged red lines among the brass posts — "but no bars."

"They're not the kind you can see."

I got to my feet. "It hurts to learn of the rift between you and Satish, but it would take a counselor with more skill than I have — and a lot more time — even to begin to close it."

Sherri seized one of my hands and placed it flat on the upper slope of her chest. She would not let go, and the heat from her bare skin moved scorchingly into my palm. "Who said I wanted to close it? Who said I wanted anything other than to escape?"

"I know exactly how you feel," I said.

To my relief, she laughed and let go. "You bear only a passing resemblance to your daddy, Will, but you've inherited his wit."

Obviously, she thought she was complimenting me. I nodded curtly to acknowledge it. "I still need to see Satish."

She waved a hand magnanimously. "Go on, then. You don't have to ask my permission. But if you decide to visit Golconda again, make sure your only motive is to cuckold my husband."

I neither spoke nor moved.

"A joke, Will. A harmless little joke." She barked a sudden shrill laugh. "Or maybe not."

"Good night, Sherri. Thanks for your time."

Without raising her voice, Sherri Gupta spoke a single word over her shoulder — "Rahel" — and the exotic woman who had ushered me in appeared beside the settee.

"Ma'am?"

"Rahel, show Mr. Keats out."

Deftly and inscrutably, Rahel did.

CHAPTER 19

In the old riverside section of Columbus, only ten or fifteen minutes from Golconda, I had trouble finding a parking space on Broadway, at least one within moderate walking distance of the Gag Reflex. Ordinarily, at six or later you can easily negotiate the streets and sidewalks downtown: with the shops and banks all closed, people have fled to their homes. But this evening everyone seemed inclined to linger. In spite of the cool spring air, several diners sat outside the Olive Branch Café, cramped fashionably at small sidewalk tables, and pedestrians of every age group, from senior citizens to body-pierced teens, strolled idly by, arm in arm, as if the whole world had taken a lovers' holiday. The size of the crowd reminded me of the hordes that often descend on the Springer Opera House, three or four blocks away, at the opening of a popular contemporary musical like *Sweeney Todd* or *Big River*.

At the unexpected cluster of people in front of the Gag Reflex, I moved aggressively toward the door. A man's voice rebuked me: "Hey, what's your rush? The place hasn't officially opened. You can't get in yet."

When I ignored him, he repeated, "You can't get in, I told you."

While continuing to work my way through the crowd, I mentally scolded myself in advance for my obscene impertinence, but nonetheless threw my voice into the space occupied by an elderly woman near my heckler.

"Sir! Please put that pitiful thing away and zip your fly!"

While the heckler and his nonplused accuser tried to sort their problem out, I reached the trim glass door and its adjacent picture window. Twisting and rattling the handle revealed the truth of the heckler's admonition. A handbill in the glass announcement case read:

DOOR OPENS AT 7:00 P.M.
SPECIAL TRIBUTE PERFORMANCE PROMPTLY AT 8

Forty minutes before I could get inside. I leaned my head against the door and muttered my frustration.

"Blast it, Gupta," I said under my breath, "let me in!"

A hand touched my shoulder. I turned to confront Denise Shurett, Skipper's agent.

"Satish can't hear you, Will. He's upstairs in a back dressing room with tonight's surprise guest. However . . ." She held up a long-handled key for my admiration, smiled, then inserted it in the lock and let us in. Resecuring the door with an interior deadbolt, she said, "Didn't expect to see you here this evening."

"Probably because no one bothered to issue me an invitation."

Denise started up the wide steps, each one painted to resemble a scuffed piano keyboard. I smelled stale beer and ghostly cigarette smoke, highly seasoned chili, and both overboiled peanuts and scorched popcorn. I fell in close behind Denise to avoid looking up her skirt as she ascended the steep stairs.

"Who did Gupta entice to this alleged tribute as surprise star?"

"Guess," Denise said.

"Myra Doone?"

"She pulled her back last week and's laid up."

"Okay. Gupta's lured Johnny Carson out of retirement."

"You wish."

"Bill Clinton, with a wooden Al Gore on his lap?"

Denise stepped onto the landing at the top of the stairs and turned around, confronting me one stair down. For the first time in our lives, we stood eye to eye. "No, dummy. One last chance, but think before you speak."

I thought before I spoke. "Dapper O'Dell?"

Denise's eyes and nostrils widened simultaneously. "Not at all funny, Will. Do you want me to tell you?"

"Please."

"Pablo Cabriales."

That news nearly sent me reeling back down the steps. "Denise, you're kidding."

She shrugged. "I never kid about paying engagements. It's against the agent's code of honor. Satish is discussing terms right now with Pablo. And trying to convince him to slant his act for a bunch of Skipper-worshipping Columbusites."

We walked out into the middle of the club's uneven hardwood floor, with scuffed saloon tables all around us and beer signs glowing on the walls. A shallow dais on the street side of the room suggested the diving platform of an ambivalent suicide.

Why would Pablo Cabriales, star of the hit sitcom "In the Shade" and frequent target of my father's long-festering resentment and verbal abuse, return to such a dismaying, downscale venue? Had Gupta promised him a restored Cadillac, a controlling interest in Chat-Val Realty, or half the proceeds from the sale of Golconda? In a moment of sheer paranoia, I imagined that Gupta had lured the star from Hollywood with the irresistible bait of Dapper O'Dell.

Denise asked about LaRue and Kelli. She asked about me. She listened to my perfunctory replies and then rattled on with unabashed enthusiasm about Pablo's talent, his endearing impulsiveness, his generosity in coming to pay tribute to Skipper. As she prated, I pondered the anomalies in the whole bizarre situation.

First, Gupta had arranged this rare appearance — potentially a sellout — so quickly that the club had had very little time to publicize it. Second, Cabriales and my father had never really liked each other. Third, Cabriales seldom traveled without a sycophantish retinue, and I would have seen some of these people by now. Fourth, except when it came to old cars and Golconda, Gupta usually pinched pennies as firmly as Skipper once did. Fifth, Cabriales did cutting-edge stuff in his stand-up shows, nothing Skipper's fans would appreciate. Sixth . . .

I interrupted Denise: "What exactly brought Cabriales here? How did those people downstairs find out he'd perform here tonight?"

"Word of mouth. A hint on last night's Channel Nine news.

They never revealed the mystery performer's identity, though, just that it would be someone big. No one except you, me, and Satish knows. And Pablo, of course."

"Okay, fine. That's half an answer. But what's Cabriales's motive for agreeing to Gupta's offer?"

"Gratitude, simple gratitude. Can't you accept that?"

"I'd rather hear it from the Hispanic Hunk himself. Let's go ask him."

Denise snatched at my jacket sleeve as I took a step toward the dressing rooms. "Satish wouldn't like you to barge in uninvited, Will. You know how he is when he's negotiating."

"I've got some negotiating to do with Gupta too, Denise. And besides, Cabriales might not mind seeing me again. He was once very friendly to me, after his last show here, when I went back-stage to compliment his performance. And I *am* the son of the dead icon we're supposedly paying tribute to tonight."

I broke away from Denise and strode through the half-kitchen at the head of the stairs and to the right-angle hallway on which lay the club's business office and two cork-lined dressing rooms with Salvation Army furnishings. Only one door out of three was closed. I knocked softly, with admirable restraint, and said, "Mr. Gupta, it's Will. May I talk to you?"

Denise Shurett stood at the end of the hall, her lips pursed and her hands on her hips. She shook her head in disappointment and marched out through the kitchen.

"Will, an important guest and I are discussing weighty affairs," said Gupta's voice. "I must hopefully ask you — "

Before Gupta could finish, the door swung inward and Pablo Cabriales hugged me to him and wrestled me mirthfully into the room. Squeezing me in his sweaty arms as if he were a nutcracker and I a stubborn almond, he cried, "*Hijo de ventrilocuo! Hijo de mi pobre consejero muerte!*" We almost fell down, but Cabriales switched his grip to my shoulders and manhandled me over to the tatty couch where Gupta sat.

"Guillermo! You look great!"

I could not say the same about Cabriales, despite his almost unaccountable delight at my arrival. His usually fine, blown-dry hair looked coarse and oily, sallow pouches hung beneath his eye sockets, and small cracks fissured his lips. His faded jeans, light-blue denim workshirt, and cheap brown boots, along with his ethnic good looks, gave him the appearance of a clichéd migrant laborer, but a romanticized and heroic one. Rolled sleeves revealed some kind of rash or fever-mottling on the undersides of his forearms. The sweat on his forehead and upper lip — missing his almost trademark mustache — tended to confirm his lapse into sickness. As always, Cabriales exuded plenty of energy, the kind found in many fidgety schoolkids, but tonight he deployed it in a febrile and uncertain way.

Gupta did not look pleased to see me. "Our surprise performer this evening, Will. Undoubtedly, we shall sell out the house."

"Hey, don't count your take yet, Satish." Cabriales dropped into a wobbly easy chair near the makeup table. "I feel fucked. Not good fucked, you know. Really, really bad fucked."

"What's the matter?" I asked him.

"*Quién sabe?* The lousy flight, maybe. Damn plane went up and down like a Matamoros whore. Or maybe it was the food. Even in first class, we got the deadly pink rubber chicken. Little chewy erasers, you know? I should've carried on some Taco Bell, man. That's the only kind of food us greasers can stand, right?"

"In an hour you'll feel better," Gupta said.

"In an hour, you could be staging *my* tribute!"

"No. You'll get better. You just need to rest."

"I'm starting to think that a nice fluffy hospital bed might offer the best rest. Three or four pretty nurses to wait on me. You get my drift, man?"

"Please don't talk that way, Pablo. You'll jinx us."

"No jinx, Satish. Just the truth."

Gupta turned away from the sweating Cabriales, as if to deny the reality of his condition. "What do you want with me, Will? I don't have much time this evening."

Cabriales interrupted, addressing me. "If I *do* go on, *hermano*, I want *you* at a front table, the very best one. With your very best girl. I'll get her so hot for you, *amigo*, you'll have to use oven mitts to take her to bed!"

"My very best girl is home with her daughter, nearly an hour away. And I doubt seriously she'll drive down on the spur of the moment."

Cabriales smirked. "So, you just find yourself another girl."

Gupta took me by the elbow. "We should let Pablo rest."

Unsteadily transplanting himself to the vacant couch, Cabriales said, "Yeah, rest, good idea. You plan everything down to the wire, just as you always do, Satish, and I'll take a little nap."

Gupta pushed me through the door and closed it quietly behind us. "It amazes me to see you here tonight, Will."

"Especially since you did your damnedest to keep the whole evening a secret from me. After all, why would I wish to attend a special tribute to my father, featuring a very funny national celebrity?"

Clasping his hands at his midriff, Gupta said, "Please forgive me, Will. There was no secrecy intended. A week ago Skipper fell dead on our stage, and the past seven days have completely disordered my thinking."

"Except when it comes to booking premium talent for the Gag Reflex."

"Please. I do apologize for not telling you. Sincerely." He gestured me on down the hall to the business office. "If not our modestly advertised tribute performance, what brings you here this evening?"

I sat down in the ladderback chair across from his particleboard desk — furniture so in contrast to the magnificence of Golconda that I wondered if Gupta actually relished maintaining his own little tenement space to go slumming in. He clearly had paradoxical tastes for both splendor and squalor.

"I wanted to talk to you about Lawrence Budge."

"Who?" The desk chair into which Gupta had lowered himself had brass casters and wide lacquered armrests — his one indulgence here.

"The Lawrence Budge who drove Skipper's hearse. The Lawrence Budge you spoke to privately the day of the funeral. The Lawrence Budge who shot his own dog. The Lawrence Budge who rented a house from you."

Gupta decided to quibble. "Not from me personally, Will. From the company. What is your interest in the man?"

"Guess," I said, echoing Denise.

He frowned, squinting in irritation. I thought that he had almost made up his mind to speak to me when the telephone rang. He picked up the handset and commenced a long discussion, a quasi-argument with a beer-and-wine distributor. I waited for the conversation to end, but Gupta deliberately protracted it. Losing patience, knowing that the man could not escape me, I got up and wandered back out into the club proper.

Denise Shurett sat at the bar, nursing a glass of white zinfandel. A bartender, three waitresses, some kitchen personnel, and a sound technician had all appeared. Denise was calculatedly teasing the crew-cut bartender. I sat down beside her. Beneath the surface normalcy of the club, beneath the drinking and the humdrum banter and the shapeless expectations of the early evening, a strange heat had begun to spread, as if Cabriales's fever and Gupta's unease were parching the very floorboards and converting our chatter into schizophrenic gibberish.

CHAPTER 20

ifteen minutes later, Gupta emerged from his office. He stopped at the end of the bar and announced to everyone that to preserve the goodwill of the customers on the sidewalk, the Gag Reflex would now open. He sent a waitress down the steps to unlock the door and stationed himself at a card table at the top of the stairs to collect a five-dollar cover charge. It amused me that the rajah of Golconda insisted on taking the cover charges and making change himself.

I left Denise and stood behind Gupta as he stashed and returned bills from a battered cigar box. I tried to talk to him, but the business of counting greenbacks and perfunctorily greeting familiar customers so engrossed him that I gave up and returned to the bar. Every stool except the one that Denise had saved for me had filled. Already a haze of cigarette smoke drifted through the room as a jazz trio — pianist, drummer, bass player — diddled languidly away at "Bye-bye, Blackbird." Soon laughter and loud conversation turned even the exchange of small talk into an operatic shouting match.

At length, Gupta relinquished his moneytaking and hand-stamping chores to a waitress and withdrew through the kitchen. Denise turned to me and yelled, "I have to go talk with the Nabob. In private, Will." Acquiescing in yet another delay out of respect for her, I nodded, and Denise slipped off her stool to join Gupta in the back. A shaven-headed soldier only just barely eighteen immediately claimed her place.

Adrienne would not have enjoyed this scene. It was too loud for either listening or talking, too dark for pleasurable people-watching, and too smoky for anyone but fire-jumpers with parachute packs and shovels. *I did not enjoy this scene.* Amazing. The son of show-business people, at thirty-four I had developed the stay-at-home sensibility of an agoraphobic librarian. This realization did not altogether dismay me. I had *worked* to separate myself from the gaudy milieu that had nourished my parents and my enigmatic father in particular. To sit at the virtual center of the Gag Reflex, and to gag reflexively at my reluctant presence at its heart, seemed to me tonight a significant triumph.

A tap on my shoulder signaled Denise's return. She shouted something. I touched my ear and shook my head. She spoke with her mouth less than an inch from the hinge of my jaw: "*Come to the back.*" I put tip money on the bar and followed her.

Pablo Cabriales lay supine in his dressing room, knees up and one forearm across his sweaty brow. The ripped sofa sagged under not only his physical weight but also his infirmity and petulance. Satish Gupta regarded him despairingly, his clasped hands hanging before him like a wrung-out dishcloth.

"Will," Denise said, "give us your opinion. I can't convince Satish on my own. Isn't it obvious that Pablo needs a doctor?"

"Yeah," said Cabriales through parched lips. "Think how bad it would look if Primetime Pablo died in this shitty matchbox."

I said, "You wouldn't be the first comic who did."

Silence. Gupta turned his abashed gaze my way. Denise grimaced. Cabriales stared up at me open-mouthed. Then he rolled his head toward one end of the sofa arm and very slowly back toward the other. A ratchety laugh escaped him, then another and another.

"Oh yeah, Guillermo, oh yeah. I can testify to that. Died here one night myself already, way back when. Every gag falling to the floor like a poisoned pigeon. But once is enough. More than enough." He pinned Gupta with a needlelike stare, then coughed, gulped, and shuddered. "I just can't wow 'em tonight the way you hoped, you mercenary *maricon*. I . . . just . . . can't."

"Do you want me to take him to the hospital?" I said.

"No," Gupta said. "Denise has volunteered to do that, very kindly."

"Then what else do you need me for?"

Cabriales pointed a shaky finger at me. "Satish has a big favor to ask you, Little Skip. I think you should do it." A cough, and a slow back-handed swipe at the crusting saliva on his lips. "Time for the chip-block to come home, no? Whaddaya say, Guillermo? Hit the boards in your daddy's name? *Una cosa grande*, eh?"

I started to protest. Denise grabbed my arms and treated me to a long exhalation of her wine-scented breath. "Who better, Will? You're the natural focus for their emotions, the only son — "

I broke away. "Skipper had three other sons he loved better, not to mention a wooden crone for a second daughter. Line up the survivors on stage and let the crowd applaud. As for me, I don't *perform*."

"Of course you do." Denise's enthusiasm never flagged. "Maybe not to rouse paying customers to laughter, but certainly to draw wounded or frightened kids out of their shells. And you can definitely belly-talk. Skipper taught you how, and you're better than three-quarters of the professional vents out there these days."

"At your father's viewing," Gupta said, "you made me briefly believe that his corpse had animated Dapper. Most gruesomely effective."

I faced him. "You didn't like my act then, Satish. But now that money's involved, I'm suddenly a valuable commodity."

Satish looked genuinely wounded. "It is not just the money, William. It is the honor of the club, my good name, and the memory of your father."

"You're all talking crazy. I don't have a dummy. I don't even have a *routine*."

"You don't have to do a routine," Denise said. "Just demonstrate a few techniques, reminisce about your dad — "

"That could prove more than *anyone* bargained for."

Cabriales spoke. "Do it, Guillermo. Do it for the Skipper." He laughed weakly at the word play. "Do it for me as well. I promised Satish, and now I . . . I can't." He drew his lips back in a grin of pain and feebly massaged his lower abdomen.

I pivoted back toward Gupta. "I'll do it on two conditions."

"Anything, William."

"First, you quit stonewalling me on Budge and come across with some credible answers to my questions."

"But I've — " Gupta cut short his own demurral. "You have my word. What else?"

"Union wages. Whatever you offered Pablo."

Cabriales snorted. "Now you hit him where it *really* hurts, *chico*!"

◆ ◆ ◆

I helped Cabriales down the back stairs to an alley off Broadway, and Denise brought her car around to pick him up and drive him to the Columbus Medical Center. Back upstairs, I rummaged through the closet in the business office for any sort of helpful prop. In my windmilling brain I struggled to organize a presentation that would neither anesthetize everyone nor provoke a riot.

With less than ten minutes to show time, I realized that I would have to fulfill my end of the agreement and trust that Gupta would subsequently honor his own pledge. Not the smartest negotiating I had ever done, but an almost unavoidable concession given the circumstances.

I found nothing in the business-office closet but a small pair of white plastic lips that opened and closed when you pressed an attached squeeze bulb. I felt pretty sure they would serve. I carried them with me into the kitchen.

Ike Madison, the club's long-time chef, stood at his gleaming stove, tending three or four pans simultaneously. An African American with the build of an All-Pro linebacker, he made the industrial-scale appliance look small. Sensing my presence, he flicked a swift glance my way before returning his attention to his skillets. "Mister Will Keats. Ain't seen you in a dog's age. How's it hanging?"

"Don't ask. Listen, Ike, I need to borrow something from you."

"Long as it ain't money. That Gupta hardly pays a body enough to keep a flea alive. Not to slander the dead, but I can't say your daddy weighed us down with riches either."

"Not news to me, Ike. Why don't you try to get on at the Columbus Hilton?"

Ike laughed uproariously. "Good one, Will. Good one. Now, what you need?"

"A large fruit or vegetable. A zucchini, maybe."

"How 'bout this?" Madison shifted a pan of chili to lower heat, walked a few steps to a plastic sack next to the refrigerator, squatted painfully, and extracted an immense purple eggplant with enough bumps and weals on its surface to satisfy a phrenologist. "Will this do?"

"Absolutely."

At my direction, Madison carved an oblong hole straight through the eggplant's bulbous half, and we inserted the plastic lips into it so that the hose and air bulb passed out the other side. We cut a yellow slip from a waitress's pad into two notched eye-shapes and glued them on with dabs of syrup. I had my dummy.

Madison touched the eggplant on its pate with a long-handled wooden spoon. "I dub thee Sir Flyin' Purple People-Eater." He laughed boomingly and turned back to his chili pan.

Nothing now stood between me and the prospect of making a total fool of myself in front of scores of strangers.

◆ ◆ ◆

"Ladies and gentlemen, I take great pleasure in presenting to you this evening as our special Skipper Keats tribute performer, exactly one week after my esteemed partner's horrifying collapse on this very stage, Skipper's only son" — a lie of course, although Gupta probably did not know it — "*Will Keats!*" Uncharacteristically and unconvincingly flamboyant, Gupta stretched out my name Ed McMahon fashion.

I walked out from the back, carrying my contrived dummy in my arm like a football but keeping him concealed under a dark-blue dish towel. Applause began tentatively, but quickly mounted in volume and intensity. Patrons acknowledged my loss and vied warmly with one another to recognize it, but they also exchanged dubious glances. I was hardly the celebrity hinted at on Channel Nine. Whether I could hold their interest beyond that first forebearing minute or so remained a doubtful prospect.

During the endless walk out, my knees wobbled and my pulse raced. By the time I stepped onto the dais, sweat drenched my flanks. I stared out through the roiling blue fog at eighty to a hundred haloed silhouettes — more people than had watched my father die, more even than the fire code allowed. My hands shook discernibly — everyone in the room could see — as I reached out to grasp the microphone.

"I'm Skipper Keats's son, yes. But I'm also a last-minute stand-in for a much better performer. Namely, Pablo Cabriales."

A murmur like that at a spectacular burst during a fireworks exhibition swept through the club. Some people applauded. Two or three — kinetic shadows — stood up as if to spot a lurking Cabriales.

"Unfortunately, the man you all wanted and deserved to see took ill about ninety minutes ago. He's in the hospital now. Nothing too serious, so far as we know, but he simply couldn't drag himself out here to perform for you. And believe me, he tried. When he finally admitted he couldn't do it, he nominated me as his replacement. I asked him to lend me his mustache, but he refused." That got a few laughs, and I relaxed a little. "If any of you want your money back, either now or at the end of my act, please apply to the cashier. If enough of you demand a refund, you might be able to pick Mr. Gupta up by the heels and shake the change from his pockets."

More laughter. After letting it die down, I changed my tone. "You know, I really wonder whether I should be standing here before you at all. My father's life crashed to a fitting if undignified end on this very spot a week ago, and I'm still in mourning. A tribute like this — it's usually a mixture of dutiful reverence and obligatory laughter in the face of death, of tears and a hilarity that comes from thumbing your nose at the everlasting dark. Tonight, frankly, I just don't know if I'm up to it."

I paused. My predicament registered with everyone in the club. No one spoke. No one lifted a bottle of beer. No one even fluttered a napkin. Smoke curled through the footlights and beer-sign glow like an intricate drifting web, linking every patron with my figure on the stage. When the expectation and tension in the room had acquired a nearly palpable heft, I spoke.

"So that's why I brought a little friend to help me out." I whisked off the towel, still firmly grasping the squeeze bulb out of view. "Say hello, Perp." I swung the white-lipped figure in a gentle arc as if to survey the crowd.

"*Whoa! Out of the frying pan and into the fire!*"

The voice I projected from the eggplant was a raspy baritone instantly identifiable as Ike Madison's. A couple of the silhouettes near the bar nudged each other, and someone female in the kitchen doorway whooped like a lottery winner. The rest of my audience, surprised, joined in.

"This is Perp," I said. "Can y'all say Perp?"

"Peerrrrp!" three-quarters of the audience cried.

"Short for Purple," I told them. "Or maybe short for Perpetrator. Perp likes to commit assaults on logic."

"*That's true. Can't deny it. Just the other day, when a woman asked me if I were a fruit or a vegetable, I told her I was neither.*"

"Neither? What did you claim to be then?"

"*A factory.*"

"A factory?"

"*Sure, just like those big barns where they keep all the laying chickens. An egg plant.*"

I won't pretend that out of a lopsided eggplant I created a character for the ages. But I succeeded in amusing the gathered Columbusites for nearly an hour, and on two or three occasions I even elicited guffaws that rocked the building's flimsy shell. With Perp as my interlocutor, I told four or five gentle and respectably outrageous stories about Skipper and his adventures with Dapper, Simon, Letitia, and Davy Quackett. Meanwhile, Perp ridiculed my pretensions as both storyteller and son of a quasi-celebrity. I parried as best I could. At length, physically spent, I lowered my voice so that everyone in the club had to strain to hear it:

"Perp, you have certain underground connections, don't you?"

"*You mean my roots? Oh, yes. Yes indeed. I'm a regular man of the soil.*"

"Right. Well, as a fellow with his fundament planted firmly in the earth, what do you think might happen to a wooden figure whose family had him buried?"

A hush enveloped the loft. I let it stretch like taffy before Perp spoke up to snap it:

"I think he just might take root. His limbs might burst through the ground and send out branches. He might just spring forth as a huge, magnificent tree, an oak or a willow or a sycamore. Something magical."

No one laughed. No one was supposed to. I placed Perp on the unused stool beside me and covered him with the blue dish towel. Whoever was operating the spots killed those focused on me and trained a lone beam on the towel-draped eggplant. Ridiculous, of course, a kind of bathos.

But it worked.

Speaking out of the darkness, I said, "I think maybe he already has, Perp. I think maybe he already has." Without any pre-arranged cue, the spotlight operator killed the remaining beam, and darkness shrouded the entire dais.

After two or three stunned beats, applause welled up. It was not wild or jubilant, not the manic noise that would have celebrated Cabriales's energetic act, but I had never heard anything like it in this shabby loft. It had very little to do with me and everything to do with the irrational regard of these people for a second-rate vent who had earnestly loved his ludicrous profession. Chills netted and shook me.

CHAPTER 21

When the footlights around the dais came on again and a tubular track light at the far end of the bar directed a pool of immaterial yellow on the rearmost tables, I saw every patron standing and applauding. Their antic silhouettes now had dimensions and shadows, and faces as well. It took me a moment to resolve these faces out of the glare and smoke, but when I did, most bore somber expressions, even if quirkily smiling. I recognized almost no one. I lowered my head and stepped off the dais.

My performance — if it even qualified as one — had lasted close to an hour. It wasn't even nine o'clock. The jazz trio would have to come back out and do a couple of sets to satisfy those patrons demanding a bona fide night out on the town. Many people, though, had apparently gotten what they had come for. A small surge of them moved toward the head of the stairs — not to obtain refunds, but to descend to Broadway, reclaim their cars, and head home.

Suddenly, in the midst of this tidal movement, I looked up. Five or six bodies away from me, closer to the door than I, a blunt-faced man in a baseball cap and a green windbreaker with an upturned collar floated into view, turned sideways, and floated on. This apparition unsettled me. For two or three seconds, my mind riffled through matches for his semifamiliar face. Then it clicked. I had just seen Lawrence Budge.

"Mr. Budge!" I shouted. "Lawrence Budge!" I struggled toward him. Bodies intervened. "Let me through, please. Let me through!" But the surge toward the stairs had its own agenda and peristaltic rhythm. I could flail within it but make no headway. Maddeningly, Budge appeared immune to this law. I watched in frustration as he gained the staircase and began to bob down it like a cork on a roaring cataract.

"Let me through!" I demanded, and, amazingly, the crowd responded, perhaps to the near panic in my voice. The logjam broke, and I gained the top of the staircase. Fixated on Budge's cap, I pelted down the smudged piano-keyboard treads.

I hit the chill of the street only a few seconds after he did, hesitated in quest of my bearings, and saw my quarry running. He had crossed the median and the far lanes of traffic and was heading north toward the River Club and the City Mills Dam. I plunged into the moderately heavy flow of cars and trucks and zigzagged after him. Brakes squealed, faces contorted, and one driver's curses snagged me like burrs.

I was several years younger than Budge, who had probably last run like this as a grade-schooler attempting to escape a bully's fist or an affectionate little girl's kisses. As a hearse driver and a couch potato, the man spent most of his waking hours on his posterior. His lungs, I assumed, would soon start to feel like ripped inner tubes, and I would catch him easily.

I sprinted past a bar called the Old City Jail Drinkery. Budge, blundering around startled pedestrians, labored north up this same sidewalk toward the intersection of 11th Street. I left behind a credit company and a shoe store, following him almost gleefully, adrenalin and self-righteousness my fuel.

I had come within six or eight feet of Budge when I collided with a burly, plaid-clad tourist, cameras draped around his neck. The gawker had stepped into my path to get a better view of the fleeing Budge. I ricocheted off this human oil drum, a camera jabbing my chest, then toppled backwards onto my butt and the heels of my hands. In an unobscured slice of my vision, I saw Budge pelt around the corner toward the river.

The tourist hoisted me to my feet as if I weighed no more than a child. "You okay, mister?"

"Yeah, thanks," I said, then darted on, wiping my skinned and bleeding palms on my trousers as I ran. At the corner that had concealed Budge's flight, I saw seven or eight strolling soldiers about fifty yards down the 11th Street sidewalk. Budge had apparently picked up both momentum and a second wind on this vague downslope to Front Avenue and the old W. C. Bradley Company building. He was not among the soldiers.

I halted, feeling dazed and light-headed. From Front Avenue, Budge could have gone only three ways, including down the cobbled-brick ramp that led to the Riverwalk. From this vantage, I could see a glinting wedge of the Chattahoochee flowing beneath the undulant hills and lush trees on the Alabama bank. Primordial river smells pervaded the entire waterfront.

Pick a direction, I told myself, and *move*!

I put on some speed, wishing that earlier I had changed out of my oxfords into tennis shoes. The slap of leather on pavement and then on cobbles echoed like gun shots. I rushed through the strolling recruits, a couple of whom shouted jocularly after me. Still no sight of Budge.

To the right of the staircase and the wheelchair ramp that led down to the Riverwalk, a young woman sat on the shadow-shrouded grass with a sketchpad. She faced the Mill City dam, a line of low cascades glimmering dully in the starlight. A battered leather handbag and a wide-mouthed cup of drawing tools rested beside her outstretched legs. What an unlikely hour to try to draw the river, I thought. But I approached her anyway and stopped just behind her right shoulder. Breathlessly I said, "Excuse me, but did a guy in a baseball cap run by here?"

No answer. Was she deaf? Then, reaching to tap her on the shoulder, I noticed with a start the golden patina of her skin and realized that I had just asked a life-sized human sculpture for information. A dummy, of sorts. Angry at both myself and whoever had placed the statue there, I moved to the head of the wheelchair ramp.

Over a hundred yards long, the incline featured a switchback halfway down and an extension that continued south toward the Dillingham Street Bridge. On this extension, struggling to remain inconspicuous, a solitary figure leaned heavily on the rail and hitched downward toward the water. I could not make out the color of his jacket; he wore no cap but could have easily discarded or lost it. If he were Budge, he must have thought he had shaken me. Or maybe exhaustion had slowed him to this laggardly pace.

I took off my shoes and set them side by side in the grass at the top of the ramp. Then I hurled myself toward Lawrence Budge, running in my stocking feet as silently as any ancient Creek Indian and exulting in the chase. I had covered at least sixty yards before Budge glanced back and saw me. He accelerated impressively and brushed clumsily past a young black couple holding hands.

As Budge neared the concrete terraces north of the Dillingham Street Bridge, a blue heron lifted from one of the steps and skimmed low over the dark waters toward the dam. I too passed the bewildered lovers, but more adroitly, and then set my calves on fire pursuing Budge upslope to the underpass and on beneath the bridge.

I collared the gasping man on the east side of a highly stylized momument to Christopher Columbus, fittingly enough on the side labeled CHAINS. Although we had both pushed ourselves virtually to the limit, I still had the strength to yank him onto his back and to twist him around on the inlaid bricks. Desperately, he thrust a hand inside his jacket, and I instinctively kicked. A pistol — the same one with which he had murdered Orcus? — flew out of his grip and skittered across the walkway. Outraged, I dropped down heavily and straddled his chest. I bunched the fabric of his shirt in my fists.

"Don't hurt me!" Budge cried. "Don't hurt me!"

"Listen, Mr. Budge, you pulled the pistol. I just want to talk. What were you doing in my daddy's club tonight?"

"I . . . I didn't know you'd be there."

"I imagine you didn't." It occured to me suddenly that any witnesses to this altercation, civilians or police, might assume me the bad guy. Hauling Budge up with me, I got to my feet. Despite his mewling resistance, I dragged him back to the bench under the Dillingham Street Bridge, where I persuaded him to sit. His throat pulsed, and his eyes bulged up at me like miniature balconies on Golconda itself. Standing over him, I said, "All right, let's hear your sordid little story."

"I'll tell you, but then you've got to let me go."

"Hardly. You stole Dapper. You shot your dog."

Budge gave me a submoronic fish stare. "I didn't want Orcus to suffer. We were always together. When I had to run — "

"Thank God you didn't have to leave a *wife* behind, right? Let's forget Orcus for now. What about Dapper? You can't convincingly deny that you took him."

"No. I did it for the thousand bucks, just like you guessed. I never figured anyone would find out."

"And you ran because I discovered the theft. Why'd you come back?"

"To tell Gupta that you knew and to hit him up for some more money. Just a little start-up scratch."

"So you swear that Satish Gupta has Dapper?"

"Sure. I gave him the stupid puppet the same Sunday I stole it."

"And what did Gupta do with him?"

"How should I know? Maybe he buggered him. Who knows what gets a big shot like Gupta excited?"

Ever since capturing Budge, I had braced myself for an escape attempt. I had not expected him to cry. Now his tears flowed, as earnest and unforced as a nun's prayer. Although I felt little sympathy for him, my right hand — independent of my distaste and embarrassment — began to pat Budge consolingly between the shoulder blades.

"Please, Mr. Keats," he managed between his sobs, "you've got to let me go. You've got to."

"Why's that, Lawrence?"

"I've got nothing now. No dog, no job, no friends. Why would you want to . . . to put me in jail?"

I stopped patting Budge on the back. With my clasped hands between my knees, I studied the river.

"Mr. Keats?"

The river, wide and fragrant and luminous, kept flowing south in the dark.

"Mr. Keats . . . ?"

"Go," I said. "Get out of town. Please don't ever let me see you again."

CHAPTER 22

The jazz combo still held the stage at the Gag Reflex. They were playing an oddly syncopated Thelonius Monk number, not well but loud. About twenty people remained in the streetside performance space, while an equal number drank and bantered in the barroom. Denise Shurett still occupied her stool. Gently, I squeezed the back of her neck between my thumb and forefinger.

"What happened, Will? Are you okay?"

"Gupta hasn't left yet, has he?"

"He's in his counting house."

I could picture Gupta sifting through the loot in the cigar box like Scrooge McDuck rummaging in his bank vault. Not an uplifting image. At all.

I left the bar and went through the kitchen. Ike Madison gave me an amiable nod and a thumbs-up sign. Two other employees congratulated me on my stage turn. I smiled politely and trudged straight past them to the business office.

Gupta had locked his door — whether against me or his employees or a gang of club invaders, I couldn't say. I rattled the knob. "Satish! Let me in!"

The door opened an inch or two on its chain, revealing a sweaty segment of Gupta's face. "Oh, William, excuse my caution." He shut the door, loosed the chain, then swung the door wide. "Please, enter."

I brushed past him and imperiously took a seat. Gripping the chair arms, I felt the abrasions on my palms keenly.

Gupta returned to his desk. "You did very well tonight,

William. Your father would have urged me to hire you."

I shook my head. "Have you figured out yet why I wanted to talk to you about Lawrence Budge?"

"I confess that I find the outlines of your concerns a little unclear."

"I find *that* a little hard to believe. Right after my impromptu tribute performance, I ran into Lawrence Budge himself."

A tic developed at the corner of Gupta's eye. He fiddled with an account ledger.

"Ran him down, I should say. Imagine. Despite your strongest admonitions, Satish, he showed up here at the Gag Reflex — in your own little playground. When he saw me take the dais, he must have panicked. But trying to remain inconspicuous, he wait-ed until I'd finished to hightail it down the stairs." I made an illustrative scooting gesture with my hands and winced in pain.

"That's quite an ugly scrape you have there." The tic at Gupta's eye belied his outward calm.

I fetched out a handkerchief and wrapped it carefully around my worst wound. "Once I'd cornered Budge, he didn't really want to talk to me anymore than you do now. Not surprising, given that you waded hip-deep together through the same foul shit to deprive the Keatses of my father's dearest possession."

"Skipper wanted to deprive you of it himself." Immediately, Gupta fell silent; his twitch intensified to the point that he cov-ered it with his hand.

I got out of my chair and leaned over the blotter on his desk. "I'll take that as an admission of sorts." Gupta refused to look at me. "All right. Maybe you'd like to know that I prevailed upon Budge to make a confession of his own. You paid him a thousand dollars to steal Dapper for you. Budge told me only minutes ago, and I have no reason not to believe him."

"William — "

"Except that you betrayed the trust of an old friend of thirty years. Who wants to believe that, Satish?"

Gupta closed the ledger in front of him. "I'm sorry."

"What?"

Finally he looked up. "I am most sorry, William." The quaint formality of his diction pled for sympathy. The foreigner in an unhappy bind. The poor immigrant down on his luck.

"Sorry?" I said. "You mean like a bartender who's just run out of somebody's favorite brand of beer?" To my surprise, my hands ached to seize Gupta's head and bang it against the wall. I controlled them — barely. "If you want to appease me, return Dapper. Simple as that. Otherwise, I'll call in the police."

He grimaced. "If I may inquire: how did you discover that Dapper was missing?"

"Not relevant. We had a bargain, Satish. I went on for Cabriales, and you stopped bullshitting and stalling. For both our sakes, don't make me turn this whole business over to the authorities."

Gupta sighed and stood up. He spread his stubby brown hands on his blotter and leaned toward me as if faintly dizzy, putting our faces only inches apart. Despite his bulk and solidity, he looked suddenly meek and vulnerable. He essayed an apologetic grin, but it immediately resolved itself into another sick grimace.

"All right, William," he said. "I will fulfill my end of our bargain."

"How?"

"Come with me, and I'll take you to your precious Dapper."

◆ ◆ ◆

Gupta directed Denise Shurett and the bartender to close up the Gag Reflex at midnight, still two and a half hours away, and led me down the backstairs into a small courtyard where he had parked his Lexus. He drove me to my own car so that I could follow him in it to Golconda.

As I motored along behind him, my excitement and anxiety mounted. Chiefly, I worried that Gupta might try to peel off for parts unknown. He dared no such maneuver, however, and from the lights and traffic we gradually transitioned into the tranquil residential district bordering Lake Oliver, and from this broad patchwork of trees and shadows into the actinic clarity of Golconda.

Once in the parking atrium, Gupta and I both noticed that the '57 Cadillac no longer occupied its accustomed slot. When we emerged from our own vehicles, Gupta said nothing, but his discomfort was evident. He herded me doorward.

"In, in," he said. "Let's reach an amiable ending to this misunderstanding."

The Indian woman I had seen just that afternoon, Rahel, greeted us in the foyer. Gupta introduced her as his niece from Hyderabad, and asked her where his wife had gone.

"Mrs. Gupta left shortly after this gentleman visited," Rahel said nervously, nodding at me. "She said she was going out for a few grocery items. But that was many hours ago."

Gupta patted Rahel's shoulder. "She has perhaps taken in a movie or stopped to talk with one of her bridge group, ignorant of the hour. There is no need to worry."

Rahel bowed and withdrew. Gupta gestured me ahead of him through the ribbon-partitioned drawing room. We passed through a library similarly cordoned, up a cordoned staircase, and into a cordoned entertainment room.

At length we entered a bedroom, conspiculously Gupta's alone, without a single strip of red ribbon anywhere. The canopied bed looked like the altar in St. Peter's in Rome. It featured deep sliding drawers in its base, eerily suggestive of the crypts at the mausoleum. Gupta knelt in front of the second drawer from the foot of the bed and prepared to put a key in its lock. At the same time, he and I noticed that the drawer already protruded at least a half inch.

"Oh, faithless woman!" Gupta blurted.

"An unfortunate family failing, apparently."

Gupta did not reply, but quickly pulled the drawer fully open. Inside lay nothing but a dummy-sized dove-grey top hat and a small audio recorder of recent vintage. Gupta gaped at these items incredulously.

Without looking at me, he said, "I put him safely in here. You see the hat. No one else knew."

"Highly unlikely, Satish. Or else Dapper would still be there."

Gupta stood and kicked the drawer shut. Although it rocketed inward, it struck and sprang back out a foot or more. "Damn her!"

"Let's calm down, Satish. Your pitching a fit won't make Dapper miraculously reappear. Maybe Sherri left you a message on the recorder." I bent to retrieve the cheap Japanese machine.

Satish's shoulders slumped. "No, no. If my suspicions are correct, that machine contains only unspeakable sorrow." He crossed the room, pulled back a corner of the brocaded draperies, and gazed out the window at Lake Oliver's cream and pewter surface.

"I've made a career of listening to sad stories," I said, pushing the PLAY button. A run of static ensued, and then, as if from leagues away and decades past, or as if from the afterlife, my father's voice resolved out of the strident white noise:

"*. . . lations! My most morbid congratulations!*"

"*Yes,*" said the distance-thinned, and younger, voice of Satish Gupta. "*I deserve them.*"

"*Because it all came off exactly as you planned?*"

"*I never imagined that Thaddeus would chose the theatrical end he did — but yes, I suppose the whole affair has concluded satisfactorily.*"

"*Then pat yourself on the back. I'll give you full credit for Thad's blowing his brains out on the Dillingham Street Bridge.*"

"*Don't assume me quite that greedy, Skipper. I'll quite happily share it with you.*"

The real Satish Gupta, the one standing morosely by the window, said, "Turn that off."

As if in response, my father said. "*Wait a minute, Satish. I wasn't the one who schemed to blackmail Sermak.*"

"*But you never really objected, did you? You thought it an altogether expedient way to push him out of the business. You despised his corner-cutting and his ineptitude and his greed as much as I did, and you begrudged not a penny of the money I paid that private detective to document Thaddeus's private indiscretions.*"

"*Satish — *"

"*Indeed, you seemed to relish those photographs of him in various indelicate conjunctions with high school boys.*"

"*Not at all,*" Skipper said. "*I merely regarded them as insur-*"

ance if Thaddeus balked at our other incentives to yield his share of our business. I never expected you to threaten to go to Evelyn with the photos."

"Turn that off!" Gupta said again. He dropped the curtain and faced me with his hands ambiguously fisted by his sides. I ignored his demand.

"Oh, no. You never expected that," his younger self said. *"But of course we both knew that only by exposing his secret to Evelyn, whom he cherished above even that terrible compulsion, would he ever relent. So it troubled you very little to let me carry the threat to him, and thus before he committed suicide, our humiliated friend gave over his shares in our partnership, as we both wished."*

"He gave over much more than that."

The younger Satish Gupta's chuckled sardonically. *"Indeed, indeed."*

The tape unspooled silently for several seconds. I was about to switch off the machine when Sherri's voice emerged from the white noise.

"No wonder you stole Dapper. Now I've taken him back, this little image of the only man I ever really loved, and maybe I should thank you for the opportunity. Thank you, then. But don't expect me to say it in person and don't come looking for me or I'll reveal what you've worked so hard to keep hidden all these years. Goodbye, Satish. Take down the ribbons, for every inch of Golconda is yours now."

I shut off the machine. "Want me to rewind? Need to hear any part of that again?"

Gupta looked down. "That will not be necessary, William. For many years I have known the first part by heart, and the rest is quite fresh."

I gestured at Gupta with the recorder. "What's behind all this, Satish? How did you ever let this damning conversation get on tape? It's practically a self-indictment for murder."

"Your father was an extremely clever man, Will. One day after Sermak's suicide we sat in my car, speaking as you heard us. I never thought our words would go beyond the confines of that vehicle. Unfortunately, I did not count on one sly eavesdropper right under my nose. Dapper."

"Skipper had the tape machine inside Dapper?"

"Yes. Most assuredly yes. And once I had concluded my foolish gut-spilling, he manipulated the device inside Dapper to play my words back to me, as if they issued from Dapper's own lips."

"So you paid Budge to kidnap Dapper for the tape? It's remained hidden in Dapper for a quarter of a century?"

"And still is. What we listened to is obviously only a copy."

"So Sherri has the original. Where do you think she's gone?"

"I have lived with that woman for many years, loving her faithfully even as she spurned and betrayed me, and yet about her inner life I still know next to nothing. I have no idea where she might flee under such circumstances."

"Who might know?"

Gupta dropped wearily into a wingback chair as if his strings had been cut. "LaRue. Your own mother, William. She and Sherri have always shared a great deal — including, more than just briefly, your father, the honorable Skipper Keats."

I recalled Sherri's words from the tape — *"this little image of the only man I ever really loved"* — and understood at once that Gupta had spoken the unhappy truth. "I think you enjoyed telling me that, Satish."

"Alas, you mistake me. Or I would have told you long ago."

Too many revelations. I dropped the duped tape in a pocket. "I'll keep this. But tell me one thing: Why didn't you destroy the original when you had the chance?"

He shrugged. "It retained some utility. I felt it compromised Skipper also to some degree."

"In Sermak's suicide?"

"Not just there. In Skipper's integrity as a vent."

"I don't understand."

"The tape on which he captured my confession also contains several of the most popular Keats and O'Dell routines. To be more precise, Dapper's lines alone. The lines a failing talent could no longer convincingly cast forth."

"You're claiming Skipper faked his act? That he triggered

Dapper's spiel off a tape? That's bullshit, Satish."

Gupta shrugged again, more eloquently. "As you wish."

My father's culpability and putative on-stage trickery could wait until I had Dapper back. "I'm leaving to look for Sherri. Would you like me to tell her anything from you?"

"Only that I continue to love her and would gladly take her back if she recants this latest betrayal."

I could only shake my head. "I wouldn't hold my breath, Satish."

"Rahel will show you out." He escorted me into the hall, where Rahel appeared and conducted me down the stairs and through the ribbon-divided rooms to the parking atrium.

Out in the drive, opening my car door, I heard an upper window slide open. Gupta thrust his head and shoulders out and waved goodbye, as if I were leaving after a midsummer garden party. "Thank you for subbing for Cabriales, Will. I will mail your check on Monday."

◆ ◆ ◆

Starved, I returned to the Beallwood Connector and stopped at a burger stand. Three cheeseburgers and a milkshake later, my watch read 11:15. I drove immediately to Skipper's Keep to talk to my mother.

LaRue received me in her bedroom. Stacks of pseudospiritual tomes tottered on her nightstand, and she clutched one volume with a finger inserted as bookmark. She greeted me with a smile and patted the parti-colored satin sheets next to her. I sat down on the end of the bed and cocked my head at her.

"You look frazzled, Will. Is everything okay?"

"Sherri Gupta has left her husband. She drove off this evening without a word of warning. Does that surprise you?"

LaRue freed her finger and set the book aside. "Actually, I've seen it coming for years."

Everything we knew that the other also knew went discreetly unspoken. At length, though, I broke the silence: "Satish thinks you might know where she's gone."

"Tell him to look for her in a cottage on Hurricane Cove on Center Hill Lake."

"And where's that, Mama? Here in Georgia?"

"Oh no. Middle Tennessee, north of Smithville, on the Caney Fork River. Beautiful country."

"What makes you think she'll be there?"

LaRue unburdened herself with a surprising degree of peace: "Skipper used to rendezvous with Sherri there. The affair lasted five or six years. I tolerated it because I loved them both. And they were quite careful never to conduct any of it here in Columbus or in Muscogee County."

I sat flabbergasted. LaRue had no idea that Skipper had sired a half-brother for me and Kelli in an illicit relationship with Evelyn Sermak, but she had full knowledge of an extended affair between Skipper and Sherri VanHouten Gupta?

"Mama, why would you voluntarily tolerate an affair?"

"They both cared for me. I thought that eventually guilt would prompt them to break it off. They didn't, of course, and that hurt quite a lot. I even got angry. But I didn't tattletale to Satish or pour sugar in the gas tanks of Sherri's antique automobiles."

"Why didn't you confront Skipper?"

"I finally did just that."

"After five or six years?"

"Skipper had many obligations and pressures in those years. I didn't want to complicate matters for either him or you."

"*Me?*"

"You wouldn't have enjoyed a divorce, Will, any more than I. Once you'd safely graduated high school and gone off to North Carolina to college, I gave him an ultimatum. Belatedly, he came to his senses."

"What kind of ultimatum?"

"I've told as much of this story as I care to this evening. I find such talk, only a week after Skipper's death, borderline sacrilegious. Besides, Skipper's spoken so sweetly to me in my recent dreams that I can't hold that old grudge against him forever."

"It sounds to me as if you forgave him long ago."

"If he comes to you in your dreams as he has to me, you'll

forgive him too. I pray that for you, Will."

I thought of Shawndrell Tompkins and his disconcerting vision of his late grandfather. It came to me that in all the apocalyptic activity of the afternoon and evening, I had forgotten to phone his mother. If I could just track Sherri down before she disappeared forever with Dapper, perhaps I could again fully devote myself to my real calling. If I still had a job.

"Give me a kiss before you go, Will."

What could I do except obey?

◆ ◆ ◆

From the kitchen phone downstairs, I placed a call — but not to Shawndrell's mother.

"You said to telephone you no matter how late."

"Uhnnnn," said Adrienne.

"So do you want to hear the full report?"

"Morning," she mumbled, and hung up.

Just as well. I doubted my ability to compose any narrative that made sense.

CHAPTER 23

The moon projected shadows of the magnolia foliage outside my bedroom window onto the floors and walls. The shadows swayed. A squirrel scampered over an attic joist. Sleep eluded me. A kind of full-body seasickness had overtaken me; it sprang from a surfeit of knowledge about myself and others, and it shook me from crown to sole.

Subbing for Pablo Cabriales, I had discovered that I could do a passable stage turn. I had learned who had stolen Dapper — stolen him not once but twice. I had heard from LaRue's own lips a confession that my father had for years conducted an extramarital affair with his partner's wife. Astonishingly, though, what most unsettled me was the revelation that for well over two decades my father had concealed a recording device inside Dapper's toggle-filled thoracic cavity and used tapes of Dapper's lines to hoodwink his audiences — and his own family members — into believing that he had perfect lip control. What chutzpah. No wonder he had seldom bothered to practice in later years. And what confidence in his own dexterity with the PAUSE button it had required to work before a live audience alternating one's natural, real-time voice with prerecorded wisecracks.

It staggered me how many lies Skipper had lived, how many illusions he had engineered and imposed, on both others and himself. Insofar as I could judge tonight, he had not conducted any part of his life with integrity. Even the charities to which he had made large donations, it now seemed, had benefited not from his goodwill and concern but instead from inchoate guilt. This man had given his contaminated seed to me, and now I lay abed lamenting his disgraceful weaknesses and mulling strategies to atone for them.

Eventually, the magnolia shadows faded, my attic squirrel ceased to prowl, and a host of different birds began their chipper sunrise racketings. Facing a six-hour drive to Hurricane Cove, Tennessee, to put period to the whole nightmarish week since Skipper's death, I resisted getting up until the last possible minute.

When I did untangle from my bed, I stumbled over to the telephone and called Adrienne. As usual, breakfast putterings and Olivia's chirpy singing provided background counterpoint to our conversation.

The first words out of Adrienne's mouth? "You never called!"

"But I did. You just never completely woke up."

"You're claiming I pulled an out-and-out zombie act?"

"Your phrasing, kiddo, but yes."

Adrienne fell silent. Then she said, "Maybe. I do tend to fly on autopilot if you wake me after midnight. Was it that late?"

"Yes." I gave her an abbreviated account of my long evening in Columbus.

"I see. And now, after school today, you intend to drive to Tennessee. May I ask one question?"

"Sure."

"Are you completely crazy?"

"Not completely. I still love you."

"Will, you can't make this trip. With no more sleep than you've had, you'll go off the road and into the rail like a kamikaze. If by some miracle you do arrive safely, it'll be well after dark. How will you accomplish anything? You've never even visited this Hurricane Cove place before."

"Adrienne, what would you have me do? Give up when I'm on the brink of resolving this whole discouraging business?"

"No. But take a few minutes and rethink your plans. I'd like you to survive this weekend. Olivia! Will, I've got to go. She's pouring Ovaltine into the oatmeal box. Olivia!"

She hung up, and I stood there, receiver in hand, obediently rethinking.

◆ ◆ ◆

Fresh-skinned and auburn-haired, Babe Young came out onto the porch of her rambling Victorian house with her pregnancy preceding her like a wash tub of rubies. She cradled it with her bare arms, her nightgown rucked up to her knees and her freckled feet as flat as hoecakes. She looked happy and sleep-calmed and beautiful.

"Hey there, Will." She smiled with languid serenity.

"Is J.W. up yet?"

"Oh sure. Can't keep that man in bed longer than a ten-year-old on the first morning of summer vacation."

I turned my eyes to the Youngs' house. They had built a scaffolding up to the second-story rain gutters and scraped the clapboards in order to apply fresh coats of white paint. Their industry shamed me. I never devoted as much time to renovating Skipper's parents' place as the Youngs spent on their house.

Blissfully rocking her belly, Babe favored me with another slow-developing smile.

At length I said, "Do you suppose I could *see* J.W., Babe?"

"No, you can't." She giggled charmingly. "That is, he's in the shower. You can sit on the pot and talk to him, but I don't think you want to actually *see* him."

"Maybe I'd better wait."

Babe pulled the screen door open for me. "Don't be shy, Will. Go right on in."

For so large a house, the downstairs bathroom had the dimensions of a bathyscape. Sink, shower, and commode virtually abutted, and steam had fogged every glass or chrome surface. The drumming in the shower suggested an August downpour on a buckled tin roof.

Upon my knock, J.W. stuck his soapy head through a gap in the yellow plastic curtain. "Will-*yum*! Care to join me?"

"No thanks. I'll take a rain check. J.W., do you and Babe have any special plans for the weekend?"

"Maybe a do-it-yourself delivery if Cletus the Fetus comes calling and my pickup won't start. Why do you ask?"

"I'd like to rent your airplane and have you pilot me somewhere."

"Really?" He sounded pleased. "Right now?"

"No, no. This afternoon." I told him the destination and asked how long the flight might take.

"Two hours. Two and a half, tops. Unless a really mean storm comes up to ground us. Can't fly in bad weather no more, Will, now that I'm gonna be a daddy. No more crazy risks for this old hound." After a beat or two, he laughed like a hyena to emphasize his new sanity.

"So you'll do it?"

"Sure. Sounds like pure pleasure, compared to the last job you invited me on." I refrained from mentioning that even on our cemetery expedition he had appeared to enjoy himself immensely. "You buy the fuel and pay the airport fees, and I won't even charge you for my invaluable time. I'm setting only one condition."

With an abrupt knock, the water in the shower cut off. I hesitated, sensing the trap, but could not prevent myself from asking, "What's that?"

The shower curtain shot back on its rings, and J.W. stepped out with his dripping arms spread wide. "Just give me a big ol' hug in case we crash and burn!" Before I could react, J.W. had clasped me to him like an amorous bear, imprinting me from cuff to collar with his outline.

"For God's sake, J.W., I've got to go to work in these clothes!"

Babe appeared in the doorway. "So, now I see what goes on while I'm out shopping."

J.W. pushed me away and examined me with smug satisfaction. To Babe he said, "This is just some of that male bonding you're always hearing about. Now, if Will was naked too, you might have some cause to worry."

◆ ◆ ◆

By the time I reached Oakwood Elementary, my clothes had dried but remained rumpled. Once at my desk, I dialed Shawndrell Tompkins's home on the off chance of finding his mother there during the day. To my surprise and bafflement, Shawndrell himself answered — in a voice no more forceful than a gerbil's.

"Hey, pal, what's up? You sick?"

Silence for a long breath. "He come again, Mr. Kee. He come again, and this time he look dead, all-over grey and evil."

"Is your mother home, Shawndrell?"

"No sir. She done went off to her job." At a plant that processed chickens, I knew. "Mr. Kee, I'm skeert!"

"Wouldn't you feel safer here at school?"

"Yessir."

"So what prompted you to stay home?"

"*He* say not to go. He say wait right in your room, boy, I'm gonna pull you *up*."

"Would you like someone to come get you, Shawndrell, and bring you to school?"

"Yessir. But they better hurry. I can see that hook, with the worms wriggling right off it."

"Sit tight," I said and rang off.

I wanted to go after the boy myself, but instead telephoned Nick Hardwick, a truancy officer in the Toqueville office, who said he'd happily oblige. My staying proved providential, for Resa Murawski almost immediately called me for help. We rushed to Mrs. Iselin's classroom to quell the ruckus that had erupted when Talulah Grimes vomited blood and succumbed to a seizure of painful hacking. Resa led the weakened Talool away to the dispensary, while I perched on the edge of Mrs. Iselin's desk to explain the situation to Talool's classmates and to answer their questions.

Returning to my office, I saw Shawndrell coming toward me. His easy saunter totally belied his earlier apprehensive talk.

"Shawndrell, how are you feeling?"

"Just fine, Mr. Kee."

"No more bad visions?"

He hung his head. "Mr. Kee, this last time I didn't really see my paw-paw at all. In fact, I think he might be gone for good."

"Then why in the world did you feed me that whopper?" I gently knuckled his head.

"I got bus-left this morning, and didn't know *how* I was gonna get to school!"

Laughing, I said, "Getting bus-left doesn't justify lying, Shawndrell. Especially about something that means so much to you. But I'm glad you and your paw-paw have apparently decided to stay where you both belong."

"Me too, Mr. Kee."

After that I sequestered myself in my converted mop closet until lunchtime. In the cafeteria, I ran into Alice Holcrow, the music teacher, another "nonessential." She lifted an eyebrow, exaggeratedly appraising the wrinkles in my outfit. "Updated your résumé yet? Mine's already gone out to three other school systems."

"Not yet, Alice. No time."

She grew serious. "Don't wait too long, Will. I've got a hunch the axe is going to fall any day. . . ."

I had just loaded my tray with a salad and three yeast rolls when Mrs. Lapierre approached. "William Keats, you look absolutely awful. Go home right now. I won't dock your sick or personal days."

"Home now? Four hours early?"

"I'll cover for you. What's a principal for?"

I had often asked myself that same question but chose not to address the topic now. "Thank you. Thank you very much." I left my salad on the tray, pocketed the yeast rolls for later, and hurried back to my office to gather up my gear. Best act on Mrs. Lapierre's offer while it still stood.

◆ ◆ ◆

I headed neither straight home nor to J.W.'s, but to Tocqueville Middle School, where I parked and hiked through the ankle-high grass to a distant classroom. A product of the 1950s, the building exhibited a long row of windows at waist height. Adrienne's seventh-graders reacted to my appearance at these windows as if the Easter Bunny had come calling. An especially eager boy hurried to one of the windows and tilted it open.

"Hey, mister, you should report to the office if you want to see someone."

"Thank you. If I wanted to see someone in the office, I'd take your advice."

Adrienne's flushed face replaced the boy's. "Are you trying to get me fired?"

"J.W. Young said he'd fly me to Tennessee."

I could not read her expression. "You're kidding. When?"

"This afternoon. At least I won't have to drive. With any luck, I'll return by Sunday at the latest."

"If everything goes well."

"Right. Maybe I can sleep a little on the trip."

"In J.W.'s duct-taped excuse for an airplane?" Adrienne barked a laugh. "Good luck, boyfriend." Somehow she got her head all the way out the window, and we kissed.

The sound of twenty-five or so hooting adolescents persuaded Adrienne to break off sooner than I would have liked. I saluted her good-bye and hiked back across the uncut grass to my car.

◆ ◆ ◆

In Mountboro, I opened my post-office box and watched a stack of fliers, bills, solicitations, and sympathy cards cascade to my feet. I had not checked the box since a week ago Thursday. With a borrowed white plastic bin from the main desk, I carried this dubious bounty home and dumped it out on my bed. After stirring desultorily through my accumulated mail, I discarded the junk and set the bills and apparent sympathy cards aside.

Among the non-ignorable items I found an official-looking envelope with an ominous return address. Before I could stop to consider its implications, I tore the envelope open and quickly read the enclosed letter. Then I read it again. My second reading neither improved its style nor countermanded its message.

Dear Mr. Keats:
    You are hereby notified that I have not recommended
    you for re-employment by the Speece County Board of

Education and do not intend to renew your contract for the next school year. Your employment will conclude at the end of the current term.

Yours truly,
R. A. Stickney
Superintendent

CHAPTER 24

Will, if Mr. Rat's Ass Stickney's heart was on fire, I wouldn't piss down his throat to put it out."

J.W. threw my dismissal notice across the room with a flourish. It landed on the small duffel I had packed for the trip to Tennessee, but I could not summon the energy to get up and retrieve it

"I don't have a job next year," I repeated spacily.

"Buck up, hoss. I can keep you busy. The Paddens need a new roof and the Demarises some porch repairs. I can even get you a little bricklaying for the new ovens at Your Daily Bread."

"I appreciate that, J.W., but what I meant was, I no longer have the only job I ever loved."

"Can't help you there, Will. But in the money department — "

I finally stood. "For once, money doesn't speak to my predicament — except that the lack of it helped get me fired. This is about the kids. Shawndrell and Talool and the whole suffering passel of them. Just because they don't vote, they don't have a say in their own treatment? Why should they get shortchanged — deprived of hands-on help — just because some desk-bound bureaucrat with a Ph.D. wants to pare down his organizational charts?"

"Good questions, Will. But I can't answer them. All I know is, we've got to get our heinies in gear if we're going to make it to Tennessee before nightfall."

I jerked my duffel up and accidentally knocked a table lamp over. The shattering of the lightbulb seemed a practical rebuke to my indignant speechifying. I had to laugh.

"All right, J.W., let's get this wild goose chase underway."

"Amen! Only the wild ones give you a run for your money anyhow."

◆ ◆ ◆

Owing to a lingering dispute between the county commissioners and a powerful commercial landowner, the terminal building five or six miles out of town sat locked and unattended. Perched on the eaves of a rusting hangar or picking their way through the weeds next to the parking lot, noisy crows greeted our arrival. When we emerged from J.W.'s rattletrap truck, some of the birds flapped off into the nearby pines, unhappily cawing.

An apparent sinkhole brimming with collapsed concrete separated us from the only light aircraft on the tarmac. Leading me around the hole, J.W. explained that it had once contained a large underground fuel tank, but that the original operator of the facility had removed it when the county refused to kick in a fair sum for the airport's upkeep.

"How do you gas up?" I asked him.

"See that vehicle over there?" A truck with a large vatlike receptacle stood next to an outbuilding. "I bought all their AV-fuel real cheap when they had to close down. My pump runs off the truck engine. Up north, we'll need about forty bucks to refuel. You got eighty for the round trip, I reckon, even without gainful employment for next year."

"I'll borrow it from Mrs. Lapierre if I have to. What about takeoffs and landings? How do you get weather conditions and air traffic reports?"

"Sometimes you just have to overfly the field and take a look at that sorry windsock over there. I call a weather service in Tocqueville for conditions hereabouts. As for the rest of it, I just keep my eyes peeled."

Little about the facility or J.W.'s modus operandi inspired confidence, but I still trusted in my friend's uncanny resourcefulness and grit. I had to.

Taking pains, we untied and fueled J.W.'s short-bodied Cessna 172. It had a cream-colored fuselage, cream-colored wings, and glossy navy-blue pin-striping. On its nose, J.W. had crookedly hand-lettered the name *Sky Babe* in alarming crimson strokes. Although the Cessna was over forty years old, he had meticulously maintained it, and when we climbed aboard, he ran a thorough preflight, cranking the engine to 1600 RPM, checking the carburetor, and cycling the left and right magnetos. His obvious expertise settled most of my remaining doubts.

Seeming to read my mind, J.W. spoke into the voice-activated mike attached to his headset. "Hell, Will, a monkey could fly one of these suckers. *You* could fly one. Just don't put yourself in the shotgun seat if a monkey tries to *land* it."

I heard him over my own miked headset. "No worry there. I ride only with FAA-certified pilots." The vibrating cab held us as companionably as an egg carton. In a few short minutes, only an inch or so of manmade materials would separate us from our planet's hurtling atmosphere. "How high will we go?"

"Four thousand five hundred feet. You'll love it. *I* love it. It's almost better than sex."

"Maybe I'd rather sleep."

"Go ahead, if you can. If the engine sputters and we go into a dive, I won't even bother waking you. We said our good-byes this morning."

"Thanks, J.W. You're a prince."

J.W. grinned. "Just part of the whole Young Airlines package, son." Then he set us rolling. The engine buzzed like a thousand kazoos, J.W. pulled back on the wheel, and *Sky Babe* shuddered into the air. The entire landscape dropped away like a discarded candy wrapper, and I realized that only a soulless zombie would try to sleep in the midst of such exhilaration.

In the air, droning toward Tennessee, I explained that Dapper had fallen into the hands of the wife of my late father's business partner and that she had probably fled with Dapper to Hurricane Cove on Center Hill Lake. I also explained that Sherri Gupta and my father had committed adultery with each other for several consecutive years. When I was finished, J.W.'s shrill whistle filled my headphones.

"Man, they just don't make 'em like your daddy no more!

Hope to hell I can still get it up for *one* gal when I'm his age, never mind *two*."

"The affair took place some time ago, J.W., but Skipper wasn't a young buck even then. Old enough to know better, certainly."

Quietly, J.W. said, "Amen."

We flew for two and a half hours. Tennessee undulated beneath us like a neon-green ocean teeming with kelly-green volcanic cones and emerald lagoons. My bladder had slowly expanded to the size of the camera bag on the tourist who had knocked me down the other night. Otherwise I had enjoyed our flight and experienced a twinge of regret when J.W. radioed for clearance to land at the Smithfield strip.

As the Cessna executed its base and final turns for landing, I saw portions of the Caney Fork River and Center Hill Lake to the north. A fair amount of daylight remained, and we had gained an hour by crossing a time zone. I actually entertained hopes of locating Sherri Gupta before dark.

My discomfort gone, I exited the modest airport bathroom to find J.W. signing paperwork at the front desk. The manager of the Smithfield facility, a burly fellow with long but tidy sideburns and a handsome silver pompadour, heard me out patiently when I asked about rental cars. Then he tossed me a set of keys.

"You'll spot a '67 Lincoln out front. I call it our airport courtesy clunker. No charge, but you're getting what you pay for. Twenty-four hours max usage, and you bring it back with a full tank. That's it. Have fun, boys."

We climbed into the battered beige-and-peach Lincoln, a barge on wheels, and drove into Smithfield itself. Center Hill Lake, Hurricane Cove, and the rental cottage where Skipper and Sherri had once held their trysts lay several miles north along Highway 56.

"You can stay here in town, you know," I told J.W. "No reason for you to get snagged in a messy confrontation. I'll pay for a motel room for you."

Now a passenger himself, J.W. scowled ingratiatingly. "Ever stop to think you could maybe use a little backup? What if Mrs. Gupta pulls a gun, or decides to punctuate your back with a steak knife? Any gal who'd elope with a wooden lover is crazy enough to kill you. No, I won't breathe down your neck when you go face to face with your daddy's girlfriend, but don't expect me to stand farther off than a shout."

"Much obliged, J.W."

"*One* of us needs to do a little thinking, hoss, and it seems I'm nominated. Now, it's my turn to sleep, and unlike you I'm going to use the time wisely." He leaned his head against the window and very lightly began to snore.

I drove. Every other homestead beyond Smithville had a sign proclaiming it a nursery. Acres of evergreen seedlings, garden patches under improvised tents of olive-drab plastic, spic-and-span or dilapidated greenhouses. The proximity of so many greenhouses gave the landscape a fairy-tale picturesqueness. As we neared the hills through which the meandering Caney Fork River had chiseled its way, these artificial galleries vanished. Forested slopes and rugged switchbacks replaced them. Hills loomed everywhere.

"This is one big-ass lake." J.W. had awakened as we came down a slope onto a lofty bridge from which we could see distant bluffside homes, fishing boats no bigger than paper clips, and a vast lavender panorama. "How do you expect to find Dapper and this Gupta gal amidst such a muchness?"

"Ask directions?" The eeriness of driving at the cruising altitude of herons tingled the soles of my feet.

"And betray ten thousand years of male stubbornness? Son, we'd have to turn in the equipment we were born with."

Before I could reply, fate intervened in the form of a dented green road sign at the head of an angled side lane. Past this sign before it fully registered, I had to slew the Lincoln to an awkward stop. Despite his fastened seat belt, J.W. had one hand on the dash and another on the door handle.

"Will-*yum*, I don't ever want to hear nothing about my piloting from the likes of you."

I backed the Lincoln up in my empty lane and got a clearer look at the sign: HURRICANE BORDER DRIVE. This road, narrow and needle-curtained, clung to the edge of a hill and plunged into a forbidding green pit of evergreens and dogwoods.

"Do we take it?" I said.

"Where else would Hurricane Border Drive lead but to Hurricane Cove? I say go."

We went, my foot poised above the brake. In less than five minutes we had descended at least two miles and fetched up at a country store of dark logs and toothpaste-white mortar. Hurricane Border Drive kept dropping lakeward, but it spawned two other roads at this junction, both dirt-surfaced and rutted. A broad-hipped middle-aged woman in jeans and floral blouse, half-lost in the plum shadows under a roofed porch, was just locking up the log building.

"Go to it, Hercule," J.W. said.

I got out of the Lincoln. Hearing my footsteps on the gravel path, the woman said, "We're closed," without even looking at me.

"I just need directions, ma'am. Hurricane Cove?"

As I had feared she would, she nodded toward the closer of the rutted trails. "That'll take you straight there. Honk at every bend or some fool'll charge up blind on you and drop his engine in your lap."

"Thanks." I turned back toward the Lincoln, and then paused. "Do you know a woman named Sherri, a long-time visitor up here? She might use her maiden name, VanHouten, or her married name, Gupta."

The shopkeeper stiffened. "No, sir. Can't say I ever heard of a lady going by either name. But lots of my customers, even the old-timers, I don't know their names."

"Fine. Well, have a good night."

Back in the car, I nosed into the double-rutted road with its median hump of thistles, dandelions, and wire grass. J.W. cleared his throat, then said, "Can't say I approve of the last question you asked that gal, Will."

"How come? She might have known Sherri."

"Oh, I'm *sure* she did. In fact, you made her decide to unlock her store and go back in. Probably to use the phone."

"Shit! You think she's calling to warn Sherri someone's looking for her?"

"Do Catholics pull out?"

Because nothing could repair my gaffe, I concentrated on driving, periodically sounding the horn as the storekeeper had advised. Traveling at no more than ten or fifteen miles per hour, we passed widely separated cottages and more elaborate homes on either side of the road. Puzzle pieces of the lake and of whale-backed hills showed through the trees on the downslope. Most of the homeowners had set out placards naming their properties: Lazy Lake Lodge, Hurricane Hangout, Weekend on the Water. One cottage, like a miniature Golconda, had exotic paper lanterns glowing in the trees all about it. We could hear dogs barking and smell the savory tang of outdoor grilling. The weekend had arrived, and the householders on the cove had descended in force.

"So what now, Dick Tracy? Knock on every door until Sherri answers and invites you in?"

"Not necessary, wiseguy. How many antique Caddies do you imagine we're going to find down this road?"

J.W. smacked his brow. "And to think I ever doubted your sleuthin' genius."

One by one we eliminated the homes with parked vehicles other than Cadillacs. Where a garage concealed a car or none was in evidence, we checked for an audible overload of kids and animals. Boisterous deck parties ruled out other candidates. By this process we narrowed Sherri's likely hideaway to an isolated bungalow on a lakeside lot below the trail. A brand new industrial-strength Master Lock thwarted any access to the interior of the set-apart garage, and only a CONDEMNED sign would have rendered the house itself any more lifeless.

"Think this is it?" said J.W. on the lane above the house.

"I don't see any alternatives."

"Well, then, scramble on down there and knock on her door. The lady might even be willing to listen to you."

I heel-walked down the needle-cushioned slope, crossed the asphalt parking area, and carefully negotiated the steep concrete steps down to the bungalow's front door. No lights in the curtained windows. No signs of life anywhere.

I hammered on the pastel-blue door. "Mrs. Gupta! Sherri! Will

Keats here! Please let me talk to you."

No response. I climbed back up to the spookily ticking Lincoln.

"Looks like we're gonna have to lay siege to the place, William. Assuming she's really in there. I'll stake out the front door from the car here. You keep watch on the back door."

"I get to squat amidst poison ivy and snakes and the foggy, foggy dew while you relax on leather cushions?"

"Who flew you up here, Will?"

J.W. had a point. Till now, he had sacrificed a great deal more for my sake than I had for his. "All right. Just don't fall asleep."

Using his wadded-up windbreaker for a pillow, J.W. had already propped himself up against the Lincoln's driver-side door. "Fall asleep? Don't know the meaning of the words. Besides, my empty stomach will keep me up all night."

I plunged downslope, this time to find a damp mosquito-filled hole from which to keep vigil on the back door. I paused briefly and tried to pick out from a high scatter of stars the chariot of this spring's spectacular comet. The sight of it eluded me, though, and yearning for what I could not have, I registered instead a faint, irregular crickety noise. It came from the lane, inside the Lincoln, and after puzzling for a moment I identified the noise as J.W.'s stomach growling. I laughed and plunged onward.

CHAPTER 25

Sunlight streaming through a canopy of birch leaves roused me from a hypnagogic state somewhere between sleep and waking. My tongue felt like the webby membrane on the inner surface of an orange. The last time I had checked my IndiGlo watch dial, it had read 3:45. Now it read 6:18.

I rose as if I had 150 pounds of wet cement on my shoulders. All my bones ached, and my muscles shifted like dislodged slabs of curing goat cheese. I rubbed my eyes and peered at the cottage. The rear door remained closed. The nest into which I had stumbled last night lay only a few yards from the house's elevated kitchen deck, near a solitary path amidst clinging underbrush. Despite my muzziness, Sherri could not have made it past me without alerting me to her escape attempt.

I walked creakily around the house to the front door, which stood wide open. A fist clenched inside me. I leapt into the doorway and called, "Sherri, Sherri! Are you there?"

A large-screen TV, a U-shaped sectional couch, a glass-topped coffee table. A kitchen with a compact microwave whose door stood open in parody of the cottage's. An unsealed package of bagels. I checked all three square, modest bedrooms, each one with depressing knotty-pine paneling, and found the only unmade bed on the premises. Sherri did not occupy it, of course, and further searching turned up no signs of either her or Dapper O'Dell.

Outside, I found J.W. in the Lincoln, curled up like a puppy. Alternating snorts and tea-kettle whistles issued through his nose. The sight of him sleeping enraged me, and I pounded clangorously on the roof of the car, heedless of the damage to my fist.

Gratifyingly, J.W. kicked out and jolted upright, knocking his head on the steering wheel. His bloodshot eyes eventually fixed on me, perplexity yielding to embarrassment, and he hurried to jack open the car door and crawl out.

"Oh boy," he said. "Oh boy. Guess I learned to tune out my stomach's caterwauling, Will."

"You let Sherri sneak right past you!"

"Damn it, Will, nobody's perfect. Tell me you didn't doze a bit yourself."

I pointedly turned my attention to the garage. Its untouched padlock shone in the sun like a badge. Sherri had pretty clearly escaped on foot to avoid lifting the garage door and firing up the Cadillac's engine.

"I have a hunch she'll head for the lake," I said.

"Why's that?" To remove the cricks from his neck, J.W. swung his head in slow figure-eights.

I squinted through the trees at the water. "The lake signifies something to her emotionally. It dominates this entire landscape. She and Skipper obviously loved it, or they wouldn't have returned to it so often for their assignations. Maybe Sherri figures that if she can outwait us on the water, we'll give up and go home. Besides, I just can't picture her thrusting out her hip and hitching a ride on the highway."

J.W. threaded his fingers together and popped his knuckles. "Your call, Will. You know the lady better than I do. But even situating her on the lake leaves a hell of a lot of territory to cover. I say we split up."

I didn't want to split up. J.W. had fallen asleep on me, yes, but I relished his company, the haphazard security of his partnership. "Let's see what turns up in the immediate neighborhood before we make that decision. C'mon, I'll drive."

We headed back the way we had come, toward the junction with the store. At the last log residence before the roads merged, an elderly man in nothing but an Atlanta Braves cap and a voluminous pair of khaki shorts sat on a lawn chair in the early sunlight, contemplating the road and sipping from an outsized thermal cup. His leathery skin made him resemble a basking iguana.

"Good morning," I said to the man. "Did you happen to see a woman go by here early today?"

"Sure did. About forty minutes ago. The Missus Keats."

Momentarily, I pictured LaRue, and utter disorientation seized me. Then I realized that Sherri must have often masqueraded as Skipper's wife. "Yessir. Mrs. Keats. Did she happen to say where she was heading?"

"Down to the marina. I offered her a ride. She had a sizable carry-case she was toting, tilting her off-stride. Said no thanks, though. Wanted the exercise."

"How do we get to the marina?"

"Go back to Hurricane Drive Road and follow it past the store."

"Thanks, old-timer," J.W. said.

I hit the gas, and our informant raised his cup in valediction and resumed his reptilian sunbathing.

We drove through thick green defiles interlaced with birdsong until we reached Hurricane Bay Marina: a shoreline parking lot, a series of weatherbeaten floating docks, a concession stand, a floating office cabin, and a gasoline-pump island. A row of tin-roofed docking bays pointed out into the inlet toward the oil-drum buoys at its mouth. Rolling wooded hills encircled the whole marina and even the formidable expanse of lake beyond it. We walked past metal fishing skiffs and fiberglass sports boats with cocked outboards. The water sparkled everywhere, and hollow, lapping noises echoed among the connected piers. We entered the open office cabin.

Notices festooned a cork bulletin board. A glass cabinet held lures for sale and supported an antique cash register. Vacation brochures and maps filled a wire rack. The competing smells of gasoline and fish rose to us through the indoor-outdoor mats on the planking. A service bell sat on the counter, and J.W. made it jump with a quick blow of the palm. The ding pulled a hawk-faced young man with sun-bleached hair out of a back room. He wore white shorts, knee-length white socks, white sneakers, and a tucked-in white T-shirt bearing the legend GET STONED WITH A ROCKHOUND.

"Sorry, gentlemen, we don't officially open till ten."

"Have you seen a handsome woman of sixty or so this morning? A Mrs. Keats? We were supposed to meet her here."

"Oh, certainly. She arranged with me yesterday for an early rental. A Suncruiser pontoon boat. She already had the key, and I saw her take off in it about half an hour ago."

"How much you charge for one of those Suncruisers?" J.W. asked.

"One hundred dollars for six hours, and of course whatever gas you use."

"Whoa," J.W. said. "Take me to the water, mama, and watch me rake it in."

The rental agent bristled, and I hurriedly showed him a placatory twenty-dollar bill. "If you'll take this for doing business so early, we'd like to rent a boat to catch up with Mrs. Keats. Something a little less pricey though."

"I can give you a skiff for the whole day for thirty-five dollars."

"We'll take it."

The marina-keeper walked us outside to a dented silver boat. J.W. stepped down into it and confidently made his way to the outboard motor at its stern. I stood on the pier studying the skiff skeptically. A church key, I thought, could have punctured it at any point.

"Take it really slow until you get past the buoys," the agent told J.W. "You don't have a speedometer like your friend does on her pontoon craft, so just try not to create a wake."

"I know how to run an outboard," J.W. said. "Could you give us any pointers on how to find our gal?"

"Turn left beyond the buoys. She headed toward Davies Island and Burgess Falls. There's a map in that box at the prow and life jackets under the rear bench. Good luck." The agent returned over the pier to his floating office.

"Come on, William," J.W. said. "You waiting for me to pipe you aboard or for your knees to quit knocking?"

"Toss me a life vest."

"*Before* you get in? Holy mackerel, hoss, didn't you trust yourself to my piloting yesterday?" But he pulled a life vest out from under his bench and tossed it to me. I caught it and hastily pulled it on over my shirt, but made no move to join J.W. in the skiff. "Come on, Keats. Every second you stand there, the farther away 'Mrs. Keats' gets in her redneck yacht."

"J.W., I can't swim."

"Not a lick?"

"One lick, and then I sink."

"Will-*yum*, get your sorry carcass aboard. Unless the *Queen Mary* heaves up on our bow and swamps us, you won't *have* to swim. Not even a lick."

I stepped gingerly into the skiff, positioned myself on the bench up front, and gripped both gunwales for support. "You promise?"

"Hey, wasn't my daddy's name Popeye? You're safer here with me than you'd be in a coin-operated speedboat in front of Wal-Mart." J.W. dropped the outboard, started it up, and set us purring at a nonthreatening clip toward open water.

"Just get us back ashore with Dapper, and I'll even grit my teeth and hug you naked again."

For a moment, I thought J.W. had not heard me. Then he shouted, "Don't do me any favors, Cap'n. Once was plenty."

◆ ◆ ◆

After a few minutes, I relaxed enough to release my white-knuckled grip on the skiff's sides. Even when J.W., seeing us free of the inlet-marking buoy, increased our speed, I continued to enjoy the freshening morning breeze, the chop of the water, and periodic glimpses of herons, wood ducks, and belted kingfishers. Turtles occasionally poked their snouts into view along the shoreline, and splashes farther out marked the leaps of bass and bluegills. Several fishermen had come out, but so far no waterskiers, jet skis, or buzzing pin-striped sports boats.

Neither J.W. nor I tried to talk, but we carefully reconnoitered the inlets and hollows off the lake's central channel, without once sighting a Suncruiser or any other variety of pontoon boat. The map in my hand suggested that even after we churned past Davies

Island, we had several miles to search before the highest cataract of Burgess Falls intervened to halt us. Skimming along in the mesmerizing bumble and spray, I had almost ceased to care about the object of my hunt.

And then J.W. shouted, "Look!"

Deep within a complex pocket gulf to our right floated a Suncruiser. Its white hull and orange awning blazed against the forested hills. The vessel drifted at the head of a jutting ridge, moving randomly in small circles between shadow and sunshine. Had Sherri gone ashore and left her boat unmoored, or simply jumped overboard for a swim? In either case, we could see no one on the pontoon boat's deck.

J.W. said, "What's your pleasure, Cap'n?"

"I guess we'd better check it out."

We putt-putted into the ragged bay. Coming alongside the Suncruiser, which had the name *Trinidad* and a hyphenated serial number painted on its flank, I searched for signs of life. None. A ghost pontoon boat rode the shallow swells. J.W. circled the craft. And as we drew even with its prow, I saw a pale wet face in the water between the pontoons. The swimmer's eyes glittered brilliantly in the false twilight under the deck, and her slender forearm swept up out of the lake to wipe her short gray hair back from her brow.

"Sherri!" I said.

She stared out at us like a mermaid at the unexpected apparition of two brutish fishermen. Her water-refracted body bobbed almost invisibly in the murk under the boat. I signaled J.W. to cut the outboard, and silence ballooned around us until she spoke:

"What do you want, William Keats? Can't you just go away and leave me alone?"

"You took Dapper, Sherri. He doesn't belong to you."

"He doesn't belong to you either."

Her remark baffled me. "Come out of the water, Sherri. We have some talking to do."

"Back off," she said, struggling to maintain herself vertical. Then she softened her tone: "Face the center of the lake, please."

"What?"

J.W. said, "Wake up, Will. We've crashed the lady's skinny-dipping party. She needs some space."

"Thank you, observant sir," Sherri said mockingly.

We grabbed paddles and oared ourselves several feet away from the Suncruiser. Sherri swam between the pontoons to the rear of the boat and, safely out of our view, climbed the drop-down ladder next to the inboard motor. The ladder clinked metallically with her each upward step. A few moments passed, and Sherri's voice said, "All right. I'm decent."

J.W. and I both looked around. Sherri had quickly pulled on powder-blue shorts, a white cotton blouse, and a floppy tennis hat.

"Only William can come onboard. You" — she pointed imperiously at J.W. — "have to go back to the marina. Those terms are nonnegotiable."

"Lady, only dying's nonnegotiable. Everything else — at least where I come from — is on the table."

"Don't make me start screaming bloody murder." Sherri nodded at the ridge behind her. "Someone will hear, and you'll both look like opportunistic rapist lowlifes."

"Babe says that's one of my most attractive looks."

"Go on back, J.W. I never meant to involve you this deeply anyway. Go on. I'll be fine."

Grudgingly, J.W. conceded. We paddled alongside the ladder at the pontoon boat's stern, and I cautiously stepped across and clung to its rails, nerving myself to climb it. J.W. started the outboard and without another word motored straight out through the inlet.

◆ ◆ ◆

Once at the top of the ladder, I saw Dapper O'Dell occupying the pilot's seat. Sherri stood forward on the open portion of the deck, but I halted under the awning next to the wheel and gazed bemusedly down on my kidnapped sibling.

Dapper wore his eternal supercilious smirk, but Sherri had stripped him of his funereal dove-grey tuxedo and re-outfitted him in a pair of tasteful black bathing trunks and an unbuttoned white sports shirt — clothes from a toddler's department some-where. The dummy's bare arms, legs, and chest shared the pseu-do-tan flesh tones of his face, as if Skipper had once actually con-sidered toting him aboard cruise ships for poolside performances. On the long upholstered seat behind the pilot's chair lay the empty case in which Sherri had carried Dapper to the marina.

Regarding me from the foredeck, Sherri trembled, but whether from the cold April water or some unguessable emotion I could not have said. She looked waiflike rather than elderly, with bones no heavier than a sparrow's. She clutched her own elbows, as if to throttle back her trembling.

Tentatively, hardly believing that I had found him, I reached out and touched Dapper's neck. My fingers came back tacky. I rubbed them together, sniffed them, and noticed the lacquerlike gloss on Dapper's trim little body. Sherri had slathered the dummy with a coconut-scented sunscreen. I wiped my fingers on my life vest and knelt beside Dapper to examine him more closely.

"Leave him alone."

I looked at Sherri without standing. "Except for a touch, I've done just that. And after the week I've had, you should appreci-ate my restraint."

"Restraint? You're *staring* at him."

"Dapper and I go back a long way, Sherri. I don't think he minds me staring at him."

"Dapper?" Sherri said. "*Dapper?*"

I rapped his head gently with my knuckles. "Dapper O'Dell. This chip-block. This dummy. Your kidnapped sunbathing buddy."

Sherri stepped toward me. "Don't touch him again. And address him respectfully, as a father deserves to be addressed."

The hair at the nape of my neck tingled and erected. I rose slowly and backed away from the pilot's chair, but the boat offered less room to withdraw than I would have liked. Something had snapped in Sherri, and something else had col-lapsed, and I stood uncomprehending before her.

"That's right. Stay away from your father. You're a bad son. Go sit over there."

I edged to the far end of the awning-shaded upholstered seat and dropped down warily. Sherri approached the pilot's seat, equally wary of me, and lifted Dapper out of it into her arms. She cradled him against her chest and tenderly massaged his back. Inadvertently, her hand rucked his little shirt up and I glimpsed with shock the cavity between Dapper's shoulder blades, the cavity containing his headstick and other operating toggles. The cavity, I now knew, containing the hidden tumor of the tape recorder.

Sherri shifted Dapper to her hip, as Skipper had occasionally held him in performance, and nodded at the portable cooler at my feet. "Please have a beer, Will. The agent stocked that for us with some lovely imports."

"I don't usually drink this early in the day."

"Skipper wants you to have one. Don't you, Skipper?" Sherri made the dummy nod its head. Then she bent as if to hear it speak something for her only, and straightened again to relay its message: "Skipper thinks a beer might loosen you up a little."

I pulled out a bottled beer, twisted off the cap, and took an obedient sip. Sherri and Dapper looked on approvingly, their smirks almost equally wooden.

"Sherri, that historic Dennis Blitch figure — whatever you choose to call him this morning — doesn't belong to you. I've come to take him back."

"He doesn't belong to Satish either! Why would you want to return him to the man who drove Thaddeus Sermak to suicide?"

I took another careful sip of beer. "I don't. Satish stole Dapper, but Dapper belonged to my father. At this moment, Sherri, they should be lying side by side in a quiet crypt in Mountboro. That's why I've spent the past six days searching for him."

Sherri strolled out onto the open foredeck with Dapper. "I once presented myself bathed and perfumed to Satish, and he became so obsessed with a callus on my thumb that he spent the next hour moistening it and filing it down, moistening it and filing it down."

"Some women would cherish that sort of attention from their husbands." I set my beer cautiously aside. "Satish loves you."

"Some women surrender to liposuction. Some women eat clay.

Some even mutilate themselves. But only idiots kowtow to men as self-seeking and evil as my husband. You've heard the tape, haven't you? You know what he did." Sherri cooed unintelligibly to the dummy in her arms.

I leaned forward earnestly. "But Skipper held that very tape in reserve so that *he* could blackmail *Satish*. How can you despise your husband and love my father when even my father resorted to blackmail tactics?"

"Will, you have that wrong. All wrong. A kind of palsy threatened his wonderful lip control." She looked at the dummy. "Didn't it, Skipper? You feared that the loss of your skill would nibble away at your reputation, maybe even end your career. So I bought you a miniature recording device. For months on end you balked at my suggestions on how best to use it, but eventually — eventually you agreed, and no one ever suspected that your skills had deteriorated at all." She kissed the ventriloquist's figure — in her mind, a simulacrum of Skipper Keats — lightly on the forehead.

This revelation was brand-new. It suggested that Skipper's affair with Sherri Gupta had lasted much longer than my mother believed, that perhaps it had never formally ended at all. What complicated cheats the two of them had perpetrated together. . . .

I reached for my beer again and took a long scalding swallow. "Sherri, you helped Skipper deceive my mother. You — "

"LaRue never understood his genius or his fears. Not really."

"You helped him deceive his audiences over and over again. Every performance a premeditated fraud."

"No. He simply refused to go before his audiences with anything other than his best."

"His best was a two-and-a-half-decade lie."

"No! You simply resent him. You always have. And in the face of your own failures and anonymity, you continue to resent him even after his . . ." She looked with evident confusion at Dapper O'Dell, the sardonic three-dimensional caricature of her lover.

"His death?" I said. When Sherri reluctantly nodded, I pursued the issue: "And if Skipper died, as we both know he did, what must we call that dummy on your hip?"

Sherri frowned, her hostility shading into an uncomfortable perplexity.

"Tell me. What must we call him?"

After a protracted beat, Sherri said, "Skipper's soul."

How could I contest this label? And why else would Skipper have insisted on taking Dapper into the crypt with him?

I finished my beer and returned the empty bottle to the ice in the cooler. Sherri suggested that I have another. Why not? Twisting and bending while remaining seated, I rummaged out another bottle and pulled at it greedily. Adrienne would have rebuked me — not for drinking a beer or drinking it so early, but for tossing it off in a way that rendered it generic and inconsequential. For failing to pay attention.

From the bow, Sherri spoke with seeming sincerity and concern. "Poor William. You look whipped. Let your eyes rest on this beautiful pastoral landscape. Evil can't live here. Skipper and I called it our private Arcadia. Its charms will wash your own soul clean."

At a weary psychological impasse, I obeyed. Cold bottle between my thighs, I looked steadily at the water, the reflecting hills. Gradually, my gaze began to lose focus, my breathing to flatten out. The drifting of the boat, the quick downing of two beers on an empty stomach, and my accumulated fatigue lulled me into a light trance, a reverie through which the faces and confused doings of the past week flitted like bats. Regaining possession of Dapper, while still important, seemed a triumph simultaneously far off and already behind me.

Sherri walked toward me from the bow and sat down in the pilot's chair with Dapper in her lap. She started the engine with a turn of the ignition key and steered us out of the pocket gulf toward open water. The smells of spilled beer, human sweat, coconut butter, fish, and gasoline washed over me in a paralyzing olfactory flood.

Peering out from half-lowered eyelids, I asked mildly, "Where are we going?"

Sherri did not answer. With a deliberate act of will, I refocused. We had drifted into an expanse of water so wide and clear that the encompassing hills looked miles distant. Sherri no longer sat behind the wheel, but knelt in the *Trinidad*'s bow with Dapper on his back in front of her. In her hand, a small metal gasoline can with which she anointed the dummy's small body, and then her own shoulders, belly, and thighs.

Quietly, I said, "Sherri, what are you doing?" Now I regretted my brief but unwise downtime. Adrienne would have cringed at my bout of self-indulgent meditation at the behest of a calculating madwoman.

Sherri looked up at me without surprise. "Getting ready for a long-overdue ceremony."

Trying to compute how long it would take to close the twenty feet or so between us, I slowly stood up. "What ceremony?"

Sherri set the gasoline can down and lifted an old-fashioned metal cigarette lighter into view. "Don't move, Will. One flip and the fickle Skipper Keats turns into bonfire fuel."

"One flip and you'll both go up in flames." I stood stock-still. "You'll pretty likely take the entire boat with you."

"So much the better. In India, they used to burn the virtuous widow on her deceased husband's funeral pyre."

"Sherri, I don't understand what you're about here."

She thumbed the Zippo's top open and waved the lighter sinuously in front of her. "I never should have married Satish. I should have married Skipper. When he died, I should have died with him."

"Oh no," I said lamely. "Never."

"Oh yes, Will. We may have consummated our love, Skipper and I, but we never consummated the marriage that should have occurred between us. Maybe we can do it today . . . in fire." She scooped Dapper off the foredeck and, posing for me like some sort of lustful arsonist, brandished the lighter again.

Her stance and the set of her mouth terrified me. "Please don't do this," I said. "For God's sake, Sherri, think about this a little." I edged two baby steps nearer.

"Do you suppose I *haven't* thought about this?" Sherri said. "Do you suppose I've thought about anything else at all?"

At that moment, a familiar voice somewhere above the pontoon boat said, "*Sherri, put the lighter away.*"

Sherri Gupta looked up. "Skipper?"

I chose that moment to rush through the gap next to the pilot's seat and chop the upraised lighter out of her hand. It spun out and away and landed with a faint splash in the lake. I slipped and fell. Sherri, still clutching Dapper, beheld me with outrage, realizing in that very instant that I had just employed the ventriloquial distant voice that her dead lover had taught me years ago.

"You son of a bitch!" she cried.

As I was regaining my feet, before I could stop her, Sherri heaved Dapper over the side of the *Trinidad*. He hit the water on his back with legs and arms outspread. For one cruel moment he floated. Then the weight of his interior armatures and covert mechanisms pulled him under. Sherri stood beside me at the rail, and we watched him go down.

I concentrated on the dummy's face, that youthful semblance of my father's visage, now suddenly wearing an expression of helplessness and bewilderment. One eye performed a slow wink, and bubbles arose from behind the descending head as if someone had cut a diver's scuba hose. The wide red mouth wavered, the eyes fogged, and the brilliant colors of the lips and cheeks dulled under a thickening veneer of lake water. At length the entire miniature body had vanished, like a photographic image eerily undergoing the development process in reverse.

CHAPTER 26

From the marina I called Satish Gupta to inform him of his wife's condition, while Sherri herself sat nearly catatonic in the rental agent's office, only her hands moving, shredding Kleenex into her lap, a watchful J.W. by her side.

Gupta vented only a single anguished exclamation, then became all business. If we would be so good as to fetch Mrs. Gupta's car and effects, a lawyer would soon meet us with a private ambulance. So while J.W. kept vigil over the disoriented woman, I hoofed it back to her cottage, gathered up her few remaining belongings, used her keys to open the garage and start her vintage Caddy, then drove back. The ambulance and Sherri's legal guardian arrived moments after my return, and they took her away. I did not weep to see her go.

We called the airport manager to reassure him that we hadn't made off with his Lincoln, and then we set out for home ourselves. We were in the air by four o'clock that afternoon, flying at 5,500 feet, and back in Columbus by half past seven, having lost an hour by the local clock. I helped J.W. tie the Cessna down, and he drove me home. I showered until the hot water ran out, then fell into bed for a twelve-hour nap.

◆ ◆ ◆

The next day, after a phone call, Adrienne and Olivia drove down from Tocqueville, dressed in their Sunday best but carrying a duffel of comfortable kick-around clothes for relaxing after the church service I had uncharacteristically enjoined upon them. We met on the rolling green lawn of Mountboro's Methodist church. After a brief, sloppy kiss from Olivia and a long, indiscreet one from Adrienne, Adrienne held me at arm's length and scrutinized me intently.

"Checking for missing parts?" I asked her.

"Just looking for the shaved spot and the stitches on your head where the doctors inserted the piety."

"No operation necessary. It just grew there over this last hellacious week."

"After what you've been through, maybe I really should cut you some slack. Let's go inside."

As we entered the church, Olivia said loudly, "I'm the only Buddhist in my class. I'm the only Buddhist in my whole school."

People turned and either chuckled or scowled. I lay a finger to my lips and whispered, "Not a good idea to announce that here, kiddo. You won't get invited to any covered-dish dinners."

We sat on a back pew in the carpeted sanctuary. J.W. and Babe occupied the third or fourth pew in front of us, their heads together like courting teenagers. "You clean up pretty good," J.W. had told me as we found our seats, and I had returned the compliment while observing that his Sunday-go-to-meeting finery — a striped shirt, a Bugs Bunny tie, and pleated Dockers — failed to include socks. The tops of his feet and his hairy ankles had flashed defiantly between his loafers and his trouser cuffs.

Framed in the apricot, emerald, and cranberry light of the stained-glass window, the preacher — not Hutchinson Payne, my radical Baptist buddy, but a sallow man only two or three years out of the seminary — spoke for eighteen and a half minutes on God's unconditional love for all His children, presumably including Buddhists, Hindus, Muslims, Voodooists, used-car salesmen, school superintendents, and ventriloquists. Not surprisingly, he declined to say if that all-embracing affection extended to wooden manikins.

I thanked the God I only intermittently believed in for sparing Sherri Gupta's life and for bringing J.W. and me home safely. I prayed that healing of all sorts would come upon Sherri, that my mother and sister and clandestine half-brother would find their hearts' ease in their own lifetimes, and that God would have mercy on my father's soul, wherever it rested: heaven, hell, or the bottom of Center Hill Lake. I asked for daily focus for myself and an evolving character worthy of the love of the woman sitting one twitchy girl-child away. I did not know what to pray for Dapper. It seemed to me, though, that he had not deserved everlasting immersion in a lake any more than he had earned everlasting entombment with Skipper.

The service concluded — mockingly or consolingly, depending on my shifting perspective — with the congregational hymn "This Is My Father's World." Adrienne did not sing, but stood respectfully and helped support the open hymnal. Olivia, however, picked up the melody by the second verse and sang out lustily from that point on. Most of the children in the sanctuary looked back at least once to determine the source of her high-pitched and off-cadence jubilation.

◆ ◆ ◆

Later, at the Mexican restaurant, Olivia and Adrienne ordered vegetarian meals while I put away not only refried beans, Spanish rice, and guacamole, but also two chicken enchiladas and a crisp beef taco.

◆ ◆ ◆

In Mockingbird Gardens, Olivia by sheer happenstance met a schoolmate from Tocqueville, and the two girls went off with the friend's mother to play miniature golf, freeing Adrienne and me to stroll hand in hand to the beach pavilion. Once there, we sat in heavy wooden rocking chairs overlooking the manmade lake.

"What will you do next year if you can't find a counseling position?"

"I have the rest of the school year to think about that. Now that I've found Dapper — "

"Found him and lost him again."

"Right. I didn't even get to hold the little bastard one last time."

"But you found him through your own efforts, without bringing in the police or sending anyone to jail. Does that sit okay with you?"

Oddly, it did. Maybe Lawrence Budge deserved some jail time. Maybe Satish Gupta had earned himself a cell through his ancient persecution of Thaddeus Sermak and his more recent complicity in Dapper's theft. But Gupta had paid for years the moment-by-moment penalty of his unrequited love for his own wife. As for Sherri Gupta, she had received her punishment; in fact, she had borne it more or less unobtrusively for so long that over this past weekend it had virtually destroyed her.

"I guess I can live with what happened," I said. "Primarily because it showed me the reliability of those I love."

I squeezed Adrienne's hand, and we rocked for a time. I could not really tell if she admired or disapproved of my vocational complacency, but at length she noncommittally pressed that button again.

"After subbing for Cabriales at the Gag Reflex, you could go into show business. Follow in your daddy's footsteps."

I laughed. "Now *there's* punishment for you. Pulling hard time in smoky little bistros and echoey old theaters. I wouldn't wish that on . . . well, Alan Papini."

"He wished it on himself. You chose working with kids."

"And the Speece County Board of Education has taken that choice right out of my hands. Unless I can get on with another system."

"Of course you can. I'll help you update your résumé. There must be a slew of openings elsewhere in the state, especially for a man. Male elementary school counselors crop up about as often as female football coaches."

We rocked some more. On the other side of the lake, a man in a slick lavender wetsuit had gone parasailing, dangling in a harness beneath an impressive orange and yellow kite. Knots of people in shorts and T-shirts gaped at him from all around the beach. What an avocation. What exhilaration. Could you make any money doing that? Would it even matter if you could?

And then I heard Adrienne saying, "First thing tomorrow morning — "

I held up my hand. "Adrienne, stop. Listen to yourself." She wore an uncomprehendingly earnest expression, her lips pursed and a vein pulsing noticeably amid the golden hairs at her temple. "LaRue and Mrs. Lapierre together couldn't sound half as obsessed and goal-oriented as you do right now."

Taken off guard, Adrienne merely stared at me.

"Even God rested," I said. "It's Sunday. We're supposed to be relaxing. Recuperating. Lollygagging."

Adrienne lifted an eyebrow.

"Do I have to remind you of what Dapper would say? Up on stage with Skipper, vying for some sign of his master's happiness?"

Adrienne looked briefly lost. Then she caught on, and the two of us chanted that foolish catchphrase together, virtually shouting by its final inexhaustible word.

ACKNOWLEDGMENTS

Philip Lawson thanks these people for their contributions to *Would It Kill You to Smile?*:

Dwayne Fuller, a former funeral-home employee, and Gene Page, location manager of the Striffler-Hamby Mortuary, who separately provided information about caskets, mausoleums, crypts, and disinterment permits.

Nancy Mallory, who knows her BBs.

John Y. Willis, who flies, even on the ground, and who in clever disguise appears as a character in these pages.

An unsung army of dedicated West Georgia elementary-school counselors.

John Yow, fiction editor at Longstreet Press, who refused to allow the winsome Will Keats to nap on the job.

None of these people warrants blame for errors of fact, aesthetic lapses, or other implausibilities. Lay all such nits and brickbats at Philip Lawson's doorstep.

15,310